SUPERTOWN

Also by Paul Kupperberg

Emma's Landing

Kevin

Paul Kupperberg's Illustrated Guide to Writing Comics

JSA: Ragnarök

SUPERTOWN

PAUL KUPPERBERG

San Diego

SUPERTOWN

Heliosphere Books®

Library of Congress Cataloging-in-Publication Data

Names: Kupperberg, Paul, author. Title: Supertown / Paul Kupperberg. Description: San Diego : Heliosphere Books, [2021] | Summary: A superhero stirs things up when he decides to retire in Wally Crenshaw's sleepy hometown. Identifiers: LCCN 2021025268 (print) | LCCN 2021025269 (ebook) | ISBN 9781937868857 (trade paperback) | ISBN 9781937868864 (epub) | ISBN 9781937868871 (kindle edition) Subjects: CYAC: Superheroes--Fiction. | City and town life--Fiction. Classification: LCC PZ7.K9523 Sut 2021 (print) | LCC PZ7.K9523 (ebook) | DDC [Fic]--dc23 LC record available at https://lccn.loc.gov/2021025268
LC ebook record available at https://lccn.loc.gov/2021025269

Cover design by AndaV3 via 99designs.com
Jeep® image by RJA1988 via pixabay.com; Downtown image by Unknown via pixabay.com; Little boy dressed as superhero, by Jack Frog via shutterstock.com

Heliosphere Books are published by Endpapers Press, a division of Author Coach, LLC.

To Max and Robin, at long last

1

THE DIRTY GRAY CAR with the cracked rear window cruised slowly down Kane Street, the driver peering through the windshield at the houses as he passed. Whiz Kid, crouching behind the bushes, watched the car go by.

For the second time in just five minutes.

Whiz Kid had first spied the car during his daily patrol. He knew everybody who lived in tiny Crumbly-by-the-Sea, New Jersey, which is why a strange car with out-of-state license plates immediately caught his attention and raised his suspicions. Because one thing the Whiz Kid knew for sure was that no one who didn't belong in Crumbly ever came to Crumbly.

Unless, maybe, they were up to no good...?

If they were, they became Whiz Kid's business.

Whiz Kid pulled the short, red cape tighter

around his shoulders as he shifted position behind the bush to keep the slowly moving car in sight. As Crumbly's resident superhero, he made it his job to keep the town safe, which he did with daily patrols and a keen eye for trouble. He liked to think his reputation for toughness kept the criminals at bay. Why come all the way out to Crumbly to pull off a dastardly deed when you knew your only reward would be a butt-kicking, courtesy of Whiz Kid?

The driver of the gray car probably hadn't gotten the word. It slowed and pulled over to the curb, stopping under the shade of the willow tree in front of number 254, Mrs. Wicker's old house. Odd, Whiz Kid thought. The two-story Victorian stood behind a dilapidated and once white picket fence. It had been left to slowly decay after its owner, old Mrs. Wicker, died about five years ago. Whiz Kid remembered hearing that she'd had only one living relative, a nephew in New York who had no interest in taking over the place. As for selling it, well, he couldn't remember the last time a house had been bought or sold in Crumbly. And there were plenty available. Three houses were for sale here on Kane Street alone.

But Whiz Kid didn't care about the state of Crumbly's real estate market. He wanted to know about the stranger in the gray car and what business he had here.

The car door swung open and the driver stepped out onto the street. The man stood a little over six feet tall, with an average but fit build, and short black hair, as well as several days' growth of dark stubble on his cheeks. His mouth was set in a grim line and his eyes were hidden behind sunglasses. He wore black slacks, a black T-shirt, and a dark windbreaker.

At this distance, Whiz Kid found it difficult to make out his features, but the hero of Crumbly was pretty sure that he hadn't been the subject of any recent alerts. He could be a lost traveler stopping for directions. No, that didn't make any sense. Anyone needing directions would have stopped at Hootie's Service Station on Old Crumbly Road long before they hit this part of town.

The man looked up and down the tree-lined street. His eyes swept over Whiz Kid's hiding place, but the Kid didn't worry. Like any super worth the name, he had mastered the art of surveillance. When he wanted to disappear from sight, he became as good as invisible to the naked eye.

"Hey, Whiz Kid!"

A shrill, mocking voice split the still summer afternoon. Whiz Kid winced and the stranger turned his head in the direction of the shout. The young hero knew exactly who the voice belonged to and silently cursed the name of this, his greatest foe.

"What're you up to, Whiz Kid? Find any good supervillains lately?" The voice drew closer, its owner cutting across the lawn of the Schaffenberger house behind whose shrubs Whiz Kid crouched. The sound of mocking laughter trailed after the voice.

Sighing, he stood up. He threw one last look in the direction of the stranger next to the gray car. The man had taken off his sunglasses to stare at the skinny eleven, almost twelve-year-old brown-haired boy wearing a white T-shirt, sneakers, and blue shorts . . . topped with a blue domino mask over his wide blue eyes and a homemade red cape draped over his bony shoulders. Embarrassed, Wally Crenshaw pulled the mask off his face and quickly looked away, but not before he saw the man smirk and shake his head in amusement. Wally's face flashed red-hot.

"Gonna save the universe today or what?" Mike Brewer sneered. The redheaded boy stopped in front of Wally, his chunky form blocking the man from view. Mike's two constant companions, Abel Schotz and Nick McCain, a pair of tall, skinny parentheses with long blond hair who looked like they could be brothers, stood on either side of him, snickering as usual. Abel and Nick almost never spoke. They just hung out with Mike, laughing at everything he said and punching each other in the ribs and shoulders when their leader delivered one of his hilarious put-downs. But no one else found Mike Brewer funny, just a bully. Though a year older, a head taller, and twenty pounds heavier than Wally, Mike was in the same grade as him.

"Hi, Mike," Wally said, fingering the Velcro patch that held the cape closed at his throat. All of a sudden, he wished that he had gone down to the beach with his two best friends instead of staying in town on patrol.

"Glad we caught you on patrol, Whiz Boy," Mike said, glancing at Abel and Nick, who started snickering right on cue. "Somebody needs your help real bad."

Wally winced again. He knew what came next. Mike Brewer had been pulling the same gag on him in one form or another about twice a week since third grade. Abel and Nick snickered some more.

"Aren't you gonna ask me *who*, Whiz Kid?" Mike said.

"C'mon, Mike. Do we have to go through this every time?"

Mike pushed his sneering freckled face in close to Wally's. "*Ask* me," he demanded.

Wally took a deep breath. Once Mike went on the attack, he became unstoppable. Like Wally had done so many times before, he just had to let this particular episode play itself out and try to walk away with as much of his dignity intact as possible.

"Okay, Mike," Wally said in resignation. "Who?"

"You!" Mike shouted, and shoved his hands against Wally's chest, sending the smaller boy stumbling backward. He landed on his rear in the bushes that had, until a moment ago, hidden him from view. He wished he were still hidden. Abel and Nick began to hoot and laugh, punching at one another like two demented chimps. Mike turned to his friends with a grin and accepted a round of fist bumps.

Turning back to Wally, Mike raised an eyebrow as a new joke came to him. "Gotta tell you, Crenshaw," he snickered. "For a super, you're pretty *bush* league! Get it," he roared, pointing to the bush Wally sprawled in. "*Bush!* You're *in* the bushes, so you're, like, *bush* league."

"Yeah, that's pretty funny, Mike," Wally muttered.

"Bush!" Mike repeated, pointing at Wally and laughing so hard he could barely get the word out.

"Dumb!"

A new voice joined the chorus. Wally

groaned and covered his eyes. This, he thought, *this* made his humiliation absolutely complete! Bad enough he had to take abuse from Mike.

But did it have to happen in front of *her*?

Brenda Cunningham rolled to a stop on her inline skates next to Wally. Small and compact, Brenda had long, auburn hair tumbling out from under her helmet, green eyes, and a sprinkle of freckles across the bridge of her nose that made Wally—for reasons he still didn't understand—want to melt into the ground. She glared at Mike as though he were the lowest thing on Earth. "Dumb," she said again. "Don't you ever get tired of pushing people around, Mike Brewer?"

Mike grinned and tapped his chin with his finger, pretending to think the question over. Wally assumed Mike had to pretend because actual thought presented too big a challenge for him. Abel and Nick snickered.

"I haven't yet," Mike said, which set his goon boys into fresh gales of laughter.

"You are so *not* funny," Brenda said. She looked at Wally. "Are you okay?"

"Oh, sure, just swell," Wally mumbled. He couldn't meet her eyes.

"Some super you are, Crenshaw," Mike guffawed. "You think Hyperion needs a *girl* to protect him?" Abel and Nick exchanged a fresh round of high fives, laughing so hard their hands almost missed.

"Oh, grow up, Mike!" Brenda snapped. "If you had half a brain, you wouldn't keep getting left back in school."

Mike Brewer's eyes narrowed and Wally inhaled sharply. This is not good, he thought. You could call Mike just about any name you wanted, but the mere mention of his scholastic failure practically guaranteed an explosion. Even Abel and Nick fell silent at Brenda's insult, taking a step back in shock.

"*Once!*" Mike bellowed, his face turning red. "I got left back *once*! Just 'cause Mr. Finlay didn't like me!"

"*Nobody* likes you, Mike," Brenda said with a toss of her hair, a sparkle in her green eyes.

Mike took a step toward her. *Big* trouble, Wally thought, his heart pounding as he struggled to free himself from the bushes. Whether he liked it or not, if Mike went nuts, Wally would have to come to Brenda's defense. Mike would probably tear his head off and use it for a basketball, but if Brenda stuck up for Wally, Wally would have to do the same for her. Either that or she would think he was the biggest (instead of only maybe the second or third biggest) wuss in the known universe.

"Oh, cut it out, Mike," Brenda said breezily,

turning her back on him. His face had turned red and twisted with anger, but she just smiled. "You're an ape and a bully, but you're not going to hit me."

Mike growled, "No?"

"No," she said. "You wouldn't hit a girl. Especially a girl whose father is the sheriff."

Mike's head snapped back with a look of bewilderment on his face. "Oh. Right."

"Yeah, duh!" Brenda said. She looked at Wally and winked. "Come on, Wally. Let's go."

"Uh, okay," Wally said. "See you later, Mike."

Mike glared at him. "Count on it, Whiz Kid," he snarled.

Brenda had already started rolling away on her blades and Wally hurried to catch up with her. Saved. For the time being, anyway. But in a town as small as Crumbly, Wally couldn't hope to avoid Mike for very long. Only that the next encounter came later rather than sooner. Like, later this century.

"Umm," he mumbled when he caught up with Brenda.

"You're welcome," she said.

"Oh, yeah, thanks," he said. Why did he always feel like such a doofus around Brenda? Well, he knew why. Like just about every other boy in his class, he *liked* Brenda Cunningham. But, even if she hadn't already been dating someone—who happened to be his best friend, Benny Sachem—Wally could never have worked up the nerve to ask her out. There were times he could barely form a complete sentence around her. He shook his head in despair. Some super I am, he thought bitterly.

Brenda rolled to a stop at the corner and looked at Wally. "You know, Wally, if you just stood up to Mike, he'd stop picking on you."

Wally shook his head and shoved his hands deep in the pockets of his shorts. "My dad used to tell me the same thing about bullies," he said, looking down at the sidewalk. "I tried it once."

"And?"

He grinned sheepishly. "The guy knocked out my front tooth."

Brenda tried to hide her smile. "Well, okay, so maybe that's not the answer for you.

"You guys have fun at the beach?" he said, desperate to change the subject.

"Yep. The water's great this time of year. You should have come with us."

Wally shuddered. "Ugh, no thanks."

"Oh, right. Your irrational fear of swimming in the ocean."

"It's not irrational. The ocean's full of . . . stuff. And it's deep."

"So is a swimming pool. Deep, I mean, but you swim in them."

"That's different. There's nothing living in a swimming pool and I can see the bottom."

Brenda shook her head. "You know, maybe if you didn't run around town in a mask and cape playing superhero, Mike wouldn't pick on you so much."

"I'm not playing," Wally said with sudden heat.

"I know, I know. I mean, I know what a fan you are of the supers. But," she added gently, "you're just a kid. You're not one of them."

"Well, no," Wally said, hating himself for the defensive whine in his voice. "Not yet, I'm not. But those guys were just kids once themselves and they all got superpowers, didn't they? Hyperion, Blend, Swift, Fakeout . . . they all started out like normal people, right?"

"I don't know about Hyperion," Brenda said.

"You know what I mean. You never know when you're going to get zapped by gamma radiation or be exposed to the rays of a meteor or get bitten by a radioactive spider, do you?"

Brenda made a face. "Spiders, radioactive or not, are ick!"

"Come on, Brenda," Wally pleaded. "If those things could happen to those guys, why can't they happen to me?"

"Because *you* live in Crumbly. Just because you want to get superpowers doesn't mean you will. Face it, Wally, all you're going to get dressing up like a super around here is beat up."

Wally nodded helplessly. Brenda didn't understand. No one did. Come to think of it, sometimes even he didn't understand. All he knew was that for as long as he could remember, he'd wanted to be a super, to fight alongside the Justice Brigade! He didn't know how or when, but all his life he had been taught if he wanted something badly enough and worked hard enough, he would get it.

It didn't matter if no one else believed.

Only he could give it up, and that would never happen, no matter what anyone else thought.

"Come on, Wally," Brenda said, smiling brightly. "Let's go to Mr. Fenderman's and you can buy me a soda for rescuing you from Mike."

"Did not." Wally grinned. "He'd finished picking on me by the time you showed up."

Brenda laughed and took off on her blades. Wally remembered the stranger in the gray car and looked back up Kane Street. The car remained parked in front of the Wicker House, the man nowhere to be seen.

Wally narrowed his eyes. This, he thought as he took off after Brenda, would require further investigation by Whiz Kid!

2

"CRUMBLY," THE BUS DRIVER yelled. "This stop's Crumbly-by-the-Sea, New Jersey!"

Charlie Harris wondered for whom the driver had made his shouted announcement. There weren't any other passengers on the bus since it had left Red Bank hours ago, with Crumbly as its one and only scheduled stop.

When he'd first tried buying a ticket, the agent had been confused, insisting no such place existed in New Jersey. It had taken going online and showing the man the town on a map on the New Jersey government website to convince him that the town existed, followed by the problem of figuring out how to get there, and freeing up a bus to make the trip with a single passenger.

But it all had been sorted out, Charlie had been sent on his way. The difficulty of just *getting* on his way made him all the more certain that his choice of Crumbly had been the right one.

Charlie retrieved his suitcase from the overhead rack and left the bus, thanking the driver. The man didn't look up as he mumbled curses and slapped at his GPS device, which had started acting up about half an hour outside of town. It had finally failed while they were negotiating a narrow road through a swamp.

Charlie found himself on a sidewalk in what, as he recalled, had been Crumbly's downtown. He used the past tense because it had all changed so drastically. The storefronts that lined the two-block long street, most of which seemed to be closed or out of business, including a pharmacy, a five-and-dime, a diner, a hardware store, a variety store, an appliance store, men's and women's clothing, and shoe stores . . . it all reminded Charlie of a small town out of the 1950s, before the big chain stores took over all the Main Streets.

Except small towns in the 1950s usually had people living in them.

Was this Crumbly-by-the-Sea or some ghost town? Charlie frowned and started to turn to ask the driver, but the doors were hissing closed in his face even as the big bus lurched off, belching diesel fumes.

"It ain't a mistake," someone behind him said.

Charlie turned and saw an old man sitting in a chair in the shade of an awning in front of one of the stores.

"It ain't, um, isn't?" Charlie asked.

The old man nodded slowly. "Nope. You're in Crumbly, all right."

"I see. Well, I *did* want to get away from it all..."

The old man nodded solemnly. "If what you're looking for's to get away, Crumbly-by-the-Sea's about as far from whatever it is you're gettin' away from that you're likely to find."

Charlie set his suitcase down and looked up and down Main Street. The rumble of the bus that had left him off in front of Jocko's Barber Shop had already faded on the still afternoon air. Other than that, he could hear or see... nothing. Not even a traffic light. Just the grizzled old man in the white barber smock sitting in the chair tipped back against the front of the barbershop.

"You visiting?"

"Nope," Charlie said. "I live here."

The old man closed one eye and looked at Charlie for a long moment. "No," he said at last. "Don't think you do, son. I know everyone living in Crumbly and I don't know you."

Charlie laughed. "Well, I'm a new resident."

"Is that right?" The old man almost sounded surprised.

"I'm Charlie Harris," Charlie said, extending his hand.

"Any relation to Sadie Harris Wicker?"

"I'm her nephew. I'm taking over her house. Aunt Sadie left it to me when she died."

"Rest her soul," the old man sighed with a shake of his head. "Shame about her passing and all. How long's it been, five years ago? She was good folk." He looked at Charlie again, this time sizing him up from head to toe. "Her nephew, eh?"

"Uh-huh. As a kid, my family and I used to visit her in the summer sometimes, but we'd always come by boat from New York. I guess my father knew better than to take the land route. Anyway, I remember the town being a little busier."

"Oh, it ebbs and it flows, depending on the time of day. Anyway," the old man said, pointing his thumb over his shoulder at the barbershop. "Name's Feeno Mullins. Best darned barber in Crumbly. Pleased to meet you."

"Same here," Charlie said. "Just curious why if you're the best barber, Jocko's name is on the window?"

"Jocko used to be best, taught me everything he knew about cutting hair, but since he died, I reckon that makes me the best. Just haven't gotten around to scraping his name off and painting mine on yet, that's all." Feeno glanced over his shoulder, thoughtfully rubbing his chin. “Been six years. Guess I’ll get to it one of these days.”

“Right,” Charlie said, picking up his suitcase. Talk about being laid back; just chatting with the man made him sleepy.

“Well, nice to meet you, Mr. Mullins. I suppose I should be getting to the house. Could you remind me where…?”

The barber rose from his chair. “Do better than that, son. I can walk you over.”

“Oh, no,” Charlie said. “I couldn’t possibly take you away from work.”

“Not to worry. Ben Woolsey won’t be in for his weekly trim until tomorrow morning. Nothing to do till then.” Feeno pointed to Charlie’s suitcase. “That all you brought with you?”

“The movers are bringing everything else by truck. One of these days, if they can find the place.”

“That can be a problem.”

Feeno Mullins got creakily to his feet and gestured for Charlie to follow. Charlie took a deep breath and fell into step next to the old man. They turned at the corner, the end of Main Street. Also the end of the sidewalk, pavement giving way to a dirt path that wandered through a large, weed-filled empty lot and onto a blacktopped street.

"Ran out of concrete, did you?" Charlie asked as they started up Cardy Road.

"Something like that," Feeno nodded. "Ran clean out of money to *buy* concrete about the time the state changed their plans for the new interstate."

"Why'd they do that?" Charlie asked. He looked around at the houses. They were all small Cape Cod cottages set back from the street on small lawns behind a variety of fences. The houses had probably been built in the 1930s and had been, over the years, modified and individualized by their owners. Some had been extended upwards, some sideways, some with wood shingles, others with aluminum or vinyl siding. The lawns were, for the most part, mowed, and bushes trimmed, with the only exceptions being those houses with weather-beaten "For Sale" signs hanging out front.

"Some kind of political thing in Trenton." Feeno shot Charlie a glance. "That's the state capitol, you know."

Charlie nodded.

"About twenty, twenty-two years back, the state got federal money to extend the interstate," Feeno Mullins said. "They planned to build an exit straight on into town here. Crumbly's got a nice little stretch of beach, used to do a good bit of summer resort business with the people coming down to the shore and all. Someone even got started building an amusement park down by the beach.

"Then, a whole bunch of big shopping malls and industrial parks got built fifteen miles north and south of town. Lots of money in those things, I hear, tax revenue and what all, and they got the highway plans changed, moving the exits east and west of town and eliminating our access.

"As if that weren't bad enough, there's marshlands between here and the highway, home to some endangered birds and frogs. And building any kind of main road from there to here would've meant paving over the marshes, which would have killed them birds and frogs. End of story, and the end of getting all that resort and park business money coming into town."

Charlie shook his head. "Tough break," he said.

"Probably wouldn't have done us any good in the long run anyway."

"Oh, yeah? Why's that?"

"You got one of those cellular telephone devices?"

"A cell phone? Sure."

"They don't work here. Some kind of electronical or magnetic interference from . . . well, they never have figured out exactly what. Oh, we get good old-fashioned telephone and television, but only over special cable wires, but that whole . . . what do you call it? Interworld web? Nothing but static here except for a couple of hours a day. You know how the world is nowadays. No computers, no business. Well, my business don't need them. You can't cut hair on a computer. Just about did Crumbly in. Only those of us with no place else to go or those too old to bother going are left."

While Charlie felt bad for the people of Crumbly, everything Feeno had told him just made it sound better and better. In addition to being a place hardly anyone outside its town limits even knew existed, Crumbly had the added advantage of being an internet dead zone. For the first time since leaving New York, Charlie Harris felt good about his decision to run away.

"It's right up the road here," Feeno said as they turned off Cardy onto Kane Street. Like everything else Charlie had seen in Crumbly, this street looked like an abandoned movie studio back lot. He knew people lived here. He just couldn't figure out where they all were.

"Where is everybody?"

"Oh, here and there, I suppose. This time of day, things are usually pretty quiet."

Feeno stopped in front of an old Victorian house behind a ramshackle picket fence that may or may not have once been white. Charlie couldn't tell. Weeds choked the small front yard and the big trees on either side of the walk to the broken porch steps were badly in need of pruning. "Here we are," Feeno said. "The old Wicker place."

Charlie let his suitcase drop to the sidewalk. "This is it?" he asked skeptically.

"Yep."

"Aunt Sadie's place," Charlie breathed. "It looks like it's seen . . . better days."

"Yep."

Charlie looked up and down the street. His eyes passed over the dirty gray car parked at the curb, but he didn't give it a second thought. Not with what he saw standing before him. The front porch and overhang looked as though a giant foot had stepped down on it right in front of the door. Several windows were broken. Rain gutters were just barely hanging on to the façade. He could see patches of bare wood where the shingles were loose or missing. The house probably hadn't been painted in decades, and those were just the problems he could see at first glance. Heaven only knew what waited for him inside.

"Wow," Charlie said.

"Yep," Feeno Mullins said. "Sadie let the old place go a bit those last few years."

"A bit. Yeah."

Okay, fine, Charlie thought. I can deal with this. Some paint, some wood, a few nails.

I *can* deal with this.

I can.

"Best I let you get settled," Feeno said. "You need anything, just give a holler."

Charlie managed a sickly smile. "I'll be hollering."

Feeno glanced at the house. "I expect you will be."

Feeno turned and ambled back the way they had come. Charlie stood watching him for as long as he could, putting off going inside. Not that he had left himself any choice. He couldn't go back to his old life. Besides, fixing the old place up would give him something to do, take his mind off what he'd left behind.

He lived in Crumbly now. In *this* house. Such as it were.

He squared his shoulders, took a deep breath, picked up his suitcase, and reached for the front gate.

It came off its hinges in his hand.

Charlie groaned, but he kept walking, the dismembered gate in hand. He stepped gingerly over the broken wooden steps, edged around the gaping hole in the porch, and set the gate against the wall next to the door. He took the key his aunt's lawyer had sent him five years ago from his pocket and reached for the doorknob.

But before he could touch it, the door flew open, revealing a tall, grim-faced man, his eyes hidden behind sunglasses.

Charlie dropped the suitcase and jumped back in surprise, tripping on a loose floor-board and tumbling into the gaping hole behind him.

The man peered expressionlessly down at him.

"Hello, Charlie," he said in a low, rumbling voice. "I've been waiting for you."

3

WALLY RACED UP THE walk to his house, a white clapboard colonial at 34 Cole Lane. He leapt up the three stairs to the porch, making a whooshing noise to simulate the sound of flight. He landed on the porch with a thud, his fists on his hips, chin held high in his best super pose. Then, red cape swirling around his shoulders, he whirled, grabbed the screen door handle, and leapt into the house.

Wally shouted in the direction of the dining room just off the front door, which his mother, a freelance graphic artist, used as her home office. "Have no fear citizen," he yelled. "The Whiz Kid is here!"

Wally's mother appeared in the doorway, taking off her glasses and smiling. A short, dark-haired woman who favored t-shirts and blue jeans, Jamie Crenshaw wore her reading glasses on a braided chain around her neck. "Is the town safe for the good guys?" she asked.

"Yes, ma'am," he said, deepening his voice. Safe, he thought, except for goons like Mike Brewer and his henchmen. As usual, he didn't tell his mom about his run-in with Mike. What could she do? Half the parents in Crumbly had complained to Mike's father about his son's bullying ways, but nothing ever came of it. Wally felt pretty sure that brutish Manny Brewer, owner and operator of the town dump, took pride in Mike's exploits, and probably even encouraged his son's behavior.

"Good to hear." Mrs. Crenshaw looked at her watch. "There's still a few hours until dinner. You hungry?"

"Nope," Wally said, reverting to his normal voice. "Just had a soda with Brenda at Mr. Fenderman's. Anyway, I gotta get online while there's still time."

His mother glanced at her watch. "You've still got about an hour. I'm finished for the day so it's all yours."

"Thanks, Mom," Wally grinned, and flew up the stairs, taking them two at a time. His mother smiled and shook her head. Internet access remained a precious commodity in Crumbly. For reasons science couldn't explain and technology couldn't quite make up for, little Crumbly-by-the-Sea sat in a pocket of interference that, through some crossed wires in the magnetic field or a bad confluence of ley lines, made it nearly impervious to certain electronic signals. Her father had been raised in town and recalled they had always suffered from spotty radio and television broadcast signals, but it hadn't mattered so much in those days. Then came cell phones, GPS, the internet, and Wi-Fi and the lack of connectivity with the outside world became glaringly obvious.

It didn't matter whether the internet tried to come to town through copper wires or fiber-optic cables. Nothing worked. One by one, the cable and telephone companies had sent their best technicians and scientists to check out the situation. One after the other, they walked away scratching their heads, baffled. None could find a plausible explanation for the mysterious blackout zone or explain why, in spite of it, every afternoon, anywhere between three and five p.m., the signal strength in Crumbly mysteriously surged and became as strong as in midtown Manhattan. And why, by five o'clock at the latest, the World Wide Web again became as inaccessible as the moon.

But that small window of access allowed Jamie Crenshaw to stay in the house she had been born and raised in and that she had inherited from her parents . . . which now, because of the town's depressed state and remote location, had become virtually worthless on the real estate market. Jamie couldn't afford to abandon her old home, but fortunately those couple of hours a day of internet access were sufficient to allow her to stay and conduct her business from Crumbly.

On the other hand, no internet hadn't turned out to be the worst thing in the world. Without it, Wally and his friends couldn't spend all their free time with eyes glued to their computers, TV sets, and smart phones and were forced instead to rely on their imaginations, ingenuity, and each other for entertainment. Practically no one in Crumbly owned a cell phone unless their work took them out of town with any regularity. She and Wally had moved back where she had been born after her husband, Wally's dad, had died, one of the thousands of victims of the Lincoln City Invasion.

Her decision to return hadn't been based entirely on the economics of a rent-free home and low local taxes. She'd made the move for Wally's sake. He'd been through enough already and the slow, unplugged pace of Crumbly seemed to have done wonders for him in the years following his father's death.

Maybe when their financial situation, or

Crumbly's fortunes, improved they could sell the old house and move back to the city, but for the time being they were doing fine where they were.

WALLY TURNED RIGHT AT the top of the stairs and paused to give the life-size poster of Hyperion on his door a smart salute before entering his bedroom.

Or, as he liked to call it, the Whiz Kid's Secret Sanctuary and Trophy Room!

The walls were decorated with posters of all his favorite heroes, while various action figures of the supers lined tabletops and bookshelves, most of which were crammed with schoolbooks, his favorite novels, and his not inconsiderable collections of books, fanzines, magazines, and comic books about the supers. He crossed straight to his desk and sat down at the computer. He flipped open the lid, glancing as he did at the small, charred nut and bolt that sat in a small, plastic display cube on the shelf over his desk, between his scale model of Mister Justice's weapon belt and a reproduction of the Knave's slingshot.

The Whiz Kid's trophy!

He'd gotten it the day he'd decided he wanted to be a super. He had been eight years old, on vacation in Washington, DC, with his parents. They had just visited the Washington

Monument and were crossing the Mall to see the White House. All of a sudden, what seemed like every police car in the world went screaming past them toward Pennsylvania Avenue. They later learned that Doctor Psycon had hidden a bomb on the White House grounds, threatening to set it off if his fellow members of the League of Villains weren't released from prison. The bomb would also detonate if anyone tried to enter or leave the executive mansion, trapping the president inside.

Suddenly, Hyperion appeared over the Senate building. Wally would never forget the electric thrill of that moment, seeing for himself the mighty hero streaking through the air like a jet. But that sight proved to be nothing compared to what came next.

Hyperion, muscles rippling under his bright blue costume, swooped down toward the White House and, without slowing, ripped one of a row of hedges from the grounds. The crowd gasped as they saw that instead of roots, a large, metallic device trailed from beneath it. A bomb!

Hyperion sped straight up, almost faster than the eye could follow. As he flew, he whipped the bush and bomb around, like a pitcher winding up for a pitch. Then, as little more than a distant speck against the sky, he released the bomb, hurtling it higher still.

An instant later, the sky exploded in a flash of fire, the burst followed by the distant thunder of the blast.

Wally stared up into the sky, his mouth and eyes open wide with wonder. He had seen plenty of super exploits online and on TV, but to see it for real, in person, made his head spin. That moment, Wally Crenshaw decided he would one day become a super himself.

He couldn't look away from the sky until, a few seconds later, he heard a sound behind him, the sharp *plink* of metal striking concrete. He turned and saw the partially fused nut and bolt bouncing as it hit the ground. He realized, it must have come off of Doctor Psycon's bomb!

Wally quickly scooped up the treasure and shoved it in his pocket. It was still warm from the explosion, but he kept his fingers wrapped firmly around it. Hyperion had touched this! And now it belonged to *him*. He couldn't imagine, then or now, owning anything more amazing than that twisted, fused hunk of metal. His dad had grabbed him then, running with everybody else to get clear of the scene as Hyperion swept down to meet Doctor Psycon's cybernetically suited minions in the hand-to-hand finale that landed the evil doctor in prison alongside the very evil companions he had been trying to free.

Almost a year later, his dad had been one of the thousands who had died in the invasion of Lincoln City by the other-dimensional F'harah warriors. Dad shouldn't have even been in Lincoln, but the plane bringing him home from California had been forced to land there when the invaders' dimensional warps had started appearing in the skies over the United States. It had been bad luck and worse timing that he'd ended up there, at ground zero for the F'harah's demonstration of their superior alien weaponry.

One day, Wally would have souvenirs of his own exploits, but until then, this fused hunk of metal remained Wally's most precious possession.

That, and his memories of his dad.

He logged on and, after quickly checking in on Facebook, went to his favorite supers website to check the latest superhero news. Who had captured who. What villains were jailed where, and which ones had staged breakouts. Databases of all the heroes and villains. Sightings of the newest members of the super community. Costume changes. News of their exploits. And the forums, where fans like Wally could spend hours discussing the news and their favorite heroes.

WhzKid:	Hi, gang. What's new?
Hyperfan554:	Hiya, Wally.
WhzKid:	Hi, Dave. What's going on?
PrncssLil:	We were just talking about the Knave.
WhzKid:	What about him?
Hyperfan554:	He's disappeared! Hasn't been seen in two weeks.
WhzKid:	Maybe he's on a mission with the JB?
Toddmann:	Negative. Spokesman for brigade told National Mask he's not.
PrncssLil:	Hyperfan thinks he's undercover on secret mission!
Toddmann:	That's dumb. Knave doesn't *do* undercover.
Hyperfan554:	:-(Not dumb! Just a guess.
Whzkid:	Maybe recovering from his last battle with Origami?
Kewldude:	Nope. Saw him on news after that fight & he looked OK.
Toddmann:	Maybe Sledgehammer Sue finally got him! She vowed revenge last time he arrested her and she broke out of prison last month.
PrncssLil:	Maybe. Sue's pretty tough.
Kewldude:	Yeh. And Knave's pretty lame. Her sledgehammer vs. his knockout whoopee cushion? No contest.
WhzKid:	:-p I *like* Knave!!!
Hyperfan554:	Hyperion rulz!

PrncssLil:	!!!!!!Ms. Muscles!!!!!!
WhzKid:	Cmon! Knave doesn't have superpowers, just using wits & gimmicks he's taken down some pretty tough baddies!
Hyperfan554:	<grin!> Wally's always been a sucker for no-powers guys like Knave and Mr. Justice. Anybody can be a no-power.
Toddmann:	WHAT???? Comparing Mr. Justice to Knave??? No way! Mr. J the coolest!!!

Wally thought the supers were all cool. Just putting on a mask and cape and going out to fight crime made them special, with or without powers. Anyway, heroes like Hyperion and Ms. Muscles were almost invulnerable, but guys like the Knave and Mr. Justice were regular people who could be hurt. Didn't that make them *extra* brave?

Wally typed a farewell to his online friends and then went to Knave's Wiki entry.

THE KNAVE

Base of Operations:	New York City.
Alter Ego:	Unknown
First Appearance:	Five years ago.
Costume Colors:	Red, yellow, orange.

Group Affiliations: The Justice Brigade (founding member)

Superpowers: None. Competent acrobat and hand-to-hand combatant. Relies on gadgets and weapons based on toy novelty items

Known Associates: Fakeout (frequent team-ups), Aquina (suspected romantic link), Blend, Hyperion, Swift, Ms. Muscles, Mr. Justice

Known Civilian Associates: Diana Walker (reporter, New York Daily *Eagle*), Professor Harold Santiago (inventor), Charles Harris (reporter, *National Mask*)

Origin: According to a feature article and interview with the Knave by Charles Harris in the *National Mask* (July 19, 2019 issue), the Knave's father owned a company that made toys, gag gifts, gimmicks, and novelty items. The Knave's father loved his work and frequently brought home new items to test on his son. The boy came to hate his father's whoopee cushions, bamboo finger-cuffs, exploding chewing gum packages, rubber bugs, etc., and they quickly entered into an escalating war of practical jokes (the Knave admitted to once filling his father's new car with tapioca pudding). Finally, Knave devised his secret identity, using modified versions of his father's creations to become a criminal and discredit whoopee cushions once and for all. But when it came time to break the law, the Knave found himself unable to go through with his plan. Instead, he ended up fighting a gang of (non-powered) criminals who were, coincidentally, trying to rob the same bank he had targeted. One year later, the Knave became one of the founding members of the Justice Brigade.

Rogues Gallery: Sledgehammer Sue, Origami, Crimewave, The Distractor, The Fool

Wally stared at the screen. What *had* happened to the Knave? He didn't expect to find any answer here, but that didn't make him any less curious. What could make someone give up being a super? Had he been hurt? Abducted? Did he suffer from amnesia? No one seemed to know.

Wally glanced at the screen clock; he would be losing his internet connection any minute. He quickly checked his email and, before logging off, went into one last area of the website, "On the Loose," which featured updates of escaped supervillains. Some of these guys escaped from prison so frequently Wally wondered why they even bothered to lock them up anymore.

The new window opened on his computer screen, and at its top the word "ALERT!" flashed in big, red letters over the image of a man, dark, unshaven, with staring, scary black eyes. Wally quickly scanned the data under the picture.

Brendan McMahon
aka THE ACCELERATOR
Escaped yesterday, Rahway State Prison. Last seen driving gray car with New York State license plates, headed south on New Jersey Thruway.
Height: 6'1" Weight: 190 Hair: Black Eyes: Black
No distinguishing marks.

Wally sucked in his breath, his eyes going wide.

The man he had seen outside the old Wicker house. Dark hair and eyes. The right height and weight... and the car! The gray car with New York plates. And Crumbly lay to the *south* of Rahway State Prison.

"Oh, wow," Wally breathed. He wished he had gotten a better look at the man on Kane Street. He couldn't swear they were the same person... "But come *on*," he muttered out loud. He didn't have to be a super detective like Mr. Justice to figure this one out! He quickly scanned the rest of the screen.

WARNING!
Accelerator is extremely dangerous! Do not approach! If spotted, contact your local police or the US Super-Villain Task Force at 1-800-555-EVIL or on Facebook, Twitter, or Instagram. Accelerator possesses the power to speed up molecular decay around any area he touches. Though he uses this power primarily to age objects in the commission of crimes, he has been known to utilize his time-speed touch on people.

But what would bring the Accelerator to Crumbly? There couldn't be anything worth the attention of a major villain like him in town. Unless he needed a place to hide out while he worked out his next evil plot. That kind of made sense. Who would ever think to look for him in Crumbly?

Wally scrolled back up to the Accelerator's picture and hit the "print" command, waiting while his color printer spit out a hard copy of the alert. He logged out and sat staring at it.

The Accelerator. In Crumbly!

At least it seemed pretty likely. Maybe. He should probably be absolutely positive before he said anything.

"Which means," he said in his deep, super-voice, "that tonight, the Whiz Kid is on the prowl again!"

4

"LET'S DO THIS INSIDE, Charlie," the man said in a low, threatening voice.

Charlie Harris stared up at him. "I just got..." he stammered, "I mean, how'd you get here before me?"

The man reached down to give Charlie a helping hand. "I said, inside," he rumbled.

Charlie waved off the offered hand and started squirming his rump out of the hole in the porch floor. "I heard you. I just don't care," he grumbled. "Answer my question, Willard."

The man angrily yanked off his sunglasses and flashed Charlie Harris an angry glare, then glanced quickly up and down the street, as though afraid of being overheard. "Don't call me that," he snapped.

Charlie swung the left side of his rear end up onto solid ground and grunted. "I asked how you found me? Crumbly's hardly on most maps and believe me, I took the long way around getting here to make sure no one followed me."

The man leaned against the doorframe and crossed thick, muscular arms over his chest. "I didn't follow you," he said. "I... looked it up."

Charlie paused in his struggle to free the last part of his trapped right cheek from the hole and stared at the man. "Looked it up? Where?"

For the first time, the man he called Willard seemed to lose some of his confidence. "Um," he said. "Online. Where, you know, where I look stuff up."

"Like *where*?" Charlie demanded. "Did you go to a website called 'Places Charlie Harris Might Run Away To dot com' or something?"

"I have my resources."

Charlie managed to free the rest of his rear and scrambled to his feet. "You've got files on us, don't you, Willard!" he demanded.

"My name's *not*—"

"I thought so! You *do* keep files on us, don't you?"

Willard avoided his eyes.

"Tell me the truth, Willard," Charlie demanded.

The man nodded. Then he quickly turned and slid into the house. Charlie followed.

"Who?" he asked. "Which ones of us?"

The man frowned. "I don't think I should be discussing this."

"*Which* ones?"

"This is inappropriate, Charlie. I've got my—"

"None? Some? *All*?"

"I can't comment—"

"Oh, wow," Charlie said, eyes wide with surprise. "It's all of us, isn't it?

"If word got out…"

Charlie started laughing. "Yeah. If word got out to the rest of the Justice Brigade that their friend and colleague Mr. Justice kept secret files on them, they'd line up to take turns kicking the snot out of you."

"Look, Charlie," Mr. Justice said, drawing himself up to his full height. "Maybe Hyperion or Ms. Muscles could take me down. *Maybe* … but they're not here right now." He closed his left hand over his right fist, squeezing it until his knuckles popped with a sound like a string of firecrackers. "It's just you. And me. And as I seem to recall from that time Doctor Psycon turned the members of the Justice Brigade against one another, Mr. Justice can put a hurting on the Knave without even breaking a sweat."

"Oh. Yeah." Charlie grinned weakly. "I remember."

"So do we sit down and talk nicely, or does

this turn into a rerun of the Knave's most humiliating beatings?"

"Since you put it that way, have a seat, Willard," Charlie said with an elaborate bow.

Mr. Justice's hand clamped around Charlie's throat before it even registered on him that the other man had moved.

"*Ghak!*" Charlie said.

"One last thing we need to get straight, Charlie," Justice hissed. "You are not to call me *that* name."

"You mean *Willard?*" Charlie Harris' voice squeaked past Mr. Justice's vise-like grip.

"I mean," he said, his face turning red, "that *name*. You are not to use it. You are a ridiculous little man who wears pointy shoes and fights with whoopee cushions, and I will not be mocked by you. Is that understood, Charlie?"

Charlie nodded. Quickly.

Mr. Justice opened his fingers and Charlie sucked in a bunch of air. As annoyed as he felt that Justice had found him, it shouldn't have been a surprise. The dark, intense man could be counted among the world's greatest detectives, a man trained from childhood to follow in the footsteps of his father, fabled New York police detective, Lt. William W. (for William) Williams, Sr. Killed in the line of duty by an unknown assassin on his son William W. Williams, Jr.'s seventh birthday, the boy blew out the candles on his cake to seal his vow to become a cop and avenge his dad's death.

William, Jr., aced the academy entrance exam and course work and probably laughed his way through the physical requirements; he had trained his mind to focus on nothing but police work and his body to the peak of physical perfection. On the streets, Officer Williams quickly grew into a smart, brave, and resourceful cop; in his first two years on the job, he racked up an impressive arrest record, leading to his promotion to the plainclothes division, a step on the way to a detective's badge.

But Williams had a problem with police work. There were too many rules and regulations preventing him from being as efficient a crimefighter as he knew he could be. Carrying a badge meant sticking to those rules. But going out by himself, wearing a costume instead of a badge... that was another thing.

Which is when William, Jr., came up with the idea of another kind of uniform, the costumed alter ego of Mr. Justice, to continue his quest for vengeance. He spent the next six years investigating, tracking down, and bringing his brand of justice to those responsible for the death of his father.

And for some reason, Charlie thought with grim amusement, he *chose* this borderline crazy teammate to tease. Right after the founding members of the Justice Brigade—himself, along with Fakeout, Aquina, Blend, Hyperion, Swift, Ms. Muscles, and Mr. Justice—revealed their secret identities to one another, Charlie decided that Justice had a few too many Williams in his name, so he started calling him Willard. When he saw how much it annoyed Justice, Charlie just couldn't stop. Mr. Uptight-Justice tried as hard as he could not to let Charlie know it bothered him, forcing Charlie to increase his efforts. Round and round it went, until Justice's anger had spilled over during the aforementioned Dr. Psycon incident.

Justice had used that as an excuse to hand Charlie his head, making the smaller man all the more determined to rub it in. If he couldn't give Justice as good as he got in a fight, he could at least try his best to drive him crazy.

Admittedly, a short trip.

But then, I *am* the Knave, Charlie thought. A certain amount of wackiness came with the territory.

Charlie caught himself. Correction: He *used* to be the Knave. He had quit, retired from the hero business. From now on and forever, he would be just plain old Charlie Harris, writer and journalist.

"Let's talk," Charlie said, leading his ex-teammate into the house.

The inside looked every bit as desperate as Charlie had feared based on the dilapidated exterior. Covered by a fairly substantial layer of dust, floorboards were warped and cracked from exposure to the elements, let into the house through the broken windows. The walls were stained and full of holes and what wallpaper remained hung in strips peeling away from the plaster. The ceiling had collapsed in several locations, with debris floating in puddles of water from a leak that had gone unchecked for years. The furniture, timeworn but sturdy old pieces, looked like they belonged in the living room of an eighty-two-year-old woman. Which, in fact, his aunt had been.

Charlie dropped onto the arm of an overstuffed sofa and looked toward Mr. Justice. "So how did you find me, Willa— Willie."

Mr. Justice sat in a dusty easy chair. "When you inherited this house, the deed got entered in the county's real estate records. My computers periodically scan all municipal databases for certain key names. Members of the brigade included."

"To spy on your teammates," Charlie said.

"Real estate transactions are public records. I'm not spying. I'm just keeping a watchful eye on everybody." Mr. Justice pointed a finger at Charlie. "And it's a good thing I do, otherwise you would have just disappeared for good."

"As per my plan, yes, Willie." Charlie rubbed his forehead, expecting a headache in his immediate future. "Look, I told Hyperion all about it, okay? We shook hands. He said goodbye and wished me luck and everything. I quit the Justice Brigade. I quit being the Knave. I just . . . quit."

"How can you quit the quest for justice, Charlie?" the dark-haired man said.

"Three reasons," Charlie said, ticking off each point on his fingers. "First, I'm not an obsessed psychopath like *some* people. Second, in case you hadn't noticed, I am, at best, mediocre at the job."

"I noticed," Justice said.

"Thanks. And third, my favorite reason of all: It *hurts*! Criminals don't like getting caught and sent to prison. They hit and kick and throw things and try to blow me up and shoot at me and zap me with all kinds of secret weapons and death rays. One guy threw *spears* at me! I got tired of always getting hurt. I don't *like* getting hurt."

"Pain is the price we pay for justice," said the master detective.

"You pay it," Charlie said. "I quit."

"The brigade needs you," Justice said.

"Two seconds ago, you called me a ridiculous little man and made fun of my whoopee cushions and pointy shoes. Which, by the way, are pointy *flying* shoes!" Charlie sniffed.

Mr. Justice laughed without humor. "Don't act like I hurt your feelings, Charlie. We both know you're only a little better than nothing… but *anything* is better than nothing. The war on crime needs every soldier it can get."

"Wow." Charlie shook his head. "See reason number one, above, that thing about *not* being nuts? I don't care, Willie. I did my duty, now I'm hanging up my ridiculous pointy shoes and walking off into the sunset. Well, technically, I took the bus."

"You can't."

"I can and I did. Now, are we done here?" Charlie swiped his hand across the top of an end table next to the sofa. He held up his dust-covered fingers. "I am *so* behind in my housework."

Mr. Justice stood. "You can't turn your back on the brigade, Knave!"

Charlie rose and whirled around, turning his back toward Mr. Justice. "Wrong again, Mr. Justice."

Willie shook his head and glared. "This isn't over yet, Charlie. Once a super, always a super," he proclaimed, then glanced at his wristwatch.

"Yeah, it's getting late, Willie. Shouldn't you be hitting the road."

"Um, say, Charlie," Willie said. "Since it *is* getting late and it's a long drive back to New York, would you mind if, you know, I crashed here tonight?"

Charlie shook his head and sighed. "Yeah, sure, why not? Make yourself at home. But on one condition."

"Which is . . . ?"

"You don't talk to me."

"Hah," Mr. Justice snorted. "It'll be my pleasure."

Charlie nodded. He couldn't very well kick the man out, could he? Well, thinking about it, he could, but what the heck? Give the big stiff a break, then send him back to skulking around alleyways and on rooftops looking for bad guys to beat up. As long as he and the brigade were out of Charlie's life, he could stand having the guy around a few hours more.

His new life could wait until morning to start.

5

"WHAT ARE YOU TALKING about, Wally?" Benny Sachem demanded.

"The Accelerator," Wally Crenshaw hissed into the telephone. "He's here!"

"The Accelerator's at your house?"

"No, you dope, in Crumbly."

Benny Sachem didn't answer right away and, from the sounds of chewing coming over the line, Wally guessed he had caught his best friend in the middle of dinner. Wally had raced impatiently through his meal, wolfing down his food and answering his mother's conversational overtures in hurried monosyllables. The dark, angry visage of the Accelerator had burned into his brain and he could hardly wait to get over to the Wicker house and see if the picture he had printed matched the face he had seen skulking around Kane Street.

"Right," said Benny, after he swallowed. "You mean like the time you caught Riotgear checking out Hootie's gas station?"

Wally reddened with embarrassment at the memory. He frowned and glanced over at his mother as she loaded the dinner dishes into the dishwasher. "That was different," he whispered. "And you promised we weren't gonna talk about that anymore."

"Well, you promised you wouldn't drag me into any more of your super-duper games," Benny said. "Besides, Sheriff Cunningham will kill you if you report this to him. I mean, after last time..."

Wally's voice got way whinier than he would have liked it to be when he said, "How did I know the guy was a state senator? Riding that motorcycle and wearing a leather jacket, he *looked* just like Riotgear..."

"Anyway," Benny said, "I'm supposed to hang out with Brenda tonight."

"Great! We'll all hang out together," Wally said. "On Kane Street. You know, maybe around the old Wicker place. And if we *happen* to see anything suspicious..."

Benny groaned. "Okay, okay, but I'm warning you, dude, you even think of calling Sheriff Cunningham because the pizza delivery guy looks like a supervillain, I'll kill you myself."

"I promise. No sheriff. I just want to check it out."

"Okay, Whiz Kid. Let's hook up on Main Street in a half hour."

Wally smiled and hung up the phone. He had the wanted poster and now he had two witnesses to back him up if he turned out to be right.

"What are you up to tonight?" Mrs. Crenshaw asked.

"Nothing much," he shrugged on his way out the door. "Just going to hang out with Benny and Brenda." And, just maybe, he thought, capture a super-dangerous, escaped villain! Talk about kicking off his career as a super with a bang!

CHARLIE HARRIS STEPPED OUT onto the back porch of his aunt's house. Correction. Onto the back porch of *his* house.

He set his coffee mug down on the railing. It collapsed under the weight.

"Okay, so it still needs a little work," he murmured.

Well, what if it did? He had retired from the supers biz. Now he could be plain old Charlie Harris, freelance writer about the supers community for the *National Mask* and other publications. And with a sweet, freshly signed contract for a series of books about his ex-super colleagues, he had all the time in the world to fix the old place up.

Even with Mr. Justice camped out on the sofa in the parlor, finishing up the last of half a dozen frozen dinners that Feeno Mullins had brought over earlier. He'd told Charlie that since no one ever moved to Crumbly, the town didn't have an official welcoming committee, but if it did, he liked to think he would be a member of it. With that, he presented Charlie with two sacks of groceries, courtesy of Ma and Pa O'Casey at the general store. When Charlie tried to thank him, Feeno told him to tell it to the welcoming committee.

All in all, Charlie felt at peace.

Peace. A strange feeling that Charlie hadn't felt in a long time. As a kid, he'd had to put up with his father's nerve-wracking pranks, and as an adult, he constantly worried about somebody uncovering his secret identity, or about the next fight with a villain. And then he had the aggravation of trying to have a real life when he never knew what potentially fatal mission he would have to take off on with the brigade, usually in the middle of a date or when he had an article or story due. How could he meet a tight magazine deadline when he had to go running off to fight mole men at the center of the Earth or a mob trying to simultaneously rob every bank in town? He'd never stopped being surprised he kept getting assignments. It probably didn't hurt that, as Knave, he belonged to the very superhero community he covered, giving him access to insider scoops that made up for his lack of punctuality.

But that had been his old life. Now and forever going forward, he was Charles Harris, gentleman writer and peaceful resident of quaint Crumbly-by-the-Sea.

"Charlie!" Mr. Justice called from inside.

Charlie closed his eyes and sighed. "Yes, Willie?"

"Is there anything for dessert?"

Tomorrow morning, he told himself. He'll be gone in the morning. And, out loud, he said, in a tone of voice usually reserved for conversations with six-year-olds, "Who wants cupcakes and milk?"

Mr. Justice said, "Oh, boy!"

WALLY, BENNY SACHEM, AND Brenda Cunningham gathered at the north end of Kane Street to watch the dirty gray car parked at the end of the block.

"See," Wally said. "The Accelerator's car is still here."

"Cool," Benny said. "The actual Accelerator-mobile!"

Brenda poked him in the ribs with her elbow, "Cut it out, Benny. How do you know it's not?"

Benny glanced at his girlfriend, then at Wally. "You're kidding?"

Wally took the folded wanted poster from the pocket of his shorts and held it out to Benny. "All I want to do is see if the guy in this picture's the same as the guy who belongs to that car."

Benny opened the poster and looked at it. Brenda peeked over his shoulder. "New York license plates, gray car."

"Two for two," said Wally.

"Unless it just happens to be a gray car from New York," said Benny.

"Work with us here, Benny," Brenda said.

Wally started to walk down the quiet street. "Come on," he whispered to his friends.

"Where?" Benny asked.

"That's *not* working with us," Brenda said, and yanked on Benny's arm.

"C'mon, Brenda," he pleaded. "Don't tell me you believe any of this stuff."

Brenda shrugged and said, softly so Wally couldn't hear, "No. But Wally does. And if it's important to him, then as his friends it's important we believe with him. Okay?"

Benny nodded. "Okay. But I still get to make fun of him, don't I? If I don't make fun of him, he'll think I don't like him."

Even as he walked a half dozen paces ahead of his friends, Wally tried formulating a plan of action. He couldn't just go up and ring the doorbell. If that car did belong to Accelerator and Wally unmasked him, he might . . . well, *accelerate* him. They needed a distraction, something to draw the occupant inside the house outside where Wally could get a good look at him. He wished he had some firecrackers. Setting off a string of firecrackers on the front porch would get him out in a hurry. Or a siren! Yeah, a nice loud siren would sure do the trick.

"So got a plan, Whiz Kid?" Brenda asked.

Wally shook his head. "Not unless you've got any firecrackers with you. Or a siren."

Benny rolled his eyes. "Maybe you can ask Brenda's dad if you can borrow his," he said, ignoring his girlfriend's withering look.

"We just need to get a look at the guy," Wally muttered.

The slow-moving trio came up alongside the dirt-splattered gray car. Brenda glanced at it, tapping her chin thoughtfully. "We could," she said, slowly, "just knock on the door."

"We could," Wally said, his eyes practically bugging out of his head, "if we all wanted to get *accelerated*!"

"He's not going to accelerate a kid," Brenda said, as she went skipping up the front walk to 254 Kane Street.

"Brenda!" Wally hissed.

"Don't!" Benny called.

Brenda ignored them, stepping around the ragged hole in the porch and pausing only briefly to look back and throw them a sweet smile before rapping her knuckles on the weather-beaten front door. Wally and Benny, in a sudden fit of not knowing what to do with themselves, collided with one another three times before charging around to the street side of the gray car and ducking down to hide just as the front door swung open.

CHARLIE HARRIS, THE CHOCOLATE frosting from the partially eaten cupcake in his hand at the corner of his mouth, looked at Brenda and smiled. "Hello," he said.

"Hi, mister," she said. "I saw your car and thought maybe you wanted it washed."

Charlie glanced at the car, wondering why there were the tops of two heads bobbing around behind it. "Sorry, kid," he said. "It's not my car. Belongs to the guy visiting me."

"Maybe he wants it washed?"

"I doubt it," Charlie said. "Sorry. But, hey, you want a cupcake? I've got plenty."

Brenda said, "I don't think so, thank you. So could you ask your friend?"

Charlie took a bite from his cupcake. "What's your name?"

"Brenda," she said, adding, "My dad's the sheriff."

He smiled and watched the two heads hiding behind Willie's car. "And a fine, dedicated lawman he is, I'm sure. My name's Charlie Harris. I just moved in."

"Did your friend drive you here?" Brenda said. He saw her trying to peek over his shoulder for a glimpse inside.

"No," Charlie said. "Well, look, it's been nice meeting you. I'll see you and your friends around, okay?"

"Sure, okay. Well, welcome to Crumbly, I guess," she said slowly, trying for one last look.

Even as Charlie closed the door, Brenda's eyes continued to look beyond him.

"Weird kids in this town," he said with a sad shake of his head.

WALLY HAD BEEN HOLDING his breath, trying to hear the conversation between Brenda and the man at the door. He had caught only the quickest of glimpses before ducking out of view behind the car, but he'd seen enough to know she hadn't been talking to the Accelerator . . . though he had a feeling he'd seen that face before.

"I thought, Benny," Brenda's voice floated over the hood of the car, "you don't believe the Accelerator is in there."

Benny and Wally looked up. Brenda stood

with one hand on the hood of the car, smiling down at her cowering friends.

"I don't," Benny said defensively. "Wally just freaked me out."

"So?" Wally demanded.

"So," she said, "he saw you guys hiding behind the car, which doesn't belong to him but to a friend who *didn't* drive him here and, no, I didn't get a look at him. His friend, I mean."

"Then it *could* be the Accelerator in there!"

"Or, it could have been his cousin Bob," Benny said.

Wally ignored Benny again. "The guy at the door might be one of his henchmen."

Brenda looked doubtful. "I don't think so. He offered me a cupcake. Besides, he said it's his house. His name is Charlie Harris."

Wally's mouth dropped open. He blinked once. Then again.

Charlie Harris!

And then his face split into the biggest smile it could hold.

"My friends," Wally boomed in his super-voice, "the adventure has just begun!"

6

STEVE GREY STOOD ON the northwest corner of Madison Avenue and Fifty-Seventh Street in New York City, waiting for the light to change from red to green. While he waited, he glanced at his watch every few seconds and impatiently tapped his foot. Traffic crawled by. Not that they were in any great hurry. No, why should they be? the tall, well-dressed lanky man with a shaved head thought. These blasted traffic lights took forever anyway. He looked again at his watch.

Two seconds had passed.

Would this *never* end?

Steve fidgeted. Steve looked uptown. He looked downtown. He tapped his foot. The light stayed red. The second hand of his wristwatch seemed to strain toward the next second, an eternity separating every tick and tock of the clock. He tried to read the headlines of the newspaper a man held open beside him, but he'd read this paper already.

Three seconds more.

Steve growled in frustration. He couldn't stand still another second and, too fast for any human eye to see, he appeared across the street, on the southeast corner of Madison Avenue and Fifty-Seventh Street.

"Whew!"

Steve Grey could not stand inactivity, could barely even tolerate the normal pace of the world. To his senses, everything appeared to move in slow motion, but only because his senses were attuned to functioning at the amazing speeds he could reach as the hero known as Swift. Someone once joked that the last time the Silver Bullet of Speed tried timing himself, he had hit the button on the timer, circled the Earth, and arrived back to hit the button again, almost slapping his hand. Not quite that fast, he nonetheless found anything less than hyperspeed left him feeling frustrated, especially when he had to slow down to interact with the rest of the world.

The plain, steel-and-glass Wheeler-Nicholson Building remained one of the most famous structures in midtown Manhattan. It may have been dwarfed by the towering granite Empire State Building a mile south of its location, and the sparkling art deco Chrysler

Building to its east, but neither of these landmarks could rival the Wheeler-Nicholson for its famous tenants.

Seven years ago, New York's super community had gathered in Central Park following their united defeat of the villainous Sir Immorto and voted to form a team. Hyperion, Mr. Justice, Ms. Muscles, Swift, Fakeout, Aquina, the Knave, and Blend joined hands that night on the Sheep Meadow, swearing to stand forever united in the face of evil, injustice, and tyranny. A grateful city turned the midtown skyscraper, left unfinished when its builders had gone bankrupt, over to the heroes, who customized its top twelve floors to serve as their headquarters. Containing everything from a command center to sleeping quarters to a launch pad for their sub-orbital transport, the *Screaming Eagle*, the Justice Brigade set up shop in the very heart of New York.

After the fourth time the brigade's headquarters were attacked by supervillains, leading to tens of millions of dollars of damage to private property, the disruption of Fifth Avenue for a week, and the closing of the Sixth Avenue subway line for almost a month, the mayor thought better of having the team *in* town. The City Council hastily but with deep regret banned super-organization headquarters inside the city limits.

Steve strode quickly through the double glass doors of 575 Madison Avenue. New space had been found for the brigade on Goodman's Island, about twenty-five miles up the Hudson River. The former military watch post served the team far better than had the old midtown location and proved infinitely easier to defend against attack. But, while the upper floors of the Wheeler-Nicholson Building had been turned into a museum dedicated to the team the city had evicted from its confines, the brigade still routinely used the old thirtieth-floor conference room for regular meetings.

Steve glanced at the bank of elevators to his left, a shudder passing through him as he thought of the endless crawl of that little cage up its shaft, stopping on each and every floor for an eternity to load and unload slow-moving passengers...

Before he could finish that thought, he had raced up the stairwell and pressed his palm against the blank wall of the thirtieth-floor landing. The wall glowed briefly as the hidden security device scanned his handprint, and then, with a soft mechanical sigh, opened to admit the speedster.

"Let's get this meeting on the road," Steve Grey called as he stepped into the conference room. Somewhere between the words "meeting" and "on," he had changed into the sleek silver costume of Swift.

IF SOMEONE HAD SET out to create the very epitome of a superhero, odds are they would have come up with someone exactly like Hyperion: six feet tall, two hundred and twenty pounds of solid muscle, his handsome face and chiseled features always ready with an easy, reassuring smile, his very presence radiating confidence and strength. Hard to believe that when not battling evil as Earth's mightiest super, he lived the quiet life of Guy Wallace, mild-mannered pharmacist.

But looking at him standing in his formfitting, bright blue, spandex costume, and short, yellow cape that seemed to flutter behind him even in the absence of a breeze, Hyperion looked to be everything a super should be.

"Have a seat, Swift," Hyperion said. "We're about to begin."

In a bit of irony that did not escape the speedster, he saw that all but two members had arrived, making him almost late.

"Mr. Justice is on a leave of absence," Hyperion said, his super-senses picking up on Swift's look around the table. "And Knave, it's my sad duty to announce, has tendered his resignation from the team."

Swift went from the doorway to his seat at

the large round conference table in the blink of an eye. "Knave quit?" he asked in surprise.

Aquina, the aquatic heroine from an undersea kingdom that claimed a lineage stretching back to legendary Atlantis, gasped. Her skin the soft blue of the Caribbean waters and her hair like silken strands of seaweed, Aquina's beauty shone through on land or beneath the sea.

She grasped the edge of the conference table. "Resigned?" she said in disbelief. "That can't be. Charlie wouldn't... surely not without talking to *me*."

Swift felt uncomfortable for the aquatic beauty. They all knew Aquina and Charlie Harris had pursued a long-term, more off-than-on relationship. Raised in the sunken land of Aquinus, the Mighty Mermaid possessed incredible physical strength that enabled her to survive the ocean's crushing depths and a psychic link with all the fish of the sea, but making a go of it with a landlocked prankster seemed to be a power she could never master.

But that probably didn't stop her from loving him, Swift thought sadly.

"Ain't that just like that clown," Betsy Romano, better known as Ms. Muscles, snapped, pounding her black work-gloved fist on the table. "Bye-bye. Hasta la vista, baby. See ya around, sweetheart!"

Hyperion made a calming gesture with his hands. "Knave had his reasons and I'm sure," he said, casting a sympathetic glance at Aquina, "that he'll find the right time and place for all appropriate explanations and farewells."

Ms. Muscles hefted her six-foot, seven-inch frame to its full height, the thick, sharply defined muscles cording in the arm she pointed at Aquina. "You wanna know what to tell him when he comes around, girlfriend?" the genetically altered super-woman said. "You tell him—"

"—that there are plenty of other *fish* in the sea!" Blend, hooted, unable to restrain himself.

Swift shook his head, too fast for the object of his displeasure to see. Blend had been born with incredible powers of mind control, a unique psychic ability that manifested itself in his ability to cloud the minds of his opponents. In his all-white costume, he could render himself invisible to the eyes of a room full of foes, or make every individual believe they were looking at their fathers, or staring into the gaping mouth of their worst nightmares. Among the many talents the television sitcom writer and former stand-up comedian Norman Gerber lacked would be his inability to keep his mouth shut. If you needed a guy to say the wrong thing at the wrong time, you could always count on Blend.

Aquina choked back a sob and ran from the table and the room, leaving a trail of moist footprints on the floor.

Ms. Muscles glared at the master of minds. "Y'know what you are, Blend? You're an idiot!"

"I know you are, but what am I?" said Blend in a high, singsong voice.

"Can we just get back to business?" asked Fakeout impatiently. "Some of us have lives outside these costumes, y'know."

Fakeout, with the power to sidestep one minute backward or forward through time, made his living as plumber Ward Simonson and complained that the time he spent away from his business meant time spent *not* making a living, thereby earning the rather loud and vehement displeasure of his wife. While he would never dream of shirking his super-duty, even in the face of a broken pipe or a water heater emergency, he resented the brigade's every non-combative demand on his time.

"Yes, please," said Hyperion. "The point is, with Knave gone, and Mr. Justice being so, oh, what's the word . . . ?"

"Weird?" offered Blend.

Hyperion shrugged and cleared his throat. "I would have said 'stressed,' but okay. To the degree where I'm not sure we could still count on him in a pinch. That leaves us two members short of a full roster."

"Well, that's never happened before," said Swift. "I mean, the eight of us are all the membership the brigade has ever had or needed."

"We won't be shorthanded," Hyperion said. "I'm making arrangements to interview possible candidates to bolster the roster. I'll have all the pertinent information downloaded to your JB smartphones to read at your leisure. After you've reviewed them, we can meet to choose the best of the available supers before splitting up into teams to interview our choices."

The five brigade members nodded in agreement. Swift had already made it halfway to the door, relieved to be moving again after those several minutes of inactivity, when Hyperion continued, "There's one more item on the agenda before we adjourn." Muttering a curse, Swift made a U-turn back to his seat before anyone knew he had moved.

The Man of Might clicked the remote control again. The graphics on the screen dwindled to a point of light, then flashed back into a split screen divided into thirds. Police mug shots, featuring the faces of two men and one woman, filled each square.

"The Accelerator. Sledgehammer Sue. Professor Lamplighter," Hyperion intoned. "What do these three villains have in common?"

"Besides lame supervillain names?" said Blend.

"All of them escaped custody in the last two months," offered Swift to speed the meeting along, "and haven't been heard from since."

Hyperion nodded. "The USSVTF," he said, referring to the US Super-Villain Task Force, the governmental agency that coordinated local police and federal efforts in the apprehension of super-powered bad guys, "has asked for our help in tracking them down and bringing them back in."

Ms. Muscles flexed her broad shoulders under her black, sleeveless muscle shirt and cracked her knuckles. "Some action. Oh, yeah!" she grinned. The Muscular Maiden liked nothing more than a good supervillain brawl.

Fakeout scowled under his white mask. "Mr. Justice is the trained criminologist of the group."

"Fakeout's got a point," said Swift. "None of us are exactly a threat to Sherlock Holmes. We need someone with a background in criminal investigations for a job like this."

Hyperion spread his hands before him. "Sorry, my friends, but William is out of the picture. We have to work with the team we've got."

Blend looked around the table. "Uh-oh!"

"Hey, Blend," said Ms. Muscles, "you ever consider *shutting up*?"

"Thought it, rejected it," said Blend with a smile.

Ms. Muscles snarled, then reached into the weightlifter belt she wore and, with a flick of her wrist, sent the one-pound metal disc she'd plucked from a pouch flying at Blend's head. Blend laughed as the disc passed harmlessly through him. Still laughing, the image the mind-controlling hero had created for his teammates to see disappeared and the real Blend became visible sitting in Aquina's abandoned seat.

"Nyah-nyah," he said, wiggling his fingers at Ms. Muscles. "Can't hit what's not there!" Blend laughed.

Swift sighed. It seemed every brigade meeting ended like this. Of course, Ms. Muscles had overreacted to Blend. The fleet-footed hero didn't blame Betsy. In fact, with a satisfied grin and faster than thought, Swift raced from his seat and shot across the room to pluck the metal disk from the floor, then whirled to flick it back at Blend before returning to his seat.

The disc smacked Blend in the chest and knocked the still laughing hero to the floor. Ms. Muscles, at first surprised, quickly figured it out, and gave Swift a wink and a thumbs-up.

"Ow," moaned Blend from the floor.

"And," Hyperion said with a heavy sigh, "I suppose that means this meeting is adjourned."

The Man of Might slumped in his seat and put his head in his hands.

Swift raced from the room and, half a second later, emerged from 575 Madison

Avenue, again dressed as Steve Grey. Ten whole minutes at that table. Man! He thought that meeting would never end!

7

"CHARLIE WHO?" BRENDA CUNNINGHAM asked politely.

"Harris! Charlie Harris is, like, only the greatest superhero journalist alive," Wally said. "I've got *all* his books. I've seen him on TV. He's been on CNN. I can't believe he's here in Crumbly and I saw him."

"From behind a car," Benny reminded him.

Wally had not stopped smiling in astonishment since Brenda had spoken the name. If he couldn't have the life of a superhero, having Charlie Harris's would be the next best thing, almost like being a sidekick, or having a backstage pass to the Infinity Crisis set in motion by Professor Mentallo during the last presidential election.

"What would Charlie Harris want in Crumbly?" Wally muttered to himself.

"He lost a bet?" Benny said.

"He's hiding?" Brenda said.

"The other man in the house," Wally said. "Who is he?"

"Why are you asking us?" Benny said. "How are we supposed to know?"

"I'm not *asking* you," Wally said. "I was reviewing the facts of the case, including the questions that we don't have answers to. Yet."

"There's no case, dude," Benny said.

"If it is the Accelerator, then maybe he wants to surrender to Charlie."

Brenda frowned. "Why would he break out of prison to come here and surrender?"

"Yeah, right. That doesn't make sense," Wally said. He sank down to the curb, planting his chin in his hands. "Okay, maybe Accelerator's holding him hostage in there."

"Why would he do that?" Brenda asked as she sat down beside him.

"Don't encourage him, Brenda," Benny moaned.

"Um, so he can negotiate some kind of deal with the Justice Brigade?"

Brenda shrugged. "I don't know. He didn't seem very, you know, hostage-y to me. I mean, he offered me cupcakes..."

"Yeah, but maybe cupcakes are the international signal for 'I'm being held hostage by Wally's imaginary supervillain friends,'" Benny said.

"Maybe he's just interviewing him," Wally said. He had long ago learned to block out his friend's jokes at his expense. He didn't know how Mr. Justice did it, gathering all those little bits of information and clues and sorting through them to solve crimes with detective work. Especially while fighting someone like the Mock Turtle, the Mirthful Terrapin of Terror who, like Benny, never shut up. Except that Mock Turtle talked very slowly.

Brenda nodded. "That makes the most sense. A lot of guys on the run talk to the press."

"'Guys on the run'?" Benny groaned. "Where are we? In one of those stupid old black-and-white movies?"

"I like old movies," said Brenda.

"Me too," Wally agreed. He looked at Brenda and they grinned at each other.

"Swell. Let's go home and watch one. I mean, how much longer are we going to hang out here anyway?" Benny said. "Unless you can think of a way to get whoever's inside to come out so you can get a look at them, there's not much else to do, is there?"

"Get *who* out of *where* to do *what*?" demanded a familiar, sneering voice from behind.

Wally cringed. Could the fates be so cruel as to subject him to Mike Brewer's evil twice in one day? And to have it happen now, when he and his companions were about to embark on a mission.

"We weren't talking to you, Mike," Brenda snapped, not bothering to look at him.

"Yeah, but you were talking on a public

street," said Mike, strutting around in front of where Brenda and Wally sat at the curb, accompanied by the ever-snickering Abel Schotz and Nick McCain, "and since we're the public and we're using the street, that makes it our business."

"Do you even *hear* yourself?" Benny said in disbelief.

"I don't have to hear myself," Mike said. "I already know what I said. Who are we trying to get out of where?"

"Yeah, because how could Mike being involved possibly turn out bad?" Wally muttered to Brenda. He got to his feet and said, "Let's just do this later, okay, guys?"

Benny said, "Fine by me. I don't know how we were supposed to get those guys out of the old Wicker house anyway."

"Is that all you wanna do?" Mike said. He jabbed at Abel and Nick with his elbows and they responded by hooting with delight and pummeling one another. "Why?"

"No, Mike," Wally said. "Come on, no fooling around. We don't even know who those guys are. It could be dangerous. I'm serious."

"The guy writes articles about the supers. You said so yourself. What's he going to do? Poke us with his pencil?" Benny said.

"Not Charlie Harris," Wally said. "The other one. The Accelerator." Even as he said the name, he saw Mike Brewer's reaction and groaned. He clamped his hands over his mouth and thought seriously about killing himself.

"Whoa!" Mike Brewer jabbed a finger at Wally. "You saying the Accelerator, the guy who broke outta prison and fought Swift, *that* Accelerator, is in that house?"

"I didn't say anything," Wally said, his voice muffled by his hands.

"Uh, you kinda did," Benny said.

"You're not helping again," Brenda said.

"You mean," Mike said, "the Accelerator *is* in there?"

"Maybe," Wally said.

"But probably *not*," Benny added.

"Yeah," Wally agreed. "Benny's right. Probably not. We were just messing around anyway. You know how I like to pretend I'm a super and—"

"Oh, no," Mike said, poking his finger in Wally's chest. "You weren't pretending, Crenshaw. You think the Accelerator is holed up in there, don't you?"

Wally shrugged, then grinned helplessly. He didn't lie terribly well. "Well, sort of. Maybe."

"*Now* is when you're going to start believing him?" Brenda said.

"Well, yeah. He says he saw a supervillain," Mike said.

"You mean like in the last week of school?"

Benny offered. "Remember, he thought Ms. Fine in the lunchroom had been possessed by Dr. Weerdscinz and put a zombie potion into the tapioca?"

Mike snorted. "Oh, yeah. I forgot about that."

"Or the time he thought Crumbly had been surrounded by a force field that would shrink the town down to microscopic size and be stolen by the alien warlord K'lang the Clawed?"

Mike frowned in thought. "Wait, did that happen before or after he saw a flying saucer that tuned out to be a weather balloon?"

"No," Benny said impatiently. "He reported the weather balloon thing as an attack by Professor Lamplighter, the nineteenth-century criminal mastermind."

"Right, right," Mike said and laughed. "I remember that."

Wally grabbed Benny's arm. "Dude, you're supposed to be my best friend."

"Hey, I'm on your side," Benny said. "You want to get rid of them, right?"

Wally threw up his hands in surrender.

"Okay, okay," he said. "Looking back on some of those things, maybe I did let my imagination get, y'know, a little ahead of me."

"A little." Mike snorted.

"But not this time. The evidence all points to it almost definitely being—"

Brenda nudged him with her elbow.

"Okay, almost definitely maybe a slight chance that the Accelerator *might* be there. But for sure," Wally said, stepping out of range of Brenda's elbow, "the other guy is, like, the top supers journalist in the country. What's he doing here?"

"What's any of us doing here?" Benny said.

"That's a good question," Mike Brewer said. "Crenshaw's, not yours, Sachem. I mean, I seen that writer guy on TV, so he's gotta be important."

"Right, like Mickey Mouse and Goofy," Benny pointed out.

"Right!" Mike said, Abel and Nick leaning in over his shoulder like obedient dogs waiting for a command. "What's the plan, man?"

Wally blinked. "Huh?"

"The plan, bonehead. What're we gonna do about it?"

Wally looked at Brenda in confusion. "Is he asking me what I think he's asking me?"

"I think so," Brenda said, almost in awe.

Wally could not believe it. Instead of laughing at or otherwise abusing him, Mike Brewer wanted to play. With him. Wally Crenshaw, butt of every joke the class bully had pulled since third grade! Except now, no one laughed, not even his archnemesis.

In fact, Whiz Kid's greatest foe had just asked for a team-up, like he was offering to put his League of Villains under the command of Wally's Justice Brigade!

"C'mon. Quit being your usual stupid and let's do this, twerp," Mike snarled.

Wally could feel himself standing suddenly a little taller, his shoulders back, the way his mother always nagged him to stand. He didn't feel like nerdy Wally Crenshaw. He felt like a hero, like Hyperion, leader of men and idol to the masses.

"You're going to do something to mess with him, aren't you?" Brenda said suspiciously.

"Naw, I won't. I promise, cross my heart," Mike said, and Abel and Nick drew crosses on their chests. "Besides, I'm bored. It's not like there's anything else to do."

"That's good enough for me," Wally said, lapsing into his super-voice without even realizing it. "Okay, everybody, listen up . . . !"

And, amazingly, they did.

"*WHERE* IS THE ACCELERATOR?" Doctor Psycon muttered.

Stormcloud reached for the cards he had just been dealt and looked up at the man in a white lab coat floating cross-legged in the air above his head. "Darned if I know, Doc, but you're the superintelligent psychic. Why don't you figure it out for us?" He looked at his cards and his formfitting sky-blue tunic, normally placid with fluffy blue clouds floating across it, suddenly darkened and flashed gray.

"I can't tell if that means you got good cards or bad," Sledgehammer Sue said. She threw a pair of cards face down on the table. "Gimme two," she said.

Across the table from her, the top hat-wearing Professor Lamplighter dealt Sue two new cards from the deck in his white-gloved hands. "Indeed, we chose the dear doctor to lead us for his uncanny ability to deduce such intelligence at will."

"Last known coordinates," Psycon muttered. "Lone wolf tendencies. Traffic patterns. Rest stops... rest stops..."

Manika shuffled her cards rapidly, her hands a blur. "Gotta go to the potty, Doc?" she giggled in a high-pitched squeal.

Over their heads, Doctor Psycon grunted, the broad brow of his oversized forehead crinkling like tissue paper over his frown.

"Considering where he's levitating, you better hope he doesn't, Manika," Crosshair said from across the room. He wore a one-piece costume in solid black except for the vivid red marksman bull's–eye symbol over his left eye and a midnight-blue pouched belt around his waist. "Not that you aren't asking for it."

"What's that supposed to mean?" Manika said. Her head jerked rapidly in Crosshair's direction.

"Hmm, not confined to main roads," Doctor Psycon said. "Could have gone to ground anywhere. Mm-*hmm*. Maximum possible distance traveled?"

"Don't you guys ever get tired of making fun of the doctor? You know he can't hear you when he's in one of his brainstorms. He's talking to himself, being rhetorical. It's how his brain works, but you guys can't get enough of making fun when you know he can't hear you."

Professor Lamplighter smiled and adjusted his top hat. "I, for one, have never hesitated to have my fun with the doctor directly to his face, Crosshair."

"Yeah, well you and the doc are old pals, and he considers you the closest thing he's got to an intellectual equal on this planet, so I guess you get a pass."

Lamplighter, the Immortal Mastermind of Crime, bowed his head and smiled. "The doctor knows he has my loyalty and respect."

"Suck up," Manika muttered, crossing and uncrossing her legs at hyperspeed.

"Doctor Psycon is the leader of the League of Villains. He's a great man who deserves our respect," Crosshair said.

"I respect his big, bumpy head," Stormcloud snickered.

"The price he pays for having the biggest,

most advanced mutant brain in the universe," Crosshair, the Prince of Projectiles said.

"What is this 'in the universe' stuff anyway," Sue snapped, pounding her fist on the tabletop. "I mean, as far as I know, there's just us in the universe!"

"Yeah? What about K'lang the Clawed?" Crosshair challenged.

Sue made a face. "K'lang? He only pretends to be from outer space. His real name's Karl Lang and he's from Scranton, you idiot."

"Okay, so there! If Earth is all there is in the universe and Doctor Psycon is the biggest brain on Earth, it isn't wrong to say he's the smartest man in the universe, is it?"

Sue frowned at Crosshair and tapped the twenty-pound head of her sledgehammer against the palm of her hand. "You're just trying to make my head hurt," she snapped.

"Anyway, the last thing I'm going to say is, before he got arrested, Accelerator stashed the loot from our Las Vegas heist."

Stormcloud's costume flashed a sunny glow. "The Vegas job. Yeah, I liked that one," he said. "Sixty million bucks from five casinos in one neat, little package."

"That's what I'm talking about," Crosshair said. "You think any one of us could've planned a job like that without Doctor Psycon?"

"Well, with all due modesty . . ." Professor Lamplighter said with a chuckle.

Sledgehammer Sue snorted. "You would've had us escaping on horseback."

"Shooting at the cops with our blunderbusses!" Manika laughed.

"The blunderbuss is an outdated *eighteenth*-century weapon. I—" Lamplighter said.

"Not as outdated as you," Stormcloud said. "Are we playing poker here or what?"

"In a minute," Crosshair said. "You're all missing the point. Accelerator is gone and so is our sixty million. At least the doctor's trying to figure out where he is and what he's done with it. All you dopes are doing is flapping your lips and making fun of him."

"And what're you doing to help things along, Crosshair?" Sue said with a mocking laugh.

"I'm waiting for the doctor to work through his brainstorm and figure things out."

"Is it too much to hope that we can just finish our card game?" Lamplighter said. "It is your bet, Sue."

"Think you'll be able to find your way to the bathroom by yourself while the doc's in his brainstorming trance?" Sledgehammer Sue sneered as she picked up the two cards Lamplighter had dealt for her.

Crosshair picked up a poker chip from the table and examined it with a deep sigh.

Then he flipped it casually across the table, where it bounced off Sue's forehead and knocked her over backward in her chair. She lay sprawled on the floor, unconscious.

"Sue folds, Professor," Crosshair said.

Lamplighter threw his cards into the air and groaned, "I wager the Justice Brigade conducts their meetings with far more dignity than this!"

8

CHARLIE HARRIS STARTED HIS first full day as a resident of Crumbly in a life-and-death struggle with the warped windows in the house at 254 Kane Street.

Except for the broken windows, the house had been closed up for five years and smelled like dust and mildew. From the look of things, Aunt Sadie hadn't invested a lot in maintenance for a while before her death and he had no idea how much neglect he would find when he got into the repairs. Having spent his entire adult life living in apartments, all that Charlie knew about home repair was how to call the landlord to send over a repairman. But he had to start somewhere. Forcing open a few windows to let some fresh air in seemed as good a place as any.

A search of the dank, dusty basement yielded a crowbar and some other tools that he carried back upstairs.

His uninvited houseguest lay sound asleep on the dusty sofa in the living room. Willie had fallen asleep fully dressed, on his back, his knees hanging over the armrest. Snoring. Willie had always been proud of his ability to fall asleep anywhere, under any conditions, at any time. "The war on crime has no bedtime. We have to grab our rare moments of rest whenever the opportunity arises," the cracked crime fighter often said.

"Time to wake up sleeping beauty and get him on the road," Charlie muttered.

He inspected the windows closest to Willie's sleeping head. He tried to raise one, but it wouldn't budge. It had been painted shut and would require more muscle power than he possessed to pry it open.

He selected a chisel from his collection of tools and worked the beveled edge into the crack between the bottom sash and the sill. Then he hefted the hammer and, with a grin and a glance at the still snoring Mr. Justice, hit the flat end of the chisel as hard as he could. It gave off a loud, satisfying clang and shattered three of the six panes of glass.

Willie snored on through the noise.

"So much for your finely honed senses," Charlie grumbled at the sleeping figure.

"Honed enough to know the difference

between danger and a klutz with a hammer," Willie said without opening his eyes.

"You're awake?"

"I have been since you came stomping down the stairs and went to the basement."

"Great. Then you can get an early start on the road and beat the rush hour traffic," Charlie said.

Willie swung his legs to the floor and stood up, stretching.

"Aren't you going to offer me some coffee before I go?"

"No."

"Got any of those cupcakes left from last night?"

"No."

"Yes, you do. You had a package of eight. I ate three and you ate two, so there are three left."

"How do you know I didn't eat them for breakfast before you woke up?"

Willie stood before Charlie and scrutinized him through narrowed eyes. "Like I said, I've been awake since you came downstairs. I heard you boil water in the tea kettle and pour dry cereal into a bowl." He reached over and plucked something from Charlie's T-shirt. He held it up for his teammate to see. "Just as I suspected... a Rice Crispy. Now, about those cupcakes?"

"You're a regular Sherlock Holmes, aren't you?" Charlie snapped. "Fine. Have a cupcake.

Have all of them, but then you've got to go. I've got a ton of stuff to do and I don't need you hanging around bothering me."

Willie smiled sadly. "It's your guilty conscience that's bothering you, Charlie. I'm just a reminder of how you're shirking your sacred duty."

"Sheesh!" Charlie rolled his eyes and turned away, reaching for the crowbar. "You never give up, do you?"

"Justice never surrenders."

"It doesn't take a hint either," Charlie said and, instead of using the crowbar on Willie like he wanted to, he attacked the window with it.

Willie watched him grunt and struggle for a while before asking, "What are you trying to do?"

"What does it *look* like I'm trying to?" Charlie said through tightly clenched teeth.

"Open the window."

"Wow, you really are the world's greatest detective, aren't you?"

"You're never going to do it that way."

"I'm fine."

"No you're not. You've already broken one window."

"They're my windows."

"Hey, if you don't want my help, just say so."

Charlie looked over his shoulder at the

other man with his most hate-filled stare. "I don't want your help!"

"Give me that," Mr. Justice demanded, plucking the crowbar from Charlie's hand.

"Hey!"

Charlie made a grab for the tool, but Willie held it out of his reach. With his other hand, he reached into his pants pocket and pulled out a pocketknife.

"Whoa," Charlie said, taking a step back. "We're gonna play it like that, huh?"

Willie shook his head. "Don't be a dope, Charlie," he said. He stuck the crowbar under one arm and pried open the little knife's blade. "It's just a Swiss Army knife, see? You keep trying to force these open, you'll just break them. You've got to cut through all the paint first."

To demonstrate, Willie ran the sharp blade of the knife along the seam where the window met the frame.

"What makes you such an expert?" Charlie said.

"Who do you think singlehandedly remodeled the Den of Justice?"

"The den of what? You mean that apartment of yours in Brooklyn?"

"Right. The Den of Justice." Finished with the knife, Willie made a fist and rapped gently around the window, loosening it from the frame, then effortlessly slid it open. He nodded in satisfaction and, before starting on the next window, looked at Willie and said, "Since you're not doing anything, would you mind getting me those cupcakes?"

Charlie, unlike Justice, knew when to accept defeat. He turned around and headed for the kitchen.

"HEY, SLOW DOWN THERE, Swift," Jamie Crenshaw said. "There's this new thing we do with our food. It's called chewing. You ought to try it sometime."

Wally continued shoveling milk and cereal into his mouth at an accelerated pace, shaking his head as he managed to grunt between bites, "Can't. Everybody. Waiting."

"Benny can wait a few minutes so you don't choke on your breakfast."

Wally lifted his face from the bowl. "Not just Benny."

"Right. And Brenda."

"And Mike Brewer, and Abel Schotz, Nick McCain, and Olivia Snyder, maybe the Truman twins, and Mike said he'd ask Jocko Mullins and . . ."

Jamie sat back on her stool at the kitchen island with a look of surprise.

"You've certainly widened your social circle all of a sudden. Since when do you hang out with Mike Brewer and . . . and, well, *anyone* besides Benny and Brenda?"

"Since now, I guess."

Jamie frowned. "Mike isn't making you do something, is he?"

He paused from tipping the bowl to his lips to get at the last drops of cereal-sweetened milk. "No, Mom, Mike isn't making me do anything. In fact, he agreed that *I'm* the leader."

"The leader? Of what?"

Wally started to say the leader of trying to find out if one of the most dangerous supervillains in the world might be hiding out in the old Wicker house, but at the last second common sense grabbed hold of his tongue and he said instead, "Of the . . . what'd'ya call it? The... thing... where you, uh... look for stuff?"

"What kind of stuff?"

"For treasure," he quickly added. "Where you scavenge for treasure."

"You mean a scavenger hunt?"

"Yeah, that's it. I couldn't think of what it's called," Wally said lamely, trying to cover his uneasiness by gulping down the rest of his chocolate milk. Half of it splashed from the glass and dribbled down his chin.

"That sounds like fun. Who came up with that idea?"

"Uh, me?"

"You?" Jamie started clearing the breakfast

dishes. "Don't get me wrong, honey, I'm happy to hear you're getting along with Mike Brewer and his friends, but a scavenger hunt doesn't sound like his kind of thing at all."

Wally shrugged, wishing he had never mentioned Mike Brewer and the rest of the kids. He knew it would set her off on an avalanche of questions guaranteed to bury him up to his neck in what he liked to think of as protective half-truths told to keep her from worrying but which were, under any strict moral or legal definition, total lies so he could get away with doing what he knew his mother would forbid him from doing. It made him feel almost guilty enough to confess.

Almost.

"I… I guess, but he just seemed to be into… hunting scavengers with us," he said, cementing the foundation of his lie in place.

"Well, if you're scavenging, I bet you'll be able to find a lot of the items you're looking for at his dad's dump. What's on your list? I remember we had a scavenger hunt in high school," Jamie said, starting to smile at some memory of the olden days that Wally recognized signaled a long story about to follow.

"Can't tell you," he said, jumping up to deliver his glass and cereal bowl to the sink in the hopes that this unusual behavior would distract her from her story.

"Why not?"

"It's the rules. We're not allowed to get any help from parents or grown-ups."

That part, at least, came close to being true. They had sworn not to breathe a word of their plans to any adults.

"Alright," his mother said, clearly not happy with having secrets kept from her. "Just be careful, okay?"

Wally hoped his smile didn't look as phony as it felt. "Mom, we're just going to play a dumb game, okay? What can happen? Especially in Crumbly. *Nothing* ever happens here."

Jamie turned on the hot water to wash the dishes. "Right, and as your mother, I'd like to see it stay that way."

9

WALLY PACED MAIN STREET in anxious circles, pausing every couple of revolutions or so to peer around the thick bushes that blocked his view down Kane Street, and check on the progress of his plan.

Plan.

If you could call it that. Yesterday, it seemed to make perfect sense. Keep the house under constant surveillance until he got a look at whoever came out of it and seeing where he goes. Well, if he went on foot. If he got into the gray car and drove away, they had no way of following him.

You couldn't say they didn't have the old house covered. His friends were deployed up and down Kane Street, each with a specific assignment for blending in. Mike Brewer was riding his bicycle with Abel and Nick following on skateboards. Brenda and Lulu Yeung played hit the penny with a rubber ball, while Jocko Mullins and Benny Sachem watched the Truman twins, Kit and Kat, jump rope. Not even the Accelerator could be suspicious of a bunch of kids playing on the street on a beautiful summer day.

He resumed pacing, gnawing at his left thumbnail. Except the longer this took, the less it seemed like such a good idea. Wally knew he sometimes let his imagination run away from him, and with everybody looking at him yesterday like he knew what to do, he had to come up with something. Even something as lame as hanging around outside the guy's house all day.

But then, even Benny had acted it like it made sense and Benny made fun of everything. And now, he had Mike Brewer—*Mike Brewer*!—on his side instead of trying to come up with interesting new ways to torture him. Crazy, right?

And speak of the devil, Mike came zooming around the corner on his bike and skidded to a stop inches from Wally.

"Reporting in," Mike snapped with military precision. Wally didn't think he had ever seen Mike without Abel and Nick right behind him, but they just hadn't caught up on their skateboards yet. A moment later, they clattered around the corner, laughing and high-fiving.

"Did you see something?" Wally asked hopefully.

"Nope. Just reporting there's nothing to report."

"Oh. Okay."

"We better get back to our posts. C'mon, you guys," Mike said, and took off in a spray of dirt, his fiendishly cackling shadows on his tail.

Wally watched them go, shocked that not only hadn't Mike already grown bored with the game, he remained its most enthusiastic player.

Maybe this hadn't been so dumb after all. Maybe he'd just been nervous, this being his first mission. And with an untrained crew of sidekicks at that.

He took a deep breath and straightened his back. Sure, nerves. That's all. If he didn't know how the supers operated, who did? Not only had Wally read every issue of the *Justice Brigade* comic book, but true accounts of practically all their cases as well. Most of those true accounts had been written by Charlie Harris, the owner and one identified occupant of the house.

He could do this!

"I can do this," Wally mumbled in agreement with himself.

"Heads up!"

Wally jumped aside just as Mike Brewer came careening around the corner again at top speed and full voice. "Someone's coming," he called.

"Who?"

"Some guy. How do I know? But he's—"

Before Mike could finish, Abel Schotz, Nick McCain, Lulu Yeung, the Truman twins, and Jocko Mullins also came racing around the corner.

"What's the matter? Where are you going?" Wally yelled.

Jocko waved back over his shoulder, eyes wide with wonder. "A guy… he came outside," he gasped.

"Did he do anything?" Wally asked.

"Yeah," Jocko gasped. "He left the house… walking down the path."

"And?" Wally said, glancing nervously at the corner, half expecting to see the Accelerator rounding the bend.

"I dunno," Jocko said, "I didn't stay long enough to see."

"Me neither," Lulu said sheepishly. "I ran away. But only because Jocko ran."

"And we ran because Lulu ran," said Kit and Kat together.

Abel and Nick snickered and punched each other on the shoulders.

Benny appeared from around the corner, not running but walking at a quicker-than-normal pace. He shook his head in disbelief at the kids gathered around Wally.

"I can't believe you dummies," he said through clenched teeth. "Why'd you run?"

Mike stood up in indignation. "I didn't run. I'm the messenger."

Kat Truman shrugged. "We panicked."

"Where's Brenda?" Wally said.

"You guys better get out of here, quick," Benny said.

"Where's Brenda?" Wally said again.

"Since when are you giving the orders?" Mike Brewer demanded.

"Fine, whatever. But Brenda..."

"Yeah, where *is* Brenda?" Wally repeated, louder this time.

"That's what I've been trying to tell you. She's with the guy and they're coming this way," Benny said.

Wally stared at him in disbelief.

"So...?" Benny said, prompting his friend.

"Right. Coming this way. Okay. Got it," Wally stuttered. "Yeah, so, um... you guys better get out of here, quick!"

"You're the boss, Crenshaw," Mike Brewer said, giving Benny a dirty look. Benny rolled his eyes.

The others started to scatter but Wally grabbed Benny's arm.

"What am I supposed to do?" he hissed.

Benny shrugged and said with a grin, "I don't know. After all, *you're* the boss, Crenshaw," and hurried off to join the others.

Around the corner, he heard the sound of

approaching footsteps. Wally chose the closest cover and dove into the bushes.

FOR ALL HIS ANNOYING faults, Willie proved to be a handy man to have as a houseguest in a house in need of repairs. While working his way through the place opening windows, he began making a list of the many needed repairs, prioritizing them as they went along. He had set Charlie to work on clean up, then attended to some preliminary demolition, ripping out rotting wallboard and damaged flooring.

Fortunately, he discovered the upstairs to be in much better shape than the first floor, and still had all its windows intact. Willie declared them serviceable for the time being but warned Charlie that a major bathroom remodel lay in his future.

"What's wrong with the bathroom?" Charlie asked.

Willie looked at the peach-colored tile and the stained claw-foot bathtub with distaste. "It's so... 1960s," he declared.

After a morning spent working up a sweat, Willie informed him that he'd found, (a) the interior of the old house to be in better shape than appeared at first glance, (b) he could help Charlie with the more urgent repairs, and (b) they had nothing in the house for lunch.

"We can get started inside, but you're going to need professionals for the front and back porches. And you might want to get a decorator in for that bathroom," Willie said, handing Charlie a list of items he needed from the hardware store scribbled on the back of a torn piece of floral wallpaper. "And get some cold cuts. Bologna, okay?"

Charlie studied the list. "Sure."

"And mayo."

Charlie made a face. "Mayonnaise on bologna?"

"Yes. What's wrong with mayo?"

"Nothing. Mayo's okay. I'm just a mustard-on-bologna man, that's all."

"I like mustard on hamburgers."

"Ketchup. Mustard's for hot dogs."

"Not where I come from. Mayo on bologna. Mustard on burgers. Ketchup on hot dogs."

"What do you put on a cheese sandwich?"

"Mayo."

"No, ick," Charlie said. "Butter on a cheese sandwich."

Willie looked ready to hurl an indignant retort at Charlie's recipe, but shook his head and waved it off, saying, "Look, can we stop this? It's making me hungry."

Charlie agreed, adding, "But everyone makes sandwiches for himself, okay?" He washed up, changed into a clean *National Mask* T-shirt, and left Willie sawing through some water-warped floorboards. Maybe the big goon would saw through the floor and crash down to the basement.

After stepping carefully around the gaping hole in his front porch and gingerly navigating the creaking steps, he paused on the walkway to take in the view of his street and a few lungfuls of soft, salty Crumbly sea air. He found the fresh air refreshing. The view that greeted him outside his door he found strange.

When he first stepped outside, there had been a bunch of kids playing, like a scene out of a 1950s movie in small-town America. He found it hard to believe there were still places where kids skipped rope and played hit the penny on the street instead of burying their faces in phones and iPads, but he supposed living in a place without internet, Crumbly's kids were forced to make entertainment themselves.

But that heartwarming tableau of Americana turned quickly to confusion. The moment the kids spotted him they turned and ran, like he was Stormcloud about to rain bolts of lightning down on them. One of a set of twin girls even screamed.

The only one who didn't run was a girl, holding one end of a jump rope and smiling at him. He recognized her from last night.

"Good morning, Brenda, the sheriff's daughter," he called to her.

"Hi, Mr. Harris," she called back and began to gather up the rope.

"Where did everybody go in such a hurry?" he said. "Was it something I said?"

"No, I guess they're just not used to strangers. We don't get a lot of visitors in Crumbly."

"I'm not a total stranger, you know. My folks and I used to visit my aunt here every summer. This is her house."

Brenda smiled. "I remember Miss Wicker. I liked her. When I was little, she used to read to us at the library for story time."

Now Charlie smiled. "Yeah, Aunt Sadie used to read to me too. I'd forgotten all about that."

"So where are you going?" Brenda asked, joining Charlie as he started strolling toward Main Street.

"I've got some shopping to do. Need to pick up groceries and hit a hardware store."

"All we've got is Ma and Pa's general store. They'll have what you need, or they'll be able to order it for you if they don't."

They rounded the corner, passing the quivering, rustling bushes. Charlie caught a glimpse of the top of a kid's head ducking down in hiding before Brenda laughed, a little too loud, and said, "Squirrels!"

"Big squirrels," Charlie agreed.

"Yeah," Brenda said, quickly changing the subject, "You're Mrs. Wicker's nephew?"

"My great-aunt. To tell you the truth, I don't remember a lot about those visits, except that the TV reception stunk and I was always bored."

"Nothing's changed."

"That's okay. The last few years I've had enough excitement to hold me a good, long time. All I want is some peace and quiet to get my work done."

"What do you do? Your work, I mean."

"I'm a writer."

"Oh, yeah? That's so cool. What do you write?"

Charlie made a vague gesture. "Oh, I've mostly been working for newspapers and magazines and stuff, probably nothing you've ever seen."

"Like the *National Mask*?"

He plucked at the front of his T-shirt and looked at the logo. "Yeah, like that."

"And now?" Brenda prompted. "What are you writing now?"

He gave her an amused look. "You'd make a pretty good reporter yourself, young lady. That's some interviewing technique you've got."

"I'm not interviewing—"

"It's okay," he laughed. "I noticed it yesterday when you knocked on my door. You were just going to stand there and keep me talking as long as possible while you tried to get a look inside the house."

Blushing, Brenda said, "I didn't... I mean, I wouldn't..."

"Don't be embarrassed, kid. It's a compliment. Look, I'm no genius, but even I can see that my arrival's got you guys curious. Can I let you in on an old reporter's secret?"

She nodded.

"When you've got a question to ask, just ask it."

Brenda nodded again, absorbing Charlie's pearl of wisdom.

"Okay, so who's your friend with the gray car?"

"None of your business."

"But you said I should just ask my question," Brenda said, confused.

"Yeah, but nobody says I've got to answer it."

Brenda laughed. "Okay, I get it. Mind my own business."

Charlie laughed. "When the question is about something the public has a right or a need to know, your job as a reporter is to find out what's true and what's not. Sometimes people don't want you to find the truth, but that doesn't change your job, so you go over their heads, behind their backs, or get under their feet until you get what you're after."

"Is that what I should do to find out about your friend?"

"You're good, kid. But no. Remember what I

said about the public's right or need to know? I don't think anybody cares or needs to know about one friend visiting another friend to help with some home repairs. That falls under my right to privacy."

"It's complicated, isn't it?" Brenda said with a bewildered shake of her head.

"Everything's complicated," Charlie agreed. "But if you've got half a brain, and I'd say you ended up with more than your fair share, you'll figure it out."

"I'm not even sure I know what the 'it' I'm supposed to figure out *is*."

"The difference between right and wrong," Charlie said. "Once you've got that licked, the rest is easy."

"Yeah?" Brenda sounded skeptical.

"Well, easi*er*," Charlie said. "A little anyway."

10

WALLY WAITED UNTIL HE could no longer hear Brenda or Charlie Harris' voices before disentangling himself from the bushes. Plucking twigs and leaves from his hair, he peeked around the corner onto Kane Street. Empty. The only sign anyone else had been there was the jump rope lying on the sidewalk.

He couldn't believe those guys had run like that. If they were going to freak out because someone came out of a house, what good will they be if something real happens? If he wanted to make his mark as a super, Whiz Kid would need a better crew.

Except for Brenda. Nothing frightened her. She'd just marched right up to the door last night and knocked. For all she knew, a supervillain lurked behind it. Not very likely, but still!

Brenda and Mr. Harris were headed toward Main Street, which probably meant they were going to do some shopping. Whoever the mysterious visitor turned out to be, he would be in the house alone for a while.

What, Wally asked himself, would Mr. Justice do under these circumstances?

A reconnaissance mission!

He could make his way to the Wicker backyard by going around to Robinson Street and cutting between Mrs. Washburn's house and the empty lot. He would have cover behind the trees that separated the properties and then, if he found the coast clear, he could sneak up to a back window and maybe get a look at Charlie Harris's houseguest. It sounded as easy as crossing the street.

So why couldn't he make himself move?

"Let's go, Whiz Kid," he said out loud. "Brenda would've already knocked on the *front* door and introduced herself by now."

He thought about how disappointed she would be if she came back and saw that he hadn't seized the moment and gotten the job done. Wally would hate to disappoint her, especially after the way she always rooted for him.

But more, he didn't want to disappoint himself. Becoming a super—a *real* super, not just some kid pretending in a towel cape and cheap domino mask—had been his dream since he'd been little. Now, finally, he had his chance, and if he chickened out, he'd never get another one, sure as heck not here in Crumbly. And he'd have to spend the rest of his life knowing he'd been too scared to take even a small chance, let alone face off against supervillains.

Or the F'harah.

They were Wally's archenemy, the aliens from another dimension whose attempted invasion of Earth had killed thousands of people in Lincoln City before the Justice Brigade and the military could drive them back to their universe. His father always told Wally he could be anything he wanted to be, even a superhero, if he wanted it and worked hard enough. Older now, he knew his dad hadn't wanted him to be a superhero. He had just been encouraging his son to follow his dreams, whatever they were. He probably figured Wally would outgrow the superhero stuff and end up in some regular, plain job like everyone else in the world, but he would never have told him not to reach for the stars. His dad believed in people.

His dad especially believed in him.

Before he could talk himself out of it again, Wally plunged back into the bushes.

The Whiz Kid had work to do.

MR. JUSTICE WHISTLED WHILE he worked. He had finished pulling up the ruined flooring in the living room and started on a bad patch in the dining room under the window. He worked the small pry bar between the wall and the floor molding and gently pulled it loose, hoping to salvage and reuse it after the floor had been patched and refinished.

Willie Williams liked this kind of work. Unlike wreaking vengeance and/or raining justice down on the heads of evildoers, basic carpentry didn't require a lot of thought. Building or fixing up a house could be complicated, sure. But when reduced to a series of hundreds or thousands of individual little jobs that, if done in the proper sequence resulted in a finished product, it became so much simpler. Right now, the simple task required identifying and removing warped wood and waterlogged or rotted plaster. Later, and with the same focus, he would fill all those holes with new wood and fresh plaster. And so on and so forth until each and every little task had been checked off the list.

He knew he came across as an aloof, coldly analytical figure to his colleagues, but in truth, when not on the job, Willie didn't like having to think too much. Fighting crime took total and absolute focus, so much so that sometimes he thought his brain would overheat and explode. By the time he reached the end of a case, he felt totally burnt out and didn't want to think. Besides, when he didn't have a criminal to hunt or a conspiracy to bust up, his thoughts turned to things he'd rather not think about. He sometimes wondered if other people had similar dark, sad thoughts but had always been afraid to ask. He worried that if they answered no, that might prove him every bit as unhinged as Charlie and some of the others thought.

So Williams had hobbies to keep his mind occupied. Like home repair. He also painted, mostly pictures of puppies and kittens and little kids with balloons, and just last year he had taken up crocheting. But his favorite hobby had to be scrapbooking. He had a whole bookcase full of his creations back at the Den of Justice. Some of them were about him and his cases, and others covered the exploits of his teammates and their careers, but most focused on happier subjects. Holidays and special people and places. He had one whole book filled to bulging with old New York City police stations and two dedicated to the animals of the Bronx Zoo. Pictures, fancy papers, lace, stickers, stencils, scissors, and glue brought him pleasure and the sort of mindless serenity he craved after a hard day confronting evil and cracking skulls.

But just being in a happy place of mindless, repetitive labor didn't mean the detective part of his brain switched off completely. Like a soldier on the battlefield, his senses were always on the alert for danger, even when asleep. He might be lost in the delicate task of trimming out the cover of a new scrapbook, but the least bit of change in his environment caused him to snap into a state of high alert. Anyone observing him wouldn't notice a change in his demeanor, an illusion he would leave them with until they made their move. Then, he thought with a smile, came the fun part.

Not that he had much of a chance of being jumped today. He knew right away when he realized he had a visitor in the backyard that it would likely be one of the kids who had been playing quietly in the street all morning, all the while staring at Charlie's house like they were waiting for it to burst into flames. His casual glances out the window and superior peripheral vision allowed him to quickly confirm his guess. It looked like the same dorky kid he had seen wearing a mask and cape yesterday when he'd arrived. He didn't know why the dress-up, but in a small town like this, it seemed only natural kids would be curious about strangers.

Willie thought the best way to get rid of him would be to give him what he came for. His face would be meaningless to the kid, anyway; there were no pictures of him on the internet to identify him against.

On the pretense of taking a break, he grabbed a bottle of water and stepped out onto the back porch. He drank some water. He wiped his brow. Gave the kid hiding—if you could call that hiding—behind a tree at the edge of the yard a good, long look.

WHIZ KID HAD BEEN training himself to be a master of shadow and cover. From his vantage point alongside Mrs. Washburn's house, he flitted to the old oak that provided shade for the back porch, then to the small toolshed. Then, as nimble and unobtrusive as a ninja, he scurried from tree to tree until, long moments later, a single maple, barely wide enough to conceal him, shielded him from view from the Wicker house.

Wally gasped for breath and felt the sweat gathering on his face. He wished he could blame his condition on exertion. If he did find the Accelerator, Wally could literally be putting his life in danger. Frozen, his back pressed against the rough bark, sweat stinging his eyes, he thought that maybe, if he could ever make himself move again, the smart thing to do would be to just get out of there. The Accelerator didn't have any reason to hurt him. Yet. But he would if Wally got a look at him…

"Cut it out," Wally growled softly to himself. "He's not gonna see you. You're Whiz Kid!"

Yeah, right. Whiz Kid. Too scared to even *look* at a bad guy. He felt like any second Hyperion might swoop in and personally strip him of his membership in the Junior Justice Brigade fan club. To tell the truth, a little part of him hoped Hyperion did appear. That way *he* could take care of the Accelerator and Wally could go home.

But until that happened, Wally had a problem; the only way to know if he could keep going would be to look around the tree.

If he did, he might see the Accelerator.

Or the Accelerator might also see him.

Wally groaned. He couldn't keep going around in circles; either he did what scared him, or he stayed hidden behind this tree all day. Or for the rest of his life. Whichever came first.

He slowly sucked in as much air as he could, releasing it just as slowly. He did that a few more times until his heart stopped thumping in his chest, and then, wishing himself luck, he slowly turned his head, craning his neck as he inched around the trunk until the back side of the old Wicker house came into view.

It looked a lot like the backside of his house. Except in need of some nails and paint. The windows were wide open upstairs and downstairs, and the drapes were pulled back. He thought he heard some noises from inside, but couldn't quite make out what they were.

After a few seconds, he pulled his head back.

Okay. That hadn't been so bad. Maybe he could give it a few more minutes. Carefully, staying hidden, he inched around until he faced the tree and could look around it without breaking his neck.

This time, he saw movement through one of the windows, but he couldn't make out any details. His heart raced again, but this time out of excitement, not fear. He'd done it. Not playing around watching a parked car or tailing Mr. Taylor from the newspaper office on Main Street to his house without being spotted. But a for-real stakeout. Just like Mr. Justice.

Wally kept a close watch on the windows, catching unsatisfying glimpses of a man, dressed in black, going about his business. It had to be the same guy he'd seen arrive in the gray car yesterday. But did that make it Brendan McMahon, aka the Accelerator? Or, like Benny had said, Charlie Harris's cousin Bob?

The rickety, old screen door squealed as it opened onto the back porch and the tall, unshaven man stepped outside.

Wally's eyes went wide.

About six feet tall, kind of regular build. Dark hair and his eyes . . . ? Wally supposed they were dark too, but at this distance, it was hard to tell. At that distance, he couldn't tell one tall, dark-haired guy from another.

Wally tried squinting and narrowing his eyes. Hyperion's telescopic vision sure would come in handy. Or a utility belt with some binoculars in it.

Or maybe he just needed to get his eyes checked.

11

"WELL?"

Mike Brewer got in Wally's face like a bad case of zits as soon as he reemerged from the bushes at the corner of Kane and Main. After their disorderly retreat, his crew had regrouped and returned to the scene of their shame. All except Brenda.

"Well what?" Wally said, surprised at the sight of the sea of eager faces waiting for him.

"Did you see him?" Jocko said.

"Yeah, did you see the Accelerator?" Lulu demanded.

"*Wellll*," Wally said, drawing out the word.

"Don't tell me you chickened out like the rest of these guys," Mike said.

"Would it make you feel better if he was as big a wimp as the rest of us?" Benny said.

Mike glared at Benny. "What's that supposed to mean?"

"Hey," Wally interrupted. "I did."

"Ha! I knew it." Mike let out a guffaw that set Abel and Nick off on a fit of laughing fist bumps. "You never got anywhere near the place, did you?"

"No, I mean I *did* see him. The guy. The visitor," Wally said.

"And?" Benny said.

Wally shrugged.

"I couldn't tell."

Everyone let out simultaneous groans of disappointment.

"I mean, not from that distance. I couldn't get close enough to say for sure. He came right out onto the back porch and if only I'd had some binoculars, I could've made an identification."

"But it *could* be the Accelerator?" Mike wanted to know. Behind him, Abel and Nick held their breaths in anticipation.

"It could," Wally said. "Or not. I need a better look at this guy."

Benny looked up Main Street, devoid, as ever, of all signs of life.

"Maybe Brenda can get something out of Mr. Harris," he said hopefully.

Mike snorted. "I don't think you guys could get a weather report out of the newspaper." Nick and Abel celebrated their friend's wit with a howling high five.

"Then don't hang out with us, okay, Mike?" Benny said.

Mike rewarded the suggestion with another snort. "Yeah, like the Whiz Kid's gonna be able to get this done without me."

"Yeah, like I didn't go into his backyard while you were running away," Wally mumbled.

"What'd you say, Crenshaw?" Mike barked.

"I didn't say . . ." Wally said, but Benny jumped in and said, "He said *he* went into the Accelerator's yard while *you* ran away."

"You ran away too, Benny," Mike snarled. "Besides, I came back, didn't I? And he better watch out or maybe I'm outta here to take down the Accelerator without him."

"As if!" Olivia said with a giggle.

"Wanna see me?" Mike said.

"Hey, c'mon, you guys," Wally said. "We're supposed to be a team. We were doing pretty good too."

"Until Mike ran away," Benny said, just loud enough to make Kit and Kat snicker.

"What's next, smart guy?" Mike demanded.

"We haven't finished what we started," Wally said. "We still don't know if Brendan McMahon is in there."

"Why don't we just tell Sheriff Cunningham and let him check it out?" Jocko Mullins said.

"Yeah," Wally said slowly. "The sheriff's kind

of banned me from reporting anybody else for being a supervillain."

"How many people have you reported?" Lulu said.

"You'd be surprised," Benny said.

"It hasn't been that many," Wally said defensively. "Besides, better safe than sorry."

Benny nodded. "Uh-huh. And don't forget, 'if you see something, say something.'"

"Exactly!" Wally agreed emphatically, before he caught his friend's mocking tone. He tried to recover a little of his dignity by regaining some control. "So yeah. Exactly. And, um, yeah... let's get back to work?"

Everyone stared at him.

"You know you sound lame, don't you, Crenshaw?" Mike said, but he shoved off on his bicycle and started peddling down Kane Street. After a second, Abel and Nick dropped their skateboards and rolled after him. The others followed.

"*Why* is Mike still here... listening to *you*?" Benny asked as he went to join them.

Wally just shrugged.

"No clue," he said. But he sure did like the feeling.

"I'M GLAD YOU GUYS were spying on me this morning," Charlie said, taking a bite out of the crispy sugar cone that held the last of his two deliciously melting scoops of rum raisin ice cream.

"Me too," Brenda said, similarly busy trying to keep her rocky road cone from oozing down her fist and onto her arm as they walked along the path to the beach.

"I'd forgotten all about the homemade ice cream at the general store," he said. "I guess I blocked more of those vacations from my memory than I thought."

"Why didn't you like it? I mean, I know Crumbly's the dullest place on Earth, but it couldn't have been that bad for a couple of weeks."

Charlie agreed. Crumbly itself hadn't been so bad, certainly no better or worse than a hundred other little towns that dotted the Jersey seaboard. What spoiled those vacations, and every other trip he had ever taken with his family, had been his father. The trickster. The practical joker.

Darryl Harris thought the whole world one big joke and treated his son like the punch line. He manufactured and sold novelty joke items, everything from bamboo thumb cuffs and squirting flowers to sophisticated puzzle boxes. As a sideline, he helped magicians develop and build stage tricks and gimmicks. And, man, did his dad love to laugh, especially at the sight of one of his tricks catching someone by surprise. It started for Charlie at literally the moment of his birth, when his father slipped a whoopee cushion under the blanket covering the scale the nurse set him on to get his birth weight.

Darryl spent the rest of his life telling anyone who would listen that his son had come into the world not with a howl but with a fart. Even the doctors and nurses found it hysterical. And his father sure knew how to milk a joke, which Charlie learned at the age of fifteen, discovering that his middle initial F didn't stand for "Franklin" as he'd been told, but rather for "fart," which the clerk at the Department of Health had refused to register on the birth certificate. As a compromise, dad had left it as plain "F." He liked to say, "The 'art' is silent, but the fart was thunderous."

Dad did not relent in his determination to instill his love of novelty items and jokes in his son and believed the best way to accomplish that would be to bombard Charlie with them. His earliest childhood memories were of being frightened to hysterics and filled diapers by some startling sight or sound as his father looked on, doubled over in hysterics. In fact, when he thought of his dad, he always pictured him laughing, one hand holding his stomach, the other pointing at the victim of his joke. Usually Charlie.

He loved his dad, but the old man drove him crazy. Not literally, but pretty close to it. His mother had had to threaten his father with a restraining order to finally get him to back off. But that didn't happen until Charlie's eleventh birthday, by which time he had already become a nervous wreck and gun-shy around his father, who would still sometimes sneak in a practical joke on him, his prankster nature overcoming fear of his wife's lawyers. At age thirteen, Charlie woke up and realized that two could play at the prankster's game. He swiped a carton of his father's patented "Stink Up the Joint" skunk pellets, slipped them under the floor mat of dad's car, and waited for, as the package promised, the "hilarity to ensue."

And on that day forward, what his mother would come to call "the war of the half-wits" was on.

"Mr. Harris?"

Brenda's voice brought him back to the present.

"Sorry. My mind wandered off."

"I asked what you found so awful about Crumbly?"

"Let's just say spending long stretches of time with my father could be pretty stressful for me."

"Tell me about it," Brenda said with a roll of her eyes. "My dad's impossible."

"I guess it's tough being the sheriff's daughter," Charlie said in sympathy, before downing the last bite of his ice cream cone.

"Mom said it wasn't a picnic being married to him even before he became sheriff, but I think she just says that to tease him."

"No doubt," Charlie said. The sand and gravel path they were following curved through shoulder-high dunes dense with patches of tall beach grass. He could hear and smell the ocean but couldn't see it yet. "We getting close?"

"It's right around these dunes," she said with a nod. "I didn't see his truck on Main Street, so Mr. Handelman's probably home."

"Couldn't I have just called him?"

"Mr. Handelman doesn't believe in telephones."

Charlie blinked, confused. "You mean he denies their existence or just doesn't like them?"

"I don't think anybody's ever asked." Brenda pointed. "We're here."

As they came around the last dune, the beach spread out before him. As beaches went, this one was nice as any on the shore, stretching for almost a mile in either direction, with clean white sands and a great view of the shimmering Atlantic, its waters rolling in gentle waves to the shore.

"He lives on the beach?" Charlie asked in surprise.

"Daddy says except for when he's got to do business, Mr. Handelman's a hermit."

"Not a bad philosophy. Does he live in a houseboat?"

"No," Brenda said with a giggle and pointed off behind him, inland, toward the seaward side of the dunes. "He lives in a hot dog stand."

Charlie looked and saw not the dilapidated little shack he expected but an entire concession building, a low concrete bunker of a structure, painted white and with a row of windows open to the beach to sell its wares. The windows fronted a large, open interior that could be used as a dining or amusement area. They had built it atop an expansive cement pad with ample space for tables and a half-constructed bandstand at the far end. Ringing the building, which spouted a sixty-foot-tall flagpole, were several other concrete and steel structures, unfinished and left to rust in the sea air.

At first glance, the concession building seemed to be in a similar state of disuse, like maybe it had been used as the town dump, surrounded by what looked like several decades' worth of old cars, household and industrial machines, as well as parts thereof, building materials, and furniture. But a homemade banner stretched across the front of the building pointed to an actual method to the madness. *Handelman the Handyman*, it read. *Architectural and Mechanical Rarities Bought & Sold.*

"You're sure this is the best handyman in Crumbly?" Charlie asked.

"Well, he's the only one, so..."

"So he's the best." Charlie nodded. "Okay, let's get this show on the road."

But before they could go any farther, an old man with a shaved head, dressed in a World War II-era combat fatigue shirt under denim overalls popped out from where he had been concealed in the tall grass.

"Halt!" he barked. "Stand and be identified!"

And since the old man had a World War I Enfield Rifle pointed at him when he gave the order, Charlie thought it best to do exactly as he was told.

WALLY STUCK HIS HEAD into the dining room his mother used as her home office and found her bent over the drafting table.

"Hey, Mom."

She looked up from her sketching, startled. "Oh. Honey, hi." She looked at her watch. "You're home early. Is everything okay?"

"Great. I just need to check something online."

"What's so urgent?"

"Um, the score," Wally blurted out, unprepared for that question.

Jamie Crenshaw laughed. "Score? You don't care about sports."

"For Benny," he said. "Benny wants to know how the Yankees are doing."

"Then why didn't he go home and use his computer?"

Wally inwardly groaned. "We were closer to here?"

"Are they waiting for you outside? Your friends can come in. They won't bother me."

"No, it's cool. They can wait. It'll just take me a second."

"Are you hungry? I can make you a sandwich."

"No, thanks, Mom." That inner groan slowly turned to a scream.

"Are you sure? It'll only take me a minute. I have salami and—"

"No, Mom. Really. Thanks."

"Okay, but if you change your mind, I can—"

"Mom!" He may have raised his voice a little.

Jamie paused in mid-sentence.

"You're doing that Mom thing again," Wally said. "I'm okay. I can make a sandwich if I want one."

She smiled and held up her hands in surrender. "Okay, honey. I'll stop."

"Thanks, Mom. Love you," he said and turned to race upstairs.

"Love you too," she called. "But if you do change your mind about that sandwich, let me know."

She heard the bedroom door slam upstairs and smiled.

"'Mom thing,' huh? I'll show him."

WALLY SIGNED ONTO THE supers news and *National Mask* websites to see if there had been any overnight developments in the hunt for the Accelerator. Despite thousands of online tips, the authorities had nothing new to report other than that the search for the time-manipulating villain had expanded into Pennsylvania.

"Still at large," Wally read off the Super-Villain Task Force page. A spokesman said they believed that Accelerator remained somewhere in the tristate area. "This is one of the largest and most extensive manhunts in the history of the task force," the spokesperson continued. "Every law enforcement agency in the vicinity is involved, along with the FBI and National Security Agency. The Accelerator may avoid capture for a while, but he's fast running out of time."

Wally wondered what information they weren't releasing. It made sense that if they were closing in on the bad guy, they wouldn't want him to know that and give him the chance to run. He also wondered if "every law enforcement agency in the vicinity" included the Crumbly sheriff's office. If so, maybe Brenda's father knew more than the USSVTF told the press. Of course, Wally would probably be the last person Sheriff Cunningham would share any of that with, but Brenda might be able to get something out of him.

Next, Wally went on Twitter to check on what the rest of the world had to say about the supervillain manhunt. The Accelerator had been trending, but all on speculation and rumors, with sightings reported in every city east of the Mississippi and one very dubious claim from Nome, Alaska, that the villain had accelerated some guy's cow so far into the future that only a stack of packaged meat remained.

He went back to the *National Mask* and dove into the boards. With New Jersey being so close to New York, the hub of supers activity in the country, there were a lot of self-styled local watchdog groups whose members spent all day online monitoring and mapping the super community. Since the Accelerator's escape, several of these groups had gone on high alert, charting every reported sighting and rating them according to their credibility. Wally zoomed in on the map to a fifty-mile radius of Crumbly which, because of its proximity to the prison Accelerator had escaped from, continued to receive hundreds of reported sightings. Nine of them, all reported in the hours before the gray car drove into

Crumbly, five of which were rated as "credible," had been made in the town's general vicinity.

Wally scrolled through the information. Sightings of the car. One of the car and the man driving it at a turnpike rest stop only about fifteen miles from Crumbly. Some of them listed a partial license plate number, no two of which agreed. And none, Wally noticed with a frown, that matched the one parked on Kane Street.

He posted on one of the sites, contributing the license number to the information pool in the hope that it would help someone else remember something. In less than a minute, the responses started coming in, but before he could read any of them, his mother knocked at the door and walked in without waiting for a response. Wally quickly closed the window he had been browsing before turning around and saying, too quickly, "Hi, Mom."

"Hi, honey. I made you that sandwich anyway," she said sweetly.

He stared at her, speechless.

"Just kidding," she said with a laugh. "Mike Brewer's at the door. Which I'm not kidding about but which I feel I should be."

Wally closed the lid of his laptop. "Mike's not so bad," he said weakly.

"You're kidding."

He shrugged. "Yeah. I guess. I mean... yeah."

"Okay," she said. And, as he passed her at the door, she added, "How are the Yankees doing?"

"Who? Oh, yeah. They won."

"Good for Benny."

"Yep. Gotta go, Mom," he said. He kissed her quickly on the cheek and raced downstairs. Just before he slammed the front door behind him, she heard Mike Brewer sneer, "What took you so long, Whiz Kid?"

Jamie wondered what Wally and his friends were up to. She couldn't imagine. But, she thought with deep, parental satisfaction, they lived in Crumbly. How much trouble could they possibly get into?

12

CHARLIE SAID, "WHAT?"

"It's okay, Mr. Baily," Brenda said.

"I said stand and be identified," the old man said. He closed one eye as he sighted down the barrel at Charlie.

"I'm standing. Identify me!" Charlie said, throwing his hands up over his head.

"It's okay, Mr. Baily," Brenda repeated. "This is Charlie Harris. He's a friend. He's here to talk to Mr. Handelman about fixing up his house."

"Brenda," Charlie whispered out of the side of his mouth. "He's got a gun."

"It's okay," she whispered back. "It's not loaded."

"You sure?"

She nodded. "All his guns are fixed so they can't shoot, even if he did have bullets."

Charlie glanced at the black hole in the end

of the barrel pointed at him and then back at Brenda.

"You're *absolutely* sure?"

She nodded.

Charlie lowered his hands and Mr. Baily lowered the gun.

"Can't be too careful these days," the old man said. "Never know when the Commies will come calling."

"Get a lot of Communist infiltrators around here, do you?" Charlie asked as his heart rate dipped back to normal.

"Not a blessed one since I been on post, by gum," Mr. Baily cackled proudly, patting the stock of his rifle.

"Good job," Charlie said. Then to Brenda he said, "Don't tell me this is the guy who's going to rebuild my porch."

"Oh, no. Mr. Baily just helps Mr. Handelman."

The old man winked. "I swing a pretty mean hammer, too, sonny."

Charlie forced a smile. "Okay."

"Is Mr. Handelman in his workshop, Mr. Baily?" Brenda asked.

Mr. Baily saluted. "Yep. You can pass."

They did. Charlie took a glance back in time to see Baily ducking back down into the tall weeds.

"Does he always do that, Brenda?"

"Only when it's his turn to be on sentry duty," she said.

"Who's on duty the rest of the time?"

"Nobody."

Charlie nodded.

"Mr. Baily fought in the war," she said. "The one in the 1940s, I think. Daddy said about ten years ago he started thinking the war was still going on. He's pretty old, you know."

"Wow, he doesn't look that old. I mean, World War II *ended* over seventy years ago. And he's still working as a carpenter?"

"Old doesn't mean useless, young man."

The voice emerged from inside the building ahead of the speaker, a short, squat, older man, his ruddy face surrounded by a wild aura of steel gray hair and a bushy beard. He wore blue denim overalls over a clean, white T-shirt stretched across a muscular chest and thick arms.

"I never said it did, sir," Charlie said. "It's just that Mr. Baily seems a little, um . . ."

"Boomer has his awkward moments, but he's a good man. A decorated war hero," the man said. He extended his hand. "Name's Morris Handelman. What can I do for you?"

Charlie took the other man's hand and said, "Charlie Harris. Nice to meet you."

The older man seemed surprised. "Harris, you say?"

"Yes, sir."

"Sadie Harris' grandnephew, are you?"

"That would be me."

"The writer?"

"Excuse me, but have we met?" Charlie asked. Something about the way the other man asked his questions tripped an alarm in his head.

Morris's laugh didn't sound quite right to Charlie. "Met? Us? Where would we have met?"

"I've been to lots of places."

Morris Handelman seemed to catch himself and closed his mouth into a benign smile. "No, I don't think so, son. It's just that it's been a few years since we've had a Harris in town, that's all."

"Mr. Harris is moving into his aunt's house," Brenda said.

"Is that a fact?" Morris gave Charlie the once-over, as if measuring his suitability for residency. "That old place needs a bit of work, you know. There's siding that has to be replaced, probably some windows as well, that front porch has to go, and I wouldn't be surprised if you need a new roof."

Charlie nodded. "The back porch is a mess too."

"I haven't been inside since your aunt passed, but the kitchen and bathrooms were dated even then. How's your plumbing and HVAC?"

"We've only just met, Mr. Handelman. Don't you think that's a rather personal question?" Charlie joked with a smile.

Morris flashed a smile that lasted all of half

a second, just to show he got it. "Uh-huh. Sarge and I will have to come around, take a look, and work up an estimate."

Charlie pointed back over his shoulder in the general vicinity of Mr. Baily's guard post and said, "Does Sarge also come armed?"

"Boomer Baily's an old warhorse who sometimes still hears the bugler's call, but he's harmless," Morris said. "Sarge Sekowsky takes care of him now. Those two enlisted together and fought in the same infantry unit in the Second World War and have been inseparable ever since."

"Okay, then. I guess I'll see you," Charlie said.

With Brenda leading the way, they started the short walk back to town.

"I'll say this for Crumbly," Charlie said once they were out of earshot of the concealed Boomer Baily, "it's sure got its fair share of colorful citizens."

"Daddy thinks it might be something in the water."

"Maybe I should start drinking bottled water."

"It couldn't hurt," Brenda agreed.

"COLONEL FLINT," THE YOUNG technician said into her headset. "I have a hit, sir."

In the underground headquarters of the US Super-Villain Task Force deep beneath the

New Jersey Meadowlands, Colonel Darwyn Flint swept his cool, ice-blue eyes across the cavernous command-and-control center, settling on Agent-in-Training Tracy Marrs on desk number twenty-three. The tall, athletic brunette rose from her seat in front of the console, one of dozens of agents monitoring the internet and airwaves for signs of super-villain activity.

"Report," the colonel snapped into his microphone as he strode to her station.

"Anonymous request for information on an open community bulletin board, server location..."

"Skip that. Describe the RFI?"

"Yes, sir. Thread discussing the search for the Accelerator. An anonymous user posted a New York State license plate number, reportedly from a gray sedan." Agent Marrs read off the number. "I'm back-tracing the poster's location now, Colonel."

"Does the plate match the car McMahon stole?" Flint said. He had come up beside the young agent and peered at her monitor.

"No, sir."

"Then why the alert, Agent?"

"Because when I ran a check on the license plate, I thought the result didn't sound right. But when I tried to run a deeper search, I hit a firewall that redirected my request and bounced it to a page that said the URL I'd requested no longer existed."

"Go on." Flint's eyes narrowed and he swept a hand over his bristly white crewcut.

"Long story short, sir, I chased the address through dozens of servers and routers looking for its point of origin, and finally cornered it in a server farm in Thailand."

"And?" he asked in anticipation.

"I pinged the site with a touchback tone and then ran the response through an algorithm that stripped out cloned and false feedback until it isolated a single valid address." Agent Marrs said. "Us. The DSA."

This intelligence caught even the usually imperturbable Flint by surprise.

"How in the world would the Accelerator get his hands on a car registered to the Department of Superhuman Activity?"

"If I may, sir," Tracy Marrs said, "the bigger question is, why did our parent agency's database block our search?"

"Yes," Flint said, drawing out the word and stroking his square jaw in thought. He pointed to her console. "Have you located the point of origin for the original RFI?"

"Yes, sir. It's a residential internet account with Coronet Cable. The IP address belongs to a Jamie Crenshaw, age thirty-seven, widowed, graphic designer, one child. Thirty-four

Cole Lane, Crumbly-by-the-Sea, New Jersey. Her history is about as ordinary as you can get. Except her husband died at Lincoln City. She owns a six-year-old Honda Civic. There's no cellular or cable service attached to her account, but she does have a standard land-line, telephone number, 201-555-1938." Tracy tapped some keys. "That's forty-six point four miles south of here, sir."

"Thank you," Flint said thoughtfully.

Agent Marrs watched him closely, trying to imagine what went on in the amazing mind of the muscular giant. A living legend in the covert operations field, Colonel Darwyn Flint had a career allegedly stretching back to service in military intelligence and the CIA during the Korean War. Some claimed his service began even earlier, in the 1940s during the Second World War. No one knew his true age, but even the most conservative rumors had him at well into his eighties. Even though he looked like a man in his fifties, she couldn't bring herself to believe the other rumor, that an encounter with an alien substance or being bathed in an ancient magic potion had somehow given the head of the Super-Villain Task Force prolonged life.

"Awaiting orders, sir," she said.

"How much field experience have you had?" he said.

"I'm afraid not very much, sir, but—"

"That's about to change. Grab your gear and try to keep up, Agent Marrs. We're going to Crumbly-by-the-Sea."

MIKE BREWER'S FATHER WOULDN'T allow a computer in the house. He believed the internet had been created as part of a vast government conspiracy to spy on American citizens. Mike didn't know why the government would want to spy on his father or anyone else in Crumbly, but there were lots of things Mike didn't understand. And what Mike didn't understand, he didn't spend a lot of time worrying about.

Mike did understand money. And he had been thinking about it a lot since learning that an escaped supervillain might be hiding out under his nose.

And Mike figured there would probably be a reward for capturing an escaped supervillain.

Sure, Wally had started this whole thing, but he'd never make the call, that big chicken. And if Wally ever did find the guts and they did have the information that got the Accelerator caught and did get the reward, they'd have to split it between the *eleven* of them . . . unless the Truman twins counted as one? Whatever. And getting *all* of something sure beat getting one-eleventh of it, especially if that something is money.

Which all brought him, after ditching Abel and Nick back on Kane Street, to the Crumbly-by-the-Sea Library and Cultural Society Center, housed in the one hundred-and-fifty-year-old Crumbly mansion, a sprawling old colonial that stood at the high end of Main Street, its austere white façade peering watchfully down on the little town named after its founder, Josiah G. Crumbly.

Mrs. Henrietta Pinchot, town librarian and the president of the Cultural Society, greeted Mike's late afternoon arrival with a suspicious glare. Young Mr. Brewer, like his father before him, did not visit very often, and his rare appearances, usually accompanied by his two snickering shadows, were more often than not a prelude to trouble. Today, he came in alone, and instead of his customary sneer of contempt, he wore a look of thoughtful contemplation.

He went straight to the table between nonfiction and young adult fiction where the library's two communal computers sat and bent over one of the machines, going to work immediately on the keyboard.

Mrs. Pinchot allowed herself the smallest little glimmer of hope. Was it possible that Mike Brewer had found something to interest him enough that it had brought him into the library on a beautiful summer afternoon? There might be hope for the boy after all.

13

"YOU KNOW, WE COULD do this with an app, Guy."

"So you've said, Norman."

"It's easy. I've been playing around building one myself online. You know, while I pointlessly sit here for hours at a stretch waiting for an alarm that almost never rings."

"Someone's got to be on monitor duty," Hyperion said.

"That's what I'm trying to tell you: they don't. The computers do the actual monitoring. We just sit here and watch them do it," Blend said. The teammates were in the communications center of Justice Brigade headquarters in the Wheeler-Nicholson Building, Hyperion making a last-minute check on the monitors.

"We're equipped with state-of-the-art satellite and quantum communications linking us to every corner of the Earth and monitoring our solar system out to the orbit of Pluto. What good is it if there's no one here to watch it?" Hyperion said defensively.

"I told you. It's a waste of time. Instead of making us sit here like dummies twiddling our thumbs for twelve-hour shifts staring at a bunch of screens, an app could send alerts to our cell phones wherever we are."

"But... monitor duty. It's a tradition."

"We'll make a new tradition all our very own," Blend said. "One that doesn't include involuntary solitary confinement."

"Haven't there been enough changes already with Charlie quitting and William taking a leave?"

"Come on, Guy. This will be good. Besides, how often do we get alerts anyway?"

The alarm started to scream.

Hyperion smiled and exclaimed in triumph, "See!"

Blend rolled his eyes.

"We have a hit on Brandon McMahon, aka the Accelerator. Correction. Two hits. First is a civilian inquiry to the USSVTF. The second is an email to the brigade's tip line."

"I could've read that on my smartphone," Blend said.

"But would you have known that both hits are from the same location, the town of Crumbly-by-the-Sea, New Jersey?"

"You do understand how computers and the internet work, right? Whatever it says on the big screen here will be sent to the little screens on our phones at the same time."

"You can explain it to me en route," Hyperion said. "Summon the team, my friend. We're on our way to Crumbly-by-the-Sea."

"HEY!"

Crosshair came striding into the meeting room, waving his cellphone over his head. The other members of the League of Villains were seated around the giant flat-screen television to watch *Hyperion: Hero from Beyond*, the unauthorized movie biography of their foe released several years earlier. Critics and moviegoers alike had found the entire production horrible, even laughable, which made it the favorite movie of most supervillains. The league never tired of repeated viewings, making fun of the hero—not to mention the portrayals of themselves—and throwing popcorn at the screen.

Only Doctor Psycon didn't participate. He still hovered in the air, his mumbling lost in the din of the blasting Dolby Sound system while his comrades turned their mockery and scorn on the movie.

"Hey," Crosshair shouted. "I found him."

Sledgehammer Sue glanced his way. "What?"

"*Him.* I found him," Crosshair hollered, but

Sue only pointed to her ear, shrugged, and turned back to the TV screen.

Crosshair took a deep breath to yell even louder, but then he spotted the remote control in Stormcloud's lap. He popped a half-inch throwing pellet from his pouch and, without even seeming to aim, flicked it at the remote control. The pellet bounced off the "pause" button and bounced back up with just enough force to nip the tip of Stormcloud's nose.

"Ow! Hey, what's the big idea?" the Lord of Lightning snarled, grabbing his nose and jumping to his feet in the sudden silence.

"I *found* him," Crosshair said.

"Who?"

"Waldo! Who do you think I mean, you chimp? McMahon. The Accelerator," the Tsar of Targets shouted in exasperation. "He's in Jersey. Some nowhere town called Crumbly-by-the-Sea."

He had their attention now. The movie forgotten, the villains gathered around Crosshair.

"Are you sure?" Manika demanded.

"Crumbly-by-the-Sea?" Stormcloud said. "Never heard of it."

"Then I guess it don't exist," Sledgehammer Sue sneered. Then to Crosshair she said, "*Are* you sure? How'd you find him?"

Crosshair held up his phone.

"Nothing to it. I created a Google Alert for

Accelerator's name and I just got an email alert about a post on some fan forum."

Professor Lamplighter shook his head and chuckled. "Oh, imagine what fun I might have had with this technology in the 1890s."

Just then, Doctor Psycon opened his eyes, returning suddenly to reality from his deep trance. He looked down at his comrades and gasped.

"I have located him," the doctor's thin, high-pitched voice announced. "After taking into consideration the many and varied data points that are together the sum total of our knowledge of the Accelerator, factoring in the standard operating procedures of the New Jersey State Police, the Super-Villain Task Force, and the FBI and their search parameters, I have concluded that our friend will be found even now within a ten-mile radius of Hershey, Pennsylvania."

Sledgehammer Sue grabbed Crosshair's phone from his hand, holding the screen up to the hovering doctor.

"Or maybe Crumbly-by-the-Sea, New Jersey?"

Doctor Psycon settled slowly to the floor, squinting at the phone in her hand.

"My glasses," he said, patting himself. "Has anyone seen my glasses? Ah, never mind. Here they are." The doctor pulled a pair of wire-rimmed eyeglasses from his pocket and slipped them onto his nose under the bulbous dome of his head.

"Son of a gun," the doctor grunted.

"What do you think, dear Doctor?" Lamplighter said.

"Who am I to argue with Google?" Doctor Psycon said.

SHERIFF RUSSELL CUNNINGHAM HUNG up the telephone on his desk, tapping the fingers of his other hand against the arm of his wooden swivel chair. The sheriff had just fielded the fifth call of the day. Five calls. He didn't usually get five calls a week, and those were mostly nonsense, like old Mr. Wannamaker's complaining of the spies watching his television through his windows at night, or reports of raccoons overturning trashcans.

Today's calls weren't much more serious, but they sure were different. Folks wanting to know why all the children, his daughter Brenda included, were running wild in the streets. That last call had been from Mrs. Washburn, complaining that hordes of crazed youngsters were trampling through her backyard. Except Crumbly didn't have hordes of kids and those it did have weren't of the crazed, rampaging sort.

The call before that had been a report of an

abandoned car with out-of-state license plates on Kane Street. He told Mr. Pavia that if it had license plates, it probably wasn't so much abandoned as parked, but after the old man reminded the sheriff who paid whose salary in this town, he sighed and agreed to come by and take a look.

Russell Cunningham didn't mind the calls. Being sheriff of Crumbly-by-the-Sea didn't require a lot of effort. He had spent a couple of years as an army MP and six years as a police officer in Newark before returning home to Crumbly to raise his family in the safety of a small town. And even though the job didn't often require he use them, he still had his cop instincts and those told him this much deviation from routine meant something could be going on. Probably nothing serious, but something.

At least it gave him something interesting to do, he thought with a smile. He stood and reached for his faded blue cap with a fabric patch of the Crumbly's sheriff badge sewn on the peak, the one symbol of his office he ever wore. A sidearm came with the job, but he had locked the gun and holster in the office safe on the day he started and hadn't had a reason to take it out since.

As he reached for the door, the telephone started ringing again. He hesitated, assuming it would probably be just another kid or car complaint, but his sense of duty got the better of him and he picked it up on the third ring.

"Sheriff's office. How can I help you?" he said.

"Is this Sheriff Russell Cunningham?" a man asked.

"Yes, sir. How can I help you?"

"Russell *David* Cunningham?" the man said, going on to recite the sheriff's date of birth, social security number, and his army serial number.

"Who is this?" the sheriff demanded. "How did you get—?"

"Don't be alarmed, sir. I have to be sure I'm talking to the right man."

"You won't know until you tell me who you are and what this is all about."

"I'm Special Agent Roger Todd, Federal Bureau of Investigation. I'm calling to follow up on some recent activity in your vicinity."

"FBI? Activity? Is this some kind of joke? What kind of activity? Crumbly doesn't *have* activity."

"I understand it's a small town, Sheriff. That's what makes the amount of chatter coming out of it that our DRU intercepted so unusual."

"You want to give that to me in civilian talk, Agent Todd?"

"D. R. U. Digital Reconnaissance Unit. Our monitors have picked up several internet communications of a sensitive nature originating from Crumbly."

"Of a sensitive nature how?"

"Well, I'd rather hear from you before I possibly prejudice your account with that information."

"I'll tell you one thing, the way you made my head start aching within thirty seconds of answering the phone, I absolutely believe you're with the government. Look, Agent Todd, either tell me what this is about or I'm hanging up."

"I'm afraid that's classified, Sheriff."

Sheriff Cunningham hung up the phone. Then he folded his arms across his chest and waited. A few moments later it rang again. He smiled, letting it ring four more times before answering.

"Sheriff's office. How can I help you?" he said.

"This is Special Agent Todd, Sheriff. We must have gotten disconnected."

"No, sir. I hung up. I figured if you can't tell me what you want, there's no point wasting either of our time."

After a brief pause, the man on the other end sighed. "Okay. Right. The intercepts were in regard to Brendan McMahon, aka the Accelerator."

That surprised the sheriff. "The one who

escaped Trenton the other day? What would he be doing in Crumbly?"

"Judging from its limited accessibility, I'd say hiding out."

"That's nuts. How would an escaped convict get from Trenton to here of all places?" The sheriff shook his head. Then he stopped, his brow creasing into a frown, and said, "Wait. An escaped supervillain?"

Agent Todd's voice took on a hint of excitement. "Yes. He's a member of the League of Villains."

"Forget it, pal," the sheriff said with a chuckle. "I can practically guarantee you there hasn't been a valid sighting here. What you intercepted is more than probably our local little boy who's always crying super-wolf."

"What?"

"The message or email you caught? From a kid named Crenshaw, right?"

He waited while the man on the other end checked his report. "A woman. Jamie Crenshaw."

"Yeah, the account would be in her name. That's his mother." Sheriff Cunningham pushed his cap back and scratched his head under his short-cropped auburn hair. "Look, I can go have a talk with him if you want, but Wally's just a kid with an overactive imagination. He sees superheroes everywhere. He runs around town pretending sometimes, wearing a mask and cape."

"That isn't the only hit, though. We've also got a message to the Justice Brigade's email tip line, this one sent from a public computer address belonging to the Crumbly library."

"A lot of people use those computers. We don't get much internet here for some reason, so not a lot of homes have computers."

"Isn't that unusual in this day and age?"

"Maybe, but it's usual enough for us, I guess. Give me your number, Agent Todd. I'll talk to Wally and get back to you with what I find out."

"Thank you, Sheriff. I appreciate your cooperation."

At least this call explained the others he had been receiving all day. Wally had probably instigated it all, imagining he'd seen the Accelerator, then getting the other kids riled up to run around hunting for the bad guy.

"Kids," he muttered with a weary shake of his head, then hurried out before his phone could ring again.

14

THE WHIZ KID STOOD alone.

As the day dragged on, the other kids began taking off. Mike Brewer went first, slipping away and leaving Nick and Abel with no one to follow. As soon as they'd realized they were leaderless, they hurried off to find and reattach themselves to him. When Brenda and Charlie Harris still weren't back to the house after Wally had returned from checking the internet, the exodus sped up. They all had excuses ranging from chores to Benny's admission that he'd gotten bored and wanted to go.

Leaving the Whiz Kid alone.

He sat on the curb at the corner of Kane and Main Streets, by now as familiar to him as his bedroom. He kept trying to think of at least one thing that made the day not a total waste of time, but he didn't have much success. Okay, maybe Mike Brewer had taken a break from being totally obnoxious, and, yeah, in spite of how scared he'd been, Wally had made himself sneak into Mr. Harris' backyard and that felt pretty good, but as far as the mission went, it had been a bust. If only he could figure out a way to get inside that house to once and for all answer the question of the visitor's identity.

But how?

"Hi, Wally," Brenda said, coming around the corner, startling Wally. He jumped to his feet.

"Brenda! Hey. Hi. Wow, I didn't hear you," he said. "Where have you been all day?"

"With me. She's been showing me around," Charlie Harris said, rounding the corner a few paces behind her, his hands filled with shopping bags. "You're Wally, right? I'm Charlie Harris. Nice to finally meet you without a car or a bush between us. Brenda tells me you're a fan."

Wally froze the instant he laid eyes on Charlie. One of the leading experts on supers in the country. His favorite writer. Actual friends with guys like Hyperion and the Knave. Standing now right in front of him, with no place for Wally to hide, talking to him. Asking him a question. Wait, he couldn't remember the question? But he'd only asked it a second ago. Wally started to sweat, blinking his eyes, and he couldn't think of anything to say.

Brenda stepped in, saying, "The biggest. He's got your books and all the magazines your articles have been in and..."

Wally's fear of coming off as the obsessive dork Brenda described overcame his awe-induced panic and he blurted out, "The *National Mask*, I've been subscribing since I was seven."

Charlie grinned. "No kidding? Man, I could hardly even read at seven."

Wally nodded and raced on, "We were visiting in Washington, DC, when Doctor Psycon tried to blow up the White House before Hyperion and the Justice Brigade stopped them, and I picked up a piece of the bomb, a nut and bolt—nothing dangerous, ha-ha-ha—and it's like my favorite thing and I—"

"Oh, yeah?" Charlie said. "I was there that day too."

"I know," Wally said, nodding in excitement. "I loved your article about it in the *Mask*."

"Thanks. I always kind of liked the way that one turned out too."

Now that he had started talking, Wally couldn't stop. "That one's my favorite, because I saw what happened myself, you know? But I also really love the stories you wrote about the supers of Europe. They sound so cool. Do you know if the Justice Brigade and the European Union are ever planning a team-up? That'd be so cool, right?"

"Yeah, it would, but can we talk about it inside? These bags are heavy," Charlie said.

"Inside?" Wally said, surprised.

"Yep. I've got a lot of repairs to make on the old place so it's kind of a mess right now, but I'm happy to talk while I'm putting away the groceries and stuff."

Wally looked at Brenda with disbelief. She winked.

Wally shrugged and smiled and said, "Sure, yeah, that'd be great. Yeah." He held out his hands, "I can carry some of those for you, you know, if you want."

"My fingers have gone numb, so yeah, thanks."

While Charlie transferred two of the bags to Wally, Sheriff Cunningham came strolling up the street. Wally noticed he wore his blue on-duty cap. That could mean any number of things, of course. He might be looking for Brenda. Or he could want to introduce himself to Mr. Harris, the new guy in town. Or maybe he'd come to yell at Wally for something, a not too infrequent occurrence.

As it turned out, the sheriff had come for all three reasons. He smiled warmly at Brenda and said, "Hi, honey. How's it going?" She said, "Great, Daddy. This is Charlie Harris. He's moving into Mrs. Wicker's house." Charlie put down some bags and shook hands with the sheriff, exchanging a round of "nice to meet yous" and a "welcome to town/nice to be heres." Only then did the sheriff turn his eyes on Wally and say, "You. I've been getting calls about you, Wally."

"M-me? What did I do? Who's calling about me?"

"Some of the people around here, wanting to know what you guys are up to. Mrs. Washburn called to complain about the mob stampeding through her yard."

"Mob?" Wally said. "I'm not a mob. And I tiptoed."

"Who's Mrs. Washburn?" Charlie said.

"Lady who lives right here, behind you," the sheriff said.

Charlie's right eyebrow went up and he looked at Wally, who wouldn't return the gaze.

"Oh," Sheriff Cunningham said, dropping the big one, "and the FBI called."

That got Wally's attention. His eyes and mouth were wide. "The . . . the . . . ," he said uselessly.

Charlie's left eyebrow joined the right.

"The agent said you reported a supervillain sighting in town. We've talked about this before, haven't we, Wally? More than a couple of times, as I recall."

"Y-yes, sir, I know, but I swear, I didn't report anything. I just asked about the Accelerator in a chat room, that's all."

That got Charlie's attention. "You mean Brendan McMahon? What about him?"

"He escaped from Trenton yesterday morning," Wally said. "I thought for sure you knew."

"I've been offline for a couple of days," Charlie said. "And I haven't had any cell reception since I got here. What's your interest in the Accelerator, Wally?"

Sheriff Cunningham answered for him. "Young Mr. Crenshaw's a bit obsessed with the supers, Mr. Harris. Let's just say he has a tendency to be a little overzealous in his identification of suspects."

"Yeah?" Charlie said.

"Where did you think you saw the Accelerator?" Charlie asked.

"Well," Wally said, starting to squirm, "I guess, uh, well, the first time, you know, I'd have to say the first time I saw him, um, see, lemme see, I think it could have been—"

"Wally," the sheriff snapped.

"Going into Mr. Harris' house," Wally said. "Okay? I . . . I thought he looked kind of like the Accelerator, who'd escaped from Trenton, which isn't that far away, and his car's gray with New York license plates, just like the reports said the Accelerator escaped in, and . . . ," but he had run out of "ands" and probably sounded like an idiot to Mr. Harris.

Who instead said, "Yeah, I can see how you could make that mistake."

"Excuse me?" The sheriff squinted suspiciously at Charlie.

"I mean, he had a bunch of facts that led him to a certain conclusion which he followed up on. That's what I do as a journalist. And what you do in police work, Sheriff. He got it wrong, but his logic isn't so completely off."

Wally couldn't believe it. A grown-up, one of his heroes, defending him for being a dumb kid.

"I'm more concerned with the logic of getting calls from the Feds," Sheriff Cunningham said. "I know you mean well, Wally, but this has got to stop, no kidding. This is Crumbly. There aren't any supers within fifty miles of here and I guarantee you, there never will be. What do you think, Mr. Harris?"

Charlie scratched his chin thoughtfully, a smile tugging at the corners of his mouth. "Well, I doubt you'll see anyone running around town in a costume anytime soon," he said.

Sheriff Cunningham put his hands on his hips and gave Wally a hard look. "Got that, son? No supers in Crumbly. Do we understand each other?"

"Yes, sir," Wally said with reluctance. "No more supers."

The sheriff let the look linger on Wally a few moments longer before nodding. "Good," he said. "Anyway, nice to meet you, Mr. Harris. Let me know if these kids bother you too much." He winked at his daughter. "Especially this one."

"Not to worry there. Brenda's been a big help showing me around town."

"Good, glad we got that all settled," the sheriff said. "No, not quite all. I almost forgot Mr. Pavia's call about an abandoned gray car outside your house."

"It belongs to a friend of mine. It's not abandoned. It's parked."

"That's what I said," the sheriff smiled. "You have a good evening. And you, young lady, dinner's in one hour."

"See you later, Daddy," Brenda said.

Charlie waited until the sheriff had moved out of earshot before he grinned at Wally, "You and the sheriff have a history, huh?"

To hide his embarrassment, Wally started gathering up some of the shopping bags. "I guess. Yeah, sort of. He hates me."

"He doesn't hate you. He just thinks you've got too much imagination, that's all," Brenda said.

"Sure. Anyway, it doesn't matter anymore," Wally said softly.

"I'm sorry, Wally," Brenda said. "He's just doing his job."

"No, he's right. I mean, what would the Accelerator be doing anywhere near Crumbly?

I guess everybody thinks I'm just a stupid kid who runs around in a mask, pretending to look for supervillains." He looked at Charlie. "I'm sorry, Mr. Harris. I shouldn't have gotten you involved."

"First, please everybody stop calling me Mr. Harris. Every time you do, I expect to turn around and see my father, which would be kind of spooky."

"Oh, I'm sorry, mist—uh, Charlie. I didn't know your dad was gone," Brenda said sympathetically.

"No, he's alive and well and living in Florida, but I just know better than to let him sneak up behind me," Charlie said. "And second, my young super friend, I know a few of the actual supers myself and I don't think you're a stupid kid."

Wally shrugged and made an effort to smile. "Thanks, Mr. Harris. But I should get home, you know? Mom will have dinner ready soon."

Wally set the bags down on the ground and said, "I'll see you later, okay?"

15

WALLY FINALLY DRAGGED HIMSELF out of bed and down to the breakfast table after his mother's third warning that he would not get another warning. He hadn't slept very well. He couldn't believe what an idiot he must look like to everyone. No wonder Mike Brewer picked on him. Even Brenda and Benny, his best friends, were sick of his superhero games. Well, definitely Benny. Probably Brenda too. After yesterday, he wouldn't be surprised if Sheriff Cunningham had told her to stay away from him before he got her into trouble with the FBI too.

The Federal Bureau of Investigation!

Just for asking a stupid question in a stupid chat room. When did that become a federal case?

But it proved one thing: the supers weren't anything to fool around with. He always knew how serious a business it was—what he'd seen in Washington, DC, and what happened to his father in Lincoln City proved that. But he'd been so young when it all happened, it felt more like a dream or a video he once used to watch but hadn't seen for a long time. It had been almost four years since his dad had died and, while Wally's memories of him were still vivid, that part where they lost him in Lincoln City had grown hazy. He had only ever seen images of the destruction once, live on television, and then spent the next years trying to forget what he'd seen. He never wanted to think of his father experiencing what he had seen that day on TV, but for a long time he couldn't *not* think about it.

He wasn't a super and he never would be. Did he really think he'd ever be able to get back at the F'harah for what they'd done to his family and the planet? They were a militant alien race that could travel between the dimensions; he wore a cheap Halloween mask and homemade cape. He'd been fooling himself all along. No, not even that. He'd just been a little kid with a big, dumb fantasy.

He could still be interested in supers without wanting to be one. A lot of kids loved baseball but knew they were never going to be able to play in the big leagues. They loved it for the game itself. The supers could still be his hobby without being his entire life.

As he finished his cereal, Brenda knocked at the back door. As relieved as he was to see her, he remained embarrassed enough by his behavior to avoid looking her in the eye.

"Hey, Wally," she said, opening the screen. "I wanted to see how you were doing."

"Hi," he said. He scrambled to his feet, taking his bowl and spoon to the sink. "I'm okay. I'm fine. Why wouldn't I be okay and fine?"

"It's okay to be upset, Wally," she said gently.

He turned on the tap and picked up the sponge to wash the bowl.

"I'm not, Brenda, okay? I told you, your father's right. Like, how lame do you have to be to see supervillains everywhere?"

"I don't think you're lame, Wally."

He scowled. "You're my friend. You have to be nice to me."

"No I don't. Benny's your best friend and he's always mean to you."

"In a lot of ways, *you're* my best friend, Brenda," Wally said, before he even realized the words had come out of his mouth.

Brenda looked as surprised to hear them as he'd been to speak them, but before either of them could respond, someone else knocked at the door.

"Good morning. Okay if I come in?" Charlie Harris said through the screen.

Wally couldn't believe how grateful he

felt for the interruption and quickly shut off the water and said, "Oh, yeah, sure. Hi, Mr. Harris."

"Charlie, remember?" He stepped into the kitchen and looked around. "Nice place. I can hardly wait until I've got a functioning kitchen again."

"Do you want a cup of coffee? Mom's always got some on the stove."

"That would be nice, thanks. I haven't had anything but instant coffee for days."

Wally got down a mug and poured a cup from the pot on the stove. Charlie declined milk and sugar. "Real reporters drink it black," he said after a satisfying sip.

"So . . . ," Wally said.

"Yeah, sorry, just enjoying the brew. Tell your mother she makes a mean cup of coffee."

"Thank you. The secret is chicory."

They all turned as Jamie Crenshaw came into the room, her "World's Superest Mom" mug in hand.

"Hi, Mrs. Crenshaw," Brenda said.

"Hi, Mrs. C," Charlie said, extending his hand. "Great coffee. I'm Charlie Harris. I'm the new kid in town, just moved in over on Kane Street."

Jamie took his hand and they shook. "Thank you, Mr. Harris. I'm Jamie Crenshaw. Nice to meet you."

He held up his cup. “Chicory you say?”

“They carry it at the general store,” Jamie said, refilling her cup. “It’s a dried root that you brew with the coffee.”

“Charlie’s Mrs. Wicker’s nephew, Mom,” Wally said. “And you know what else?”

Jamie tilted her head and gave Charlie the once over. “Let me guess. He’s also a writer who reports on the supers.”

Charlie laughed. “Have you been Googling me, Ms. Crenshaw?”

“Call me Jamie. And I didn’t have to. I heard it through the grapevine.”

“I imagine news travels fast around here.”

“Boy, you don’t know,” Wally said with a groan.

“Let’s just say everybody watches out for everybody else’s business,” Jamie said. “Your arrival set off a round of phone calls and gossip at the general store, that’s for sure. Everybody’s wondering what brings a successful writer from New York to our little lost corner of the world.”

“As it happens, a lost corner of the world is exactly what I’m looking for. I’ve got some books to write and all I need is a quiet place in which to write them.”

“Well, you’ve found it. Sometimes the quiet around here is deafening.”

“Yeah? What’s your excuse?”

“Wally is. I grew up in Crumbly but left to

go to college in New York, then ended staying there, got married, and had Wally. Then he and I came back here after he turned eight."

"Had enough of the big city, huh?"

"You could say that," Jamie said softly.

"Oh, hey," Charlie said, realizing they were wandering into a sensitive area, "I'm sorry, I didn't mean to pry or anything."

"No, it's okay. My husband was in Lincoln City."

CHARLIE FELT HER WORDS like a blow to the gut.

He had been in Lincoln City too. With the Justice Brigade.

Where they had failed to stop the alien invaders from destroying the city.

"Are you all right, Charlie?" Jamie said.

"What? Me? Yeah, I'm fine," he said. He looked at her and then at Wally. "I'm . . . yeah, I didn't know. I'm sorry, kid."

Wally shrugged and nodded. "It's okay."

Jamie smiled and quickly changed the subject back to the safety of coffee, asking Charlie if he wanted more.

"Thanks, but I just stopped by to see if Wally would be interested in doing a little honest labor."

"Labor?" Wally said skeptically. "Is that like work?"

"*Paid* labor, kid. Brenda's already signed on to the crew."

"Oh, that's different. Sure."

"Me and my friend," Charlie said, adding, "you know, the one who's *not* the Accelerator? We're doing some work on the house and could use some muscle for dragging out the trash, sweeping up, maybe even painting if you can figure out how to use a roller. Think you can handle it?"

Wally looked at his mother. She smiled and nodded.

"Thanks, Charlie," he said. "When do we get started?"

"You kidding? You're already late. Let's go!"

THE BIG BLACK SUV stopped when it reached marsh water up to its hubcaps. Behind it, somewhere, a narrow, but serviceable tarmac road had somehow disappeared under deepening layers of mud, muck, and tall marsh grasses. Ahead of it, nothing but more water and muck and more marsh grasses. The air hummed with the sound of thousands of croaking frogs and chirping birds.

The driver's side window of the SUV slid down with a soft buzz.

"How is this possible, Agent Marrs?" Colonel Darwyn Flint said in disbelief. "How do we get lost in the swamp in a vehicle outfitted with a state-of-the-art digital satellite tracking system?"

In the seat next to him, Tracy Marrs studied the satellite tracking screen panel.

"I think it's a marsh, sir," she said. "And something's seriously wrong with the GPS. We can't acquire a signal." She tapped at the screen, adjusted controls on the dashboard, and shook her head. "I can't tell what's causing the interference, but I don't think it's being directed specifically at us."

"What sort of interference?"

Tracy flipped open another panel on the dash, this one unfolding into a keyboard, and began to type. "It's hard to say, sir. Whatever it is, it doesn't have a point of origin, and it's covering a broad range of frequencies, from common carrier waves to our shielded signals."

Lost in thought, his mouth set in a grim line, Flint tapped his fingers against the steering wheel.

"It's theoretically impossible to block a quantum signal, isn't it?" he said.

"Theoretically, sir. The signal changes frequency several million times a second and there's no way to duplicate quantum particles to tap into or block the signal."

"Which means?"

"It means we're lost, sir," Agent Marrs said with a helpless shrug.

"Yes," Flint said. "That's my conclusion as well."

The agents from the US Super-Villain Task Force sat silently, considering their options.

"Maybe we should back up and try to find the road we were on. We can take that back to the interstate and ask directions to Crumbly at the rest stop?" Tracy finally offered.

Flint nodded. A man of few words, he turned the key in the ignition. The engine groaned, made a grinding sound, then clicked and went silent.

"Agent Marrs?" he snapped.

Even as Tracy turned to the keyboard, all the displays and lights in the car went dark.

THE JUSTICE BRIGADE'S VERTICAL takeoff and landing craft, the *Screaming Eagle*, sat on the helipad atop the Wheeler-Nicholson Building in New York, its three engines idling in neutral. Hyperion manned the controls, waiting impatiently for his teammates to finish strapping in.

It had taken longer than he liked for everyone to respond to the summons after he and Blend had received the alert. Ward Simonson, aka Fakeout, told him not to bother him in the middle of the night unless it was a real emergency, and Aquina seemed to be ignoring her signal device. Both finally showed up, after dawn. If they hadn't already been shorthanded, Hyperion would have left without them, but then the team would have been literally at half-strength, a dangerous situation to put them in.

"Ready to go anytime you are," he called over his shoulder.

"Hold on," Ms. Muscles said. "Aquina had to go back downstairs for some water."

"She knows we keep water in the refrigerated compartment," Hyperion said in disbelief.

"Not for drinking," she said. "To keep her wet. She can't pour refrigerated water over her head."

"Why not?" Fakeout said. "She's from a civilization that lives at the bottom of the Atlantic Ocean. It's a lot colder down there than a chilled bottle of water."

"Why don't we just keep a tank of water onboard for her?" Fakeout asked.

"You know how much a tank of water weighs?" Fakeout said.

"I write sitcoms. You're the plumber. How much does it weigh?"

Fakeout said, "I don't know exactly. But a lot. The *Screaming Eagle* is built for speed, not to be a tanker."

"Want me to go get her? I can be back in a second," Swift said, unable to stand the inactivity.

"Nobody move," Hyperion ordered. "We'll wait for Aquina. She'll be right back."

The others continued to grumble, but a few minutes later Aquina returned, the hatch closed with the push of a button, and the *Eagle* rose straight up from the rooftop. The engines roared and, when they had gained enough altitude, Hyperion swiveled the engines to airplane mode and pushed forward on the throttle. The *Screaming Eagle* leapt into the sky and headed out over the blue Atlantic before turning south toward New Jersey.

"I'M LOSING PATIENCE HERE," Crosshair said through clenched teeth, tightly gripping the steering wheel.

Stormcloud, in the row of seats behind him, said, "You lost it an hour ago. Which would be, what? About thirty feet back."

"I'd be surprised if we've moved even that far," Crosshair said. "This traffic's insane."

"Jersey Turnpike, brother," Sledgehammer Sue said with a shake of her head. "The Garden State Parking Lot."

Professor Lamplighter carefully crossed his legs in the rear row of seats, checking the crease of his trousers.

"Sometimes I feel we were better off before technology came along and made us so impatient," he said.

"We'd be better off with *better* technology, like some kind of air transport instead of a miserable old van that used to belong to an old-age home," Manika said.

"It is simple, efficient, and unobtrusive," Doctor Psycon, riding shotgun, said. "And the windows were already blacked out when I purchased it."

"It also gets stuck in traffic," Sue said.

"A small price to pay for its benefits," the doctor said.

"The Justice Brigade's got that *Screaming Eagle*. Have you seen that thing? It's slick," Stormcloud said.

"I read about it in the *National Mask*," Maniak said. "It can take off and land like a helicopter, then fly like a jet at Mach three, with a range of over five thousand miles."

"And a price tag of several tens of millions of dollars," Psycon reminded them.

"Once we collect our money from Accelerator, we may want to think about upgrading our transportation, Doc," Crosshair said, peering at the endless river of traffic stretching out before them.

"Yeah, there ought to be enough spare bucks for a spiffy set of wings. Especially since there won't be enough left of Accelerator for him to take his split," Sue said, patting the hammer in her lap.

"Perhaps," Doctor Psycon said.

16

WALLY HAD TO ADMIT to being both a little disappointed and a lot relieved that Charlie Harris's visitor hadn't turned out to be the Accelerator after all. Having Charlie come to live in town was cool enough; getting to hang out with Charlie was beyond anything he could have ever imagined. He was actually talking about the supers with a guy who *knew* the supers.

He was sure his head was about to explode, but in a good way. He had so many questions, he didn't know where to start. Brenda suggested he calm down and breathe but Wally couldn't stop himself.

The hole in the front porch had been patched with several boards and surrounded with yellow and black NYPD warning tape.

"That would be William's handiwork,"

Charlie said, stepping around the patch. "He's a very cautious guy."

"I'll say. Does he always carry police warning tape around with him?" Wally said.

"He believes in being prepared. I think he used to be a Boy Scout." Charlie opened the door, letting his two new helpers in ahead of him. "Willie, I'm home," he called. "We've got company."

Wally heard the sound of hammering from somewhere in the rear of the house, which stopped at the sound of Charlie's voice. Then he heard footsteps before the tall, grim-faced man Wally had spied on from the backyard appeared in the hallway. The man put on a smile at the sight of Charlie's young companions, but Wally thought it had to be about the phoniest smile he had ever seen. Like something he had practiced in front of a mirror without ever having seen one himself. He didn't look very friendly at all.

Or anything like Brendan McMahon.

"Hello," he said.

"Willie Williams, this is Brenda and Wally," Charlie said. "I'll leave it to you to sort out who's who. They're going to help out around here. Thought I'd have them clear out the demolition debris and then get them started on the basement. Old Aunt Sadie was apparently quite the pack rat."

"GREAT," WILLIAM SAID WITH clearly false enthusiasm. He recognized the boy as the one who had sneaked into the yard to spy on him yesterday. He hadn't seen the girl before but assumed she had been the one who had come to the door the afternoon he'd arrived. Both were just curious children, but he thought the girl shouldn't be underestimated.

"Hi, Mr. Williams," the two kids said, more or less in unison.

The unpracticed smile still plastered on his face, William turned to Charlie and said, "Can I talk to you a minute, Charlie?"

"Can't it wait?" Charlie said patiently.

"I don't think so. It's about… the foundation."

"The foundation?"

William nodded. "Of everything," he said emphatically.

"Why don't you guys wander around and familiarize yourself with the place. Watch out you don't fall through any holes in the floor, okay?" Charlie gave the other man a weary look and said, "Let's talk."

CHARLIE AND WILLIAM DISAPPEARED into another room, leaving the two young friends alone in the foyer. Shrugging at one another, they turned to do as Charlie had told them.

Since all the houses on Kane Street had been built at the same time using the same blueprints, they were already familiar with the layout, but they wandered into the dining room at the rear of the house to give the grown-ups their privacy.

"I don't think Mr. Williams wants us here," Wally whispered.

"I'm not sure Charlie wants *him* here," Brenda whispered back. "I don't think they're all that friendly, do you?"

Wally shook his head. "He's got kind of a creepy smile too."

Brenda nodded. "I wonder what's going on."

"Maybe," Wally said slowly, his face lighting up with the glow from his imagination, "maybe he's, like, a reformed supervillain who Charlie's helping out by—"

"I kind of doubt it," she said. "And maybe you should be careful with the supers stuff. After yesterday, I mean."

"I know, I know. I'm just saying. I'm over it, okay?"

"It's just not worth getting into trouble for," Brenda said, concern in her voice. "I know you love the supers, but most people don't understand it like your friends do."

"No, they don't. They all make fun of me, even Benny."

"Benny's a jerk," she said, looking surprised at the sound of her words.

"Who's a *what?*"

Brenda walked over to the other side of the room and stood looking out the window.

"Nothing," she said.

"Calling Benny a jerk's not nothing."

"It's not a big deal. We just had a little argument."

"When? About what?"

Brenda folded her arms and shrugged. "Nothing, Wally. I told you, it's no big deal."

Wally watched her suspiciously. He would be the first to admit that he had no idea what went on between boyfriends and girlfriends, but in the seven months and nine days they had been going together, he'd never known them to have a fight. True, Benny might be a jerk sometimes, but Brenda would usually just make a joke or jab him in the ribs, and he'd cut it out. He'd never seen them come even close to arguing.

But instead he said, "Oh. Okay, I didn't mean—"

She whirled to face him and asked, angrily. "I mean, what's so hard about just doing something because I ask him to?"

"Uh," Wally said, surprised.

"But, no, he just makes another dumb Benny joke."

It hadn't occurred to him before, but Wally now realized why Benny hadn't also tagged along with them this morning.

"I told him not to talk to me until he grows up."

Beads of sweat broke out on Wally's forehead. He knew he should say something to help make her feel better, but he couldn't even begin to think what that might be. He *wanted* to agree that, yeah, Benny could be a jerk, but as Benny's best friend, Wally knew he didn't mean the things he said. He couldn't help making jokes, and girls . . . well, if he knew anything about girls, they sometimes wanted guys to be serious.

Brenda waited for him to say something and that only fanned his small spark of panic. He had to say something, but what?

IN THE FRONT PARLOR, William hissed at Charlie, "Do you think it's a good idea bringing them here? I don't trust that kid. He's been spying on me since I got here."

"Relax, Willie," Charlie said. "They're nice kids. Someone new comes to town, they're bored, they play spy games. What are you so worried about?"

"Our safety, for one thing."

"We're safe. We're in Crumbly. You know the town's motto?"

William stared at him, waiting.

"It's right there on the sign into town, 'Welcome to Crumbly-by-the-Sea, Where Nothing Ever Happens.'"

"This isn't funny."

"It could be, if you weren't such a stiff."

"There's no laughter in the face of injustice," William said, sounding like a man reciting an oath.

"And there's even less in the company of a stiff. Look, my house, my guests. You don't like it, leave. In fact, why are you still here anyway? Don't you have to get back to the city and singlehandedly save Western civilization from being overrun by the vast criminal hordes?"

"The brigade can take care of things while I'm away for a few days," William said defensively.

"What's going on, Willie? I told you, I've resigned, hung up my pointy shoes for good. You're not going to get me to change my mind."

"We'll see," William said, trying to sound mysterious.

Charlie shook his head, studying his colleague. "No. If you had something up your sleeve to get me back, you'd have pulled it out by now. This isn't about me anymore, is it, buddy?"

"You couldn't be more wrong," William said, laughing unconvincingly, then turned abruptly on his heels and strode from the room. Charlie let out a heavy sigh and followed.

17

MORRIS HANDELMAN CLAMORED UP a ladder against the back wall and onto the roof of his beach-front bunker. The monitors on his five-dimensional quasar doppler radar had sounded the alarm warning of an approaching aircraft, still thirty miles north of town but closing fast. Of course, aircraft of all kinds passed regularly through Morris' monitored airspace, but he had programmed his sophisticated array to sort through routine commercial and private traffic and only alert him when it found vehicles of unknown type or design or which were moving too fast or were on suspicious flightpaths.

This unidentified flying object had launched from the middle of Manhattan, which seriously limited the possibilities of its origin. At the speed they were moving, it would be overhead in minutes. He reached for the binoculars dangling from his neck and raised them to his eyes to scan the sky. Even though his cloaking devices were supposed to render him and the town effectively invisible to electronic detection, he always worried that someone might have invented something better. A small chance, true, but there were no absolute certainties in life.

He finally spotted it, a speck against a cloudless blue sky that quickly grew in his lens until he could see it with his naked eye. His very practiced, expert, naked eye that told him the airship had indeed been headed straight for Crumbly all along.

"Yep, it's them alright," said Morris Handelman, the man once known as the supervillain Giz-Mo.

SHERIFF RUSSELL CUNNINGHAM SAID, "Let me get that for you, Mayor," and reached into his pocket for his wallet. He smiled at Ma Casey across the counter of the general store and said, "Make that two coffees, Ma. And you got any of those homemade donuts today?"

Mayor George Cole turned and smiled his appreciation. "Why, thank you, Russell. Good morning."

"Just made them fresh this morning, Sheriff," Ma Casey said. She reached for a paper cup to fill from the pot of hot, dark coffee in her hand. Ma was a solid, squat woman in a sensible dress, worn work boots, her graying blond hair worn up in a fashion that had last been popular in the 1960s. She had a kindly face, a quick smile, and clear blue eyes that missed nothing.

"Can I tempt you too, your honor?" the sheriff said.

"With one of Ma's donuts? Always, m'boy, always." George Cole's sunny smile grew even brighter. "Though it's not every day we see you indulge." Both the mayor's sweet tooth and the sheriff's battles with his waistline weren't any secrets in town.

"It just feels like a donut kind of day," the sheriff said with a satisfied smile.

The sheriff took his first, satisfying sip of coffee and waited patiently while Ma put two of her delicious, soft donuts on paper plates, dusting them both with powdered sugar. But before he could reach for his warm, sweet reward, the general store began shaking, and he knew right then and there that he'd been wrong.

It wasn't going to be a donut kind of day after all.

FEENO MULLINS STEPPED BACK from the barber chair and carefully eyed his handiwork. He had spent the last several minutes carefully working his hand clippers over the bristling plateau of gunmetal-gray hair on top of the tanned, bullet-shaped skull before him. Next, he lathered up the hair on both sides of the man's head with shaving cream and now stood holding a straight razor. Feeno tried to be extra careful cutting Sarge Sekowsky's hair. The retired Marine took pride in a proper, military cut. He liked it short and shaved, a bristly crew cut on top with cleanly shaved temples and sideburns. He called it "whitewalls," and he had worn it that way since he'd first enlisted decades ago.

Feeno tilted Sarge's head to the right and started to carefully scrape the razor around his ear.

"Heard about the new fella?" the barber said.

"The one taking over the old Wicker place?" Sarge said, his voice a gravelly baritone.

"Is there a second new fella?" Feeno asked.

Sarge grunted. "Heard, haven't met him yet."

"Seems nice enough."

"We'll see."

Feeno wiped the razor on the towel folded over his arm and leaned in to continue his work when the air suddenly filled with a high-pitched mechanical whine. He stopped, the sharp blade poised over Sarge's left ear.

The sound grew louder and closer. By the time the two men raced out the barbershop door to investigate, the plate glass window had started vibrating from it.

The big airship, painted matte black, its three giant turbo-engines swiveled toward the ground, fell toward them from the northern sky.

"Well," said Sarge. "That's different."

"Yep," Feeno said in agreement.

INSIDE THE WICKER HOUSE, WALLY and Brenda were busy at their first task, gathering up and hauling out to the driveway all the ruined drywall and flooring that Charlie and Mr. Williams had torn out.

Charlie's visitor hadn't been very happy when he returned from their private chat and walked past the kids and into the other room, where he threw himself into his work in sullen silence. The conversation seemed to have had the opposite effect on Charlie, who came out with a big smile and a plan of action. He issued them heavy work gloves, instructed them to be on the lookout for stray nails, and presented them with a trash barrel for hauling the debris outside.

They had been at it almost an hour when the house started to shake.

Wally had a load of wallboard from the dining room balanced on top of his head when he felt it. At first, he thought someone was using a jackhammer, but the noise that accompanied the shaking sounded all wrong, not the rat-a-tat of construction equipment, but like the muffled whine of powerful engines. Some sort of helicopter or jet or—

Mr. Williams went racing past Wally, muttering something under his breath, the only words of which the startled boy could catch were "screaming eagle." But what kind of bird made that kind of—?

Wait.

Screaming eagle? As in *the Screaming Eagle*, the Justice Brigade's supersonic vertical takeoff and landing transport?

"No way," Wally whispered to himself.

He dropped his load and ran to the window, trying to locate the source of the sound, which now seemed to come from all directions. Then he saw it.

"Way!" he gasped.

CHARLIE HAD ALREADY DASHED up the walk by the time Wally dragged Brenda to the door. They weren't the only ones lured outside by the arrival of the *Screaming Eagle*. Wally couldn't remember seeing this many of his neighbors all together since the town's Fourth of July picnic.

But no one could ignore the landing of a strange aircraft at the end of Main Street in the middle of a lazy summer day.

"What is it?" Brenda said.

"It's the Justice Brigade," Wally said. "That's their ship."

"Wally," Brenda started to say, but then stopped herself.

"What?"

She shook her head and laughed in disbelief. "I almost told you not to get carried away again."

Wally grinned. "Do I get to say I told you so?"

"Just as long as you don't say it to my father." Brenda started to laugh. "This is insane, Wally."

"Right?"

She grabbed his arm and hugged it to her. "Aren't you going crazy? What are they doing here? How can you stand it, Wally?"

Wally honestly didn't know if it was the arrival of the *Screaming Eagle* or the way Brenda held on to his arm that made him feel dizzy.

"I... I don't know," he said, his voice hoarse.

He couldn't think with her hanging on to him like that, so he pulled away, following after Charlie, who had raced ahead up the sidewalk.

"Come on. We've got to stay close to Charlie. He knows the Justice Brigade."

Brenda nodded, her face bright with excitement.

DURING HIS LAST FEW months with the brigade, Charlie had started experiencing panic attacks whenever he'd had to suit up for action as the Knave. The thrill he used to get being a superhero had been replaced with a silent dread of inevitable pain. When he started out, the bad guys would put up a good fight to avoid being caught, but there seemed to have been an unspoken agreement that kept the violence from turning deadly.

But something changed after Lincoln City; like that sudden, senseless destruction somehow gave the world permission to go nuts and forget the old rules. Crooks who used to rely on non-lethal weapons for their crimes started showing up with blasters and lasers. Charlie never would have become the Knave in the first place if he'd had to face that kind of firepower. Sure, he wanted to help, but not at the risk of having his head blown off.

As soon as he'd heard the approaching whine of the *Screaming Eagle*, he felt the beads of panic sweat pop up on his forehead. It took him a second to catch his breath and remember he'd quit the team.

Not that an appearance by the brigade didn't still put him in danger. Their showing up like this could draw the wrong kind of attention. Why couldn't they leave him alone? He just wanted to get lost in this little bit of nowhere. He understood why crazy Willie had chased after him. But Guy Wallace, Hyperion, had wished Charlie luck in his new life. And, come to think of it, how did anyone else in the brigade know where to find him? Willie certainly wouldn't have shared the information. Mr. Justice himself had been like someone on the lam from his responsibilities to the team.

All of which confused Charlie and made him very unhappy. He had to do damage control. Quick. Tell the brigade whatever he had to in order to get them out of town as fast as possible, and then tell his new neighbors...

Something.

"Good plan," Charlie muttered as he trotted down the street, every eye of every resident of every home he passed on him. Some were starting to come out onto the street and fall in line behind him, the grand marshal of a parade marching to mess up his life.

"WOW," MS. MUSCLES SHOUTED over the dying whine of the turbines. "Are you sure you got the right place this time, Guy?"

Hyperion ignored her, his attention on shutting down the ship.

"What's the old saying? *Fifth* time's the charm," Blend said.

"It's only our third stop," Fakeout said.

"Are you sure?" Blend popped his safety belt release. But before he rose from his seat he said, "Should I even bother getting up or are we just going to find out we're in the wrong place again and take right off?"

"*This* is the right place," Hyperion announced tersely. "I told you. There's something interfering with the *Eagle*'s instruments. This time, I used my super-senses to locate the town and guide us in, but someone doesn't want it to be too easy to find," Hyperion said.

"Agreed, but this isn't Accelerator's MO," Fakeout said. "I mean, he's no dummy, but he's no scientist either. He couldn't have rigged up whatever it is that's messing with our instruments."

"Maybe he had help?" Ms. Muscles suggested.

"Only guy he knows capable of this kind of science is Doc Psycon," Blend said.

"And Accelerator and Doctor Psycon have been at war ever since the Vegas job," Hyperion reminded his colleagues. "Which means we have an unknown variable in the mix. That's not good news, but at least we know to expect a surprise."

"If you're expecting it, how can it be a surprise?" Blend asked.

"At any rate," Hyperion said, peering out the ship's windscreen, "now that the dust kicked up by our arrival has settled, it looks like the local town folk have been kind enough to come out to greet us."

Blend seemed doubtful. "If I was writing

this for television, those townsfolk would turn out to be killer cyborgs from the future."

Hyperion reached for the switch to open the hatch. "I doubt we have to worry about that," he said, but then hesitated. "Still, everybody keep a watchful eye on the crowd. Just in case."

He hit the switch and the *Eagle*'s hatch hissed open, a ramp automatically unfolding to the ground.

Straightening his cape, Hyperion stepped out into the sunlight, his hand raised in greeting to the sea of faces gathering around the now silent ship. He put on his friendliest superhero smile and said, "Excuse me, but this *is* Crumbly-by-the-Sea, New Jersey, isn't it?"

18

CHARLIE ONLY RECOGNIZED A couple of the townspeople who got to the *Screaming Eagle* ahead of him, but the faces crowded in the hatch behind Hyperion were all too familiar.

He pushed his way through the gathering onlookers, most of them staring in disbelief. It wouldn't be long someone got over their shock and started asking questions. He hoped to get to Hyperion before they did.

"*What do you think you're doing?*"

Too late.

The voice booming the question over the heads of the townsfolk belonged to Sheriff Russell Cunningham, who pushed his way through the onlookers from another direction, followed by a confused-looking little man with a round face.

They made way for the sheriff, who strode up to the landing ramp and parked his foot on it, scowling at the costumed Hyperion.

"I'm Hyperion and this is the Justice Brigade," Hyperion announced.

"I know who you are," the sheriff snapped. "What I want to know is what do you think you're doing landing an aircraft on a public street? Have you got a permit for that thing?"

"Permit? This is the *Screaming Eagle*. We're the Justice Brigade," Hyperion said, clearly confused by his reaction.

"And this, to answer your question, is indeed Crumbly-by-the-Sea. And to clear up any further confusion, what you've done is illegal under local, state, and I'm pretty sure federal law. You can't just drop an aircraft down anywhere you want, especially not in the middle of *my* town," the sheriff said, still annoyed he'd left his donut when he'd run out of the general store.

"*Our* town," said the mayor, spraying crumbs from his donut.

"I'm sorry, sir, but people are usually glad to see us," Hyperion said, starting down the ramp.

"What's your business in Crumbly, sir?" the sheriff said

Hyperion nodded, glancing at the increasing number of onlookers who were joining the crowd.

"About that," he said, leaning in to speak softly to the sheriff. "Perhaps it would be better if we spoke in private, sir. This is a matter of some delicacy and—"

"Look, Mr. Hyperion, you ran out of 'delicate' as soon as you landed a jet in the middle of town. So please tell me what's going on or I'm going to have to ask you to move this thing."

"Move it? Where?"

"My first thought would be to the nearest airport."

"Where's that?"

From the crowd, someone yelled, "There's the airfield over in Wayfair, about twenty miles west."

"That's only for small aircraft," another voice responded. "Something this size, you probably gonna have to go to Newark Airport."

"It doesn't matter," a third voice added. "This is one of those vertical takeoff and landing deals. It doesn't need a runway."

"Just an airport," the first man said.

"Undoubtedly," man number two agreed.

"Or an aircraft carrier," suggested the third.

A growing look of confusion in the eyes behind his mask, Hyperion said, "Please, Sheriff."

The sheriff nodded. "Let's talk inside."

Visibly relieved, Hyperion turned to lead Sheriff Cunningham up the ramp, but before he could take a step, a man behind him yelled, "Hey, yo, wait!"

Hyperion glanced back over his shoulder at

the man who had shouted, then did a surprised double take.

"Charlie?" Hyperion said in disbelief. "What are you doing here?"

THOUGH NEVER PARTICULARLY SHY, Charlie Harris felt suddenly self-conscious as every eye turned his way. He hadn't wanted to make a scene, but a loud interruption seemed the only way to get Guy's attention before he disappeared inside the *Eagle* with the sheriff and possibly said something to mess things up for Charlie.

Hyperion appeared to forget all about the sheriff, coming down the ramp toward Charlie. "I must say, when you told me you were leaving the—"

Charlie laughed loudly and quickly grabbed Hyperion's hand, shaking it vigorously, talking over the hero. "Hey, hi, Hype, old pal! Good to see you guys. Thanks for coming all this way, you know, to . . . to . . . I mean, for that interview." Still gripping his former colleague's hand, he turned the man around to led him back up the ramp. "Yeah, that *interview* you promised me. *Before* I left New York?" They passed the baffled sheriff and Charlie hoped his smile didn't look as stupid as it felt. "Hey, Sheriff. Hope you don't mind if I talk to these guys, just for a second, okay? Thanks."

Once inside the *Eagle*, Charlie demanded in a loud whisper, "What are you doing here?"

"H-hello, Charlie," Aquina said softly from the rear of the pack.

Charlie managed not to groan out loud and turned to her with a weak smile. "Yeah, hi, Aquina. I've been meaning to email you, but the internet around here sucks..."

Sheriff Cunningham stuck his head in the hatch. "Hello?"

Charlie jumped, whispering to Hyperion, "Just let me do the talking, okay?"

"Yes, but—"

The sheriff stepped into the ship. The mayor followed him, stopping at the hatchway, content with observing from a distance. "Sorry, Mr. Harris, but I got here first," he said.

Charlie gave Hyperion one last hard look and then put on a happy face to greet the sheriff. "Yeah, sure, but you see, I left town pretty quick, so the brigade kindly agreed to fly out here to finish our interview. You know. No big deal."

"That's not why we're here," Hyperion said.

Charlie's head swiveled to stare at Hyperion in disbelief.

"Yes," Charlie insisted through clenched teeth. "It *is*."

"But it's not," the Man of Might said. "We're looking for the Accelerator."

Charlie blinked. "In Crumbly?"

Hyperion nodded.

"He's not here. I already told that to the FBI agent who called me," the sheriff said.

"What FBI agent?" Hyperion said.

"Agent Todd, I think he said. I also got a call from the state trooper barracks. Their intel has this McMahon halfway across Pennsylvania by now."

"That doesn't match with ours, sir," Swift said. "Several sources have him hiding right here in your town. That might explain the mysterious electronic interference you've been experiencing."

"We've had that since before the Accelerator was even born," the sheriff said. "They say there's some kind of atmospheric anomaly that prevents electronic signals from reaching us most of the day. You get used to it."

"Nothing at all?" Blend said. "Like *no* cable or internet?"

From the hatch, Mayor Cole said defensively, "We get a couple of hours of internet in the afternoon. Otherwise, it's a very pleasant way of life."

"Can we get back to the Accelerator?" the sheriff said.

Charlie realized that no one had mentioned Willie yet. He wondered if the brigade even knew he was also in Crumbly. And, come to think of it, he expected Mr. Justice would have shown up already. Surely the self-proclaimed world's great detective hadn't missed the *Eagle*'s arrival.

"No cause to be alarmed, Sheriff. We'll take care of him," Hyperion said reassuringly.

"You'll take care of him . . . how?" Sheriff Cunningham asked suspiciously.

"In whatever way is necessary," Ms. Muscles growled, flexing her muscles for emphasis.

"I'm afraid I can't allow that," the sheriff said.

"It's okay," Blend said. "He's one of the bad guys."

"Besides, how're you gonna stop us?" Ms. Muscles demanded.

Hyperion took a step between the sheriff and his flexing teammate. "Deep breaths, Betsy," he whispered to her. Then he smiled at the sheriff and said, "This is your town, sir, and we're uninvited guests. How do you suggest we proceed?"

"You can start by checking your facts. Believe me, if this Accelerator were here, I'd know." He jabbed a finger in Charlie's direction. "This guy barely stepped off the bus before I started getting calls. And even if the Accelerator did slip into town without anyone seeing him, there's no way he missed your arrival in this thing."

"All the more reason we should get moving,"

Fakeout said. "He might be making his escape even as we speak."

"No, no, no," the sheriff said. "There's not going to be any super-brawl in Crumbly."

"Probably not," Hyperion agreed. "He had been outfitted with power dampeners before he escaped. As long as he's got those on, he's no more super than you. We should be able to pick him up with no problem."

SWIFT HAD ALREADY COME to the end of his patience. In the time his teammates had been arguing with the sheriff, they could have finished the job and been back on their way to the city. Well, *he* could have finished the job. From the air, he'd seen the size of Crumbly; it would take him less than thirty seconds to conduct a superspeed search without anyone feeling more than a breeze from his speedy passage.

He decided not to waste any more time. While Hyperion and the others were busy with the sheriff, he took a step to the side and, in the blink of an eye, disappeared.

A BREEZE BLEW PAST Wally, ruffling his hair as he and Brenda walked through the still-growing crowd of their neighbors at the end of Main Street. Everyone had spilled into the streets. Adults and kids. Mike Brewer hovered nearby, Abel Schotz and Nick McCain, circling around him like goofy moons, and he saw Benny with a bunch of their other friends, but everybody kept a safe distance from the ship.

Charlie had sprinted ahead of them and Wally'd lost sight of him. By the time he and Brenda got close enough, he had vanished. Kit and Kat Truman were the first to reach them with the news, delivered in breathless stereo, that both Brenda's father and Mr. Harris had gone inside the aircraft to talk to the supers.

Wally and Brenda looked at each other, eyes wide. He grabbed her hand and said, "Let's go!"

19

AFTER THREE CIRCUITS THROUGH town, Swift hadn't found any sign of the Accelerator. He hadn't checked inside anybody's home, of course, but just about the entire town seemed to be on the streets, either gathered around the aircraft or on their way to it. This had to be the most exciting thing that had ever happened here.

A reconnaissance mission that should have taken a half hour, tops, had turned into a prolonged farce. Every moment of it felt like an eternity to the Mach Master and he just wanted to get this wasted trip over and done with as soon as possible.

One more time around, just so he could report to the very precise Hyperion with absolute assurance no Accelerator could be found anywhere within the town limits.

Racing past a house on one of the back streets, he caught the movement of the curtains in a front window. It could have been a breeze that stirred them, but he spotted movement behind them.

A split second later, Swift appeared as if out of thin air as he came to a stop on the porch of the house.

During which interval, the figure in the window scarcely had time to blink, much less duck out of sight.

"I'm still not fast enough to fool you, Steven," Willie said, pushing aside the curtains to nod a greeting.

"You never will be, William. What are you doing here?" the speedster said in surprise.

"Redecorating," Willie said. "You want to help?"

20

"CRUMBLY," SULLIVAN THE BUS driver yelled. "This stop's Crumbly-by-the-Sea, New Jersey!"

Penny Potter, editorial assistant for the *National Mask*, got to her feet, grateful that the long and bumpy ride from New York had ended at last, as well as anxious to get on with what she had come here to do.

Her hurried research on Crumbly-by-the-Sea hadn't revealed anything that she thought would even remotely interest a supervillain. The most interesting thing about the town turned out to be its supposed inaccessibility; when she'd called the bus company to inquire, the man taking reservations had been shocked... not only that she wanted to travel to Crumbly, but because hers would be the *second* ticket sold to the town within days of one another after years of inactivity.

The other two passengers were slower to

respond, but Penny knew they were probably exhausted. They hadn't boarded the bus at a proper stop with tickets. They'd been hitch-hiking along the muddy grooves that passed for a road through the marshes, their car having broken down some miles back. Both the man and the woman looked as though they had been through an ordeal; clad in black leather jumpsuits or uniforms of some kind, they certainly weren't dressed for hiking through dank marshlands.

Despite their odd apparel, they insisted they were just tourists. Penny knew they were something more than that, something probably linked to the very reason that had put her on that bus to Crumbly, New Jersey: the search for the Accelerator. The magazine had been tipped to the possibility that the villain's escape car had been found in the little town and, with no one more experienced available to follow up, her editor had sent her to cover the story.

All those months spent doing research and fact-checking the work of the magazine's writers had given her an almost encyclopedic knowledge of the members of the supers community. That's why the moment she saw the bedraggled duo who dragged themselves onto the bus, she knew they were *somebodies* in the world of the supers. Not the woman so much, but definitely the man. She had seen him before.

Penny spent the remainder of the ride wracking her brains for some clue to his identity. She tried going online to browse the photo morgue of the *National Mask* in the hopes something would trigger her memory, but she couldn't get a signal out here in the swamp.

At the driver's second, louder announcement, the man's eyes snapped open and he sprang to his feet, like a soldier coming to attention. He had none of the hesitation or confusion people usually experience when they're woken up suddenly in a strange place.

Penny waited until they were in the aisle before she rose to follow them out the door and onto what appeared to be the town's Main Street. Or it could have been the deserted set from an old 1950s TV sitcom.

Polly couldn't believe places like this still existed. Nobody else would either, not without pictures. Fortunately, her cellphone could still take pictures even if it couldn't at the moment make calls. But as soon as she raised it to take some shots of the empty street—including, incidentally, the man and his friend—he turned and put up his hand and shouted, "Hey! No pictures!"

"I'm taking a picture of the street, not you," Penny lied.

"You do not have our permission to photograph us, young lady," he said, sounding like a warning label. "To do so risks civil and or criminal liability and penalties."

"Who talks like that?" Penny said, speaking to the girl with him.

"He does," the girl said.

"Miss Marrs!" the man snapped. "I'll speak for this unit."

"Yes, sir," the girl said with an apologetic glance at Penny.

"There's a general store. That's usually a good place to pick up local news. Let's go," he commanded and, without waiting for a reply, did an about-face and marched off. The girl followed.

"Sorry, *General*," she muttered to his retreating back.

Then it hit her. The way he moved and spoke, this guy was military through and through. But not a general.

A colonel!

She couldn't be sure; as far as she knew, no pictures of the man existed. But his exploits were legendary... and his presence had to mean an even bigger story than she had come for.

WILLIE CAREFULLY WORKED THE blade of the scraper under the faded wallpaper in the dining room. "It's coming off easy," he said. "I thought I'd have to steam it first, you know, to soften the glue? But this stuff's so old, it's dried out and practically falls off by itself."

Swift paced the floor behind him.

"William," he said.

"After that's removed, I'll hit the wall with some sandpaper to smooth it down, then give it a skim coat of plaster."

"Cut it out, William. Will you please just tell me what's going on here?"

"I told you. I'm helping Charlie fix up his house. I recommended painting, instead of wallpaper so you want a good finish to take the paint and—"

Willie felt a sudden rush of wind that shoved him to the center of the room, then swept around and around him in a cloud of dust and a blizzard of wallpaper. When it stopped, the walls had been stripped clean of wallpaper and sanded down to a satin finish. The discarded wallpaper had been folded and shoved in a trash barrel. The plaster dust continued to snow down around them. And Swift stood beside him, arms folded across his chest.

"I would have plastered and painted it for you too, but no matter how fast *I* am, I can't make liquids move any faster than they do."

"Nice work," Willie said with an appreciative nod. "How long do you think it would take you to demolish the front and back porches?"

"Can I use your head as a sledgehammer to knock them down?"

Willie flashed a humorless grin. "I'm just having fun with you, Steve."

"You? Having fun?"

"It's the sea air. It makes me giddy."

"Look, why are you really here? It's the Accelerator, right? We can help you take him in."

"The Accelerator?"

"He's here, isn't he?"

"The Accelerator's in Crumbly?"

"Don't you know?"

"How would I know?"

"You're supposed to be the world's greatest detective, aren't you?"

"I am."

"Then you had to know,"

"But you only just told me," Willie said.

"Then *what* are you doing here?" Swift said, his head beginning to vibrate a little in exasperation, making him sound like a high-pitched cartoon mouse.

"To talk Charlie out of abandoning the pursuit of justice. But once I saw the condition of this place, I thought he could use a hand."

Swift grabbed his head to slow it down. "Charlie told you this is where he's moving? No offense, William, but after Aquina, you're probably the last member of the brigade he'd give his forwarding address."

"Don't underestimate our bond," Willie said.

"The one you guys formed when you beat him up?"

"Doctor Psycon made me do it!"

"No, no, no, Doctor Psycon only released us from our inhibitions so we could do what we secretly *wanted* to do. *You* secretly wanted to beat up Charlie."

"It's not that big a secret. Anyway, what about you? You wanted to keep running in circles around midtown Manhattan even though it created a vacuum that sucked all the oxygen up into outer space."

"I didn't want to hurt anyone, Willie. I just gave in to my need to run."

"We're getting off the point. What's this about the Accelerator?"

"We intercepted a couple of emails and postings that pointed us here, but there's something screwy about the whole Mayberry vibe, don't you think? It's like the town where time stood still."

"I like it."

"Yeah, well, I don't trust anything that stands still," the Sultan of Speed said. "Did you bring your costume?"

Willie nodded.

"You better suit up and come back with me to the *Eagle*."

"This sounds like something you guys can handle by yourselves."

"After we're done, you can star in a basic-cable, home-fix-it show for all I care, but right now, I think we should have all hands on deck."

"But I've got all this work to do..."

"No you don't. I did it for you."

"Well, I..."

"Willie," Swift said softly. "Who's trying to abandon the pursuit of justice now?"

Willie rolled his eyes and made a clucking sound with his tongue.

"Okay, okay. Give me a minute to change."

PENNY TOOK A CAREFUL look through the window of the general store. The man and woman were at the counter, both looking impatiently around the store. The man reached out and tapped a bell on the countertop, obviously not for the first time and just as obviously with the same lack of results as earlier attempts.

Penny didn't intend to wait for someone to answer a bell. She'd come to prove to her editor, Mr. Taylor, that she had what it took to be an investigative reporter. She had the instincts; she had to produce the story that would prove it.

She followed deserted Main Street in one direction, but it came to end after a single block. She turned around and doubled back, this time rewarded by the sight of movement up ahead, where the sidewalk became a dirt path, and the road turned off around a bend. Penny picked up her pace and hurried towards it.

She turned the corner and saw…

The *Screaming Eagle*?

"Colonel Darwyn Flint and the Justice Brigade, in the same place at the same time?

"What in the world is going on?" Penny exclaimed.

21

BOOMER BAILY HAD ALREADY completed his patrol around the perimeter of Morris Handelman's property and had settled in for an afternoon catching up with his favorite soap operas when the alarm sounded.

Boomer didn't even bother lacing up his boots. He just grabbed his gun and ran. He couldn't remember the last time there had been an alert. Although, to be fair, he sometimes couldn't remember what he'd had for breakfast. But he took pride that he could react almost as fast as when he had been on active duty. He knew he didn't always understand the briefing book these days, but darned if he couldn't still take care of himself in a brawl.

He found Sarge and Morris in the large utility room that had been modified to serve as a command center. Morris plugged into the main control console, surrounded by banks of monitors. From here, they could look in on any part of Crumbly and its surroundings via the pinhead-sized cameras powered by an electron battery the master tinkerer had secretly installed all over town.

"Reporting for duty," Boomer snapped.

"At ease, old buddy," Sarge said. "Morris is still assessing the situation."

Morris played with some of the dials, bringing the scene from the vacant lot at the end of Main Street up on the main screen.

"There's the first part of our problem, gents," Morris said. "The Justice Brigade's landed. Literally in our backyard."

"There's more?" Sarge growled.

A flip of a switch brought a new image up on the main screen: a long shot of Old Crumbly Road and a van parked on it, the name of an old-age home in the Bronx painted on its doors. Several individuals could be seen standing by the van. Morris twirled a dial that zoomed in on the passengers.

"Crosshair, Sledgehammer Sue, Professor Lamplighter," Sarge snarled.

"They're just outside the perimeter sensors, so I only found them after the *Eagle* tripped the first alarm."

"This is bad," Sarge snapped.

"It gets worse. Look."

Another switch and the scene changed from

the van to the interior of the general store, where a camera looked down at the counter from up in a corner by the ceiling.

"Who's that?" Boomer said, squinting at the screen.

"I don't have an ID on the woman, but he's an old friend of ours, Boomer. You remember Darwyn Flint, don't you?" Morris said.

The old soldier gasped, clutching his rifle, looking to Sarge for confirmation. "Is that really the lieutenant, Sarge?"

"He's a colonel now," Sarge said, pronouncing the rank like as though it left a bad taste in his mouth.

"Aw, Lieutenant Flint was okay," Boomer said. "Like you always said, a lieutenant's still *almost* a soldier."

"He's wearing heavy brass on his collar now, Boomer," Sarge said. "What are they doing here, Morris?"

The man once known as the villain Giz-Mo shrugged helplessly. "I don't have a clue and I think we all know how much I hate that. The only factor that's changed in the past seventy-two hours is the arrival in town of that writer for the *National Mask*, Charles Harris."

"And his friend," Boomer reminded them.

"Yes, thank you, Boomer. Of course, I did a background check on them both when they first got here. Harris inherited the house five years ago, after Sadie Wicker passed, but left it to sit empty until he showed up the other day." Morris turned to the keyboard on his console and started typing. "He recently left the *Mask* with a big book contract. I suppose he's here to write.

"The other man, according to the registration of the car with that license plate number, is William Williams, a former New York police officer, now an unlicensed private investigator in Brooklyn. He works solo, keeps a low profile. He's not even on the internet."

"It makes sense, a reporter being friends with a lone wolf PI," Sarge said.

"It does," Morris agreed, distracted by the information rolling down his screen. "But I'm afraid I've made a mistake."

"You?" Boomer stuttered. "That's impossible."

His mouth a grim, hard line under his beard, Morris said, "I wish that were true, my friend, but it's been so long since anything out of the ordinary's happened that I suppose I just got lazy." He pointed to the screen. "I'll spare you the details, but if I'd bothered to look beneath the surface, I would have found out sooner that Mr. Williams' car belongs to the Department of Superhuman Activity."

"I don't get it," Boomer said, blinking in confusion.

"Williams is working with the Feds," Sarge

explained. "But so what? Even if he is, what's got him, the task force, the league, and the brigade in such a hot hurry to be in Crumbly all of sudden? Like you said, nothing ever happens here."

"We're here," Boomer said, sounding uneasy.

"We've been here close to thirty years," Sarge reminded him. "Nobody is looking for us anymore."

"Perhaps," Morris said. "But for now, I suggest we stay out of sight and monitor the situation."

"You're the boss, Morris," Boomer said, snapping off a salute.

"It's probably also wise to institute a complete signal blackout on the entire sector until we know what's going on." He tapped at some switches on the console. "Goodbye telephone." Tap. "Television." Tap. "All radio frequencies." Tap. "Internet." Tap, tap, tap. "Adjust the distortion dome that renders us invisible to satellite surveillance and signal intercepts to maximum."

WATCHING HYPERION AND SHERIFF Cunningham argue, Charlie wondered what he had done to deserve this. He didn't ask for much. Just some peace and quiet. He had done what he could for his fellow man, both as a reporter and as the Knave, and in return, he wanted to be left alone.

"Charlie?"

The voice, as soft as a wave lapping at the shore, spoke from behind him.

"Hi, Aquina," he said and hoped the smile he plastered on his face before turning to her looked convincing. "How's it going?"

"Why didn't you tell me you were leaving, Charlie?" she said.

He glanced at the sheriff, still occupied with Guy, and whispered, "Can't this wait?"

She shook her head, splashing him with a few drops of water.

"I didn't tell anybody my plans, except Guy."

"But what about us?"

"There hasn't been an *us* for months, Aquina," he said, trying to keep his voice at a whisper. "You broke up with me, remember?"

"But then I forgave you!"

"For what? You called me an irresponsible, selfish child who you never wanted to speak to again. And then you said you hoped someone kicked me into the Bottomless Chasm of Mawkra, whatever that is. But the thing is, you were right."

"Not right, just angry," she cried softly.

Charlie stole another glance at the sheriff, who looked to be rapidly losing patience with Hyperion.

"And you got angry because you were right about me. Look, this isn't the time or the place for this conversation. Are you guys here for the Accelerator?"

"That's what Guy told us," the Beauty from Beneath the Sea said, sniffling.

"Don't you think that's kind of weird? You guys come looking for the Accelerator in a place no one even knows exists and you find me?"

Aquina burst out in tears and sobbed, "Oh, Charlie!" Then she ran over to Ms. Muscles, who put a comforting arm around her shoulders while giving Charlie a dirty look.

Bad, Charlie thought. And if the past were any indicator, things would only get worse. The Justice Brigade only served one function: punching bad guys and assorted hostile creatures until they couldn't get back up again. Even when the situation didn't call for it, one or more of its members were likely to throw a punch.

If he had any hope of salvaging the new life he wanted to build in Crumbly, he had to get rid of his former teammates. Fast. And that included Willie. Especially Willie.

"Mr. Harris," Sheriff Cunningham called. "May we speak with you a moment?"

With no idea how he hoped to achieve his goal, Charlie gave the sheriff a weak smile and went to join the conversation.

* * *

WALLY AND BRENDA FOUND Jamie Crenshaw on the front porch when they came running up the street to his house. In his excitement, Wally didn't see the concern drawn on her face as he jumped the porch steps and stopped breathlessly in front of her.

"Mom, you're not going to believe it, but the Justice Brigade... they're here. The *Screaming Eagle* landed on Main Street. It's amazing. And I saw Hyperion and Brenda's dad is inside the *Eagle* and so is Charlie and the whole town's there to see it—"

"Slow down, Wally," Jamie said, taking his face in her hands. "I saw it land. What's going on?"

"You gotta see it, Mom, it's awesome," he said, too excited to stand still. "I just came to get my souvenir, you know, from Washington? Maybe I can get Hyperion to sign it. I mean, how cool would that be?"

"Honey, is there some sort of trouble?"

Wally's shrug went up to his ears. "I don't think so. Everybody's just standing around talking."

Brenda finally caught up with the exuberant Wally, joining them on the porch.

"Don't you want to go see them, Mom?" Wally said.

"No," Jamie said. She looked at him with a scowl. "And I don't want you going back there either, Wally."

But Mom—"

"No," she said again and with finality. "It's one thing to make the supers your hobby, and I know they're the good guys, but they're dangerous to be around, honey. Wherever they are, there's trouble. You remember Washington, don't you?"

"Are you kidding?" Wally cried. "Only the most awesome day of my life."

"It was awesome because you were seven years old," Jamie said. "But terrifying to the grown-ups. This isn't a movie or a videogame, honey. This is real. The danger is real."

"But Hyperion got rid of the bomb," Wally said. "He saved everybody . . . he saved *us*."

"Yes, he did," she said softly. "That time."

Wally opened his mouth to answer but stopped when he saw his mother's face. Her fears had nothing to do with Washington or the hundreds of other times when the supers had saved the day.

It had to do with one of the times they'd failed.

In Lincoln City.

"Do you understand, honey?"

Wally looked away. He did understand. But he also didn't. But mostly he didn't want to see her so sad.

So he nodded.

"Yeah, Mom, I do," he said, barely above a whisper.

"Thank you, Wally. I don't want you getting

hurt, that's all," she said, giving him a quick hug before he squirmed out of her grasp, embarrassed in front of Brenda.

After Jamie went inside, Wally slumped into the porch swing, setting it into motion. Brenda dropped down beside him, waiting several minutes before speaking.

"Wally?"

"Yeah?"

"You okay?"

He shrugged. "I'm fine."

"You're not acting fine."

"Well, maybe it's because I'm *not* fine," he snapped. "I can't believe it. The Justice Brigade is right here and I can't even go see them. When will I ever get this close to them again? I mean, nothing interesting ever happens in this stupid town."

"What about yesterday?" Brenda said.

Wally frowned. "What *about* yesterday?"

"You had all of us on a stakeout for a super-villain, dummy."

"That doesn't count. Anyway, it turned out not to be the Accelerator after all, so we were mostly just goofing around."

"But it *could* have been him, right?"

"But it wasn't."

"But it *could* have been, and could have been is almost the same as it really being him until we found out he was somebody else, right?"

Wally gave her a sideways look. "If you say so."

They swung silently on the swing.

"Hey, Brenda? If we weren't friends, how, like, stupid would you think I am for the whole supers and, you know, Whiz Kid? I know it's stupid, but—"

"I don't think it's stupid."

"Everybody else does."

"So what? Benny's obsessed with horror movies. Kit and Kat collect Barbie dolls. Mike collects soda pop cans. You like the supers. What's the difference?"

"I guess. Except Kit and Kat don't want to *be* Barbie."

"Right. And they couldn't be even if they wanted to because Barbie's not real. But the supers are, Wally."

"So?"

"So that means it's not so stupid to dream about becoming one since people obviously *do*."

"It is for me. I'm not brave enough to be a super. Yesterday, I froze trying to work up the courage to peek around a stupid tree," Wally said miserably. "And, man, what if it *had* been the Accelerator and he saw me? What would I have done then?"

"How much you want to bet Mr. Justice didn't fight any supervillains at your age either?"

Wally chuckled. "Yeah, I guess."

"Anyway, you never thought the Justice Brigade would get within a million miles of Crumbly, but here they are. If one impossible thing can happen, so can another."

"Yeah, maybe. In another million years."

Brenda poked him in the ribs with her elbow and they both laughed.

"Hey," she said, "I just realized. Just because you can't go back to the Screaming Vulture—"

"*Eagle*! *Screaming Eagle*."

"Whatever. Anyway, just because you can't go doesn't mean *I* can't."

"Sure, rub it in."

"What I'm saying is, give me your souvenir and I'll see if I can get Daddy to get Hyperion to sign it for you."

Wally leapt on his feet faster than Swift.

"That. Would. Be. *Awesome!*" he said. "You are the best friend ever, Brenda. Wait right here; I'll be right back, okay?" He dashed into the house.

22

"STILL NOTHING, DOCTOR," CROSSHAIR reported from the roof of the van. He sat cross-legged, maintaining surveillance through his powerful telescopic sighting device, happy to finally be close to their destination after a miserably endless drive through some of New Jersey's least attractive real estate. "Looks like just about the whole town's come out to gawk at the *Screaming Eagle*."

"But no sign of our friend, Mr. McMahon," Doctor Psycon said.

"So how do we flush him out?" Stormcloud said.

Doctor Psycon raised his hands to his oversized dome and wiggled his fingers frantically around his head. "I can feel him nearby," he said with frustration, "but this interference fuzzies my perceptions and makes it all but impossible to focus on his psychic emanations."

"What could be so potent as to scramble both our electronics and your psychic resources?" Professor Lamplighter said.

"It doesn't matter. It's enough we know we have him cornered. In fact, we can even use the presence of the brigade to our advantage," Doctor Psycon said.

"You got a plan?" Sledgehammer Sue said.

"I've a plan," the doctor said. "It should offer us ample time to seek out, locate, and remove Mr. McMahon while the brigade is still surprised by our presence."

"Let's hear it, whatever it is. I'm getting antsy sitting around doing nothing," Manika said, twiddling her thumbs so fast the air hummed.

"WILL YOU ALL PLEASE just *quiet down*!" Sheriff Cunningham bellowed over the blur of voices inside the *Eagle*'s cabin.

The conversation had been confusing but calm until the man in the leather jumpsuit came charging in, claiming jurisdiction over the Justice Brigade, the sheriff, the mayor, and any villains, super or otherwise, who happened to be in the neighborhood. Hyperion responded with a roll of his eyes and told the man, who he called Colonel Flint, that he should turn around and go home because the brigade had the situation under control. The Flint guy told Hyperion to stand down, which made the woman with the bad temper and muscles take a swing at him. Flint stepped under her fist and grabbed hold of her wrist, twisting it up behind her back.

That's when the others jumped in, everybody shouting and pointing fingers and making a lot of threats. The closest thing the sheriff had ever seen to it had been when Brenda's third grade Halloween party had turned nasty over a disputed apple-bobbing incident.

Charlie also stood back and watched the moment dissolve into chaos, but unlike the sheriff, he wasn't surprised. Charlie knew that Colonel Flint and the brigade had been thorns in each other's sides for years. Flint wanted the brigade placed under his command, but the heroes were determined to stay independent of government control. "The amount of paperwork alone is reason enough to avoid it," Hyperion had once told him, to which Charlie had replied, "So is avoiding Flint."

Charlie doubted the heroes and agents even heard the sheriff over the din. It wouldn't be the first time they'd let themselves be distracted by this kind of argument, but at least this one didn't break out during an actual mission.

He came up alongside the sheriff and said, "I know how to handle this. Cover your ears."

The baffled lawman said, "What?"

Charlie stuck the thumb and forefinger of his right hand between his puckered lips and blew as hard as he could.

His piercing whistle made the sheriff wince, but it got everybody's attention and, as if a switch had been thrown, the ship went suddenly silent, and all eyes turned his way.

"Who are you?" Colonel Flint demanded.

"Just a citizen, sir," Charlie said with a grin. "Charlie Harris, the *National Mask*."

"What's a reporter doing here?" Flint said. He pointed a finger at Hyperion. "Don't you even have sense enough to keep reporters off your ship?"

"Bite me," Hyperion said.

"Gentlemen, gentlemen," Charlie said quickly. "You're fighting over nothing. The Accelerator is not—I repeat, *not*—in Crumbly. A local kid with too much imagination saw a stranger, got excited, and posted about it in a chat room, that's all."

Agent Marrs suddenly and loudly cleared her throat, startling everyone. Looking uncomfortable, she started speaking in a low mumble.

"What?" Ms. Muscles shouted. "I can't understand you."

The young woman cleared her throat again and said, "I'm sorry. I said, we also got a tip. On the task force's anonymous website. From a public computer at the library. Here. In Crumbly."

"What do you have to say about *that*, Mr. Harris?" Flint said.

"Probably another one of the kids," Charlie said. "A bunch of them spent most of yesterday trying to get a look at who's in my house."

"I can check with Mrs. Pinchot to see if any of the kids used the computer yesterday," the sheriff said.

"Who *is* in your house, Mr. Harris?" Flint said.

In his head, Charlie said, *Uh-oh*, but out loud he said, "Excuse me?"

"You said, and I quote, 'A bunch of them spent most of yesterday trying to get a look at who's inside my house.' If you were referring to yourself, you would have said 'trying to get a look at me.' Besides, I doubt even overexcited children could possibly mistake you for Brendan McMahon. So my question again, sir, Who is in your house?"

"A friend," Charlie said, trying at once not to lie but remain evasive. He didn't want to get into it with Hyperion and the brigade about Willie in front of strangers. "A friend, visiting me from New York. He's helping me with some home repairs."

Agent Marrs leaned closer to Flint and said, "His car, sir?"

Flint looked back at her with a blank stare.

"The registration? To the DSA?"

"The car with the New York license plates," Flint exclaimed, as though he just remembered it. "We traced its ownership back to the Department of Superhuman Activity."

"Which brings up the question of how McMahon would get his hands on a DSA car?"

"Excuse me?" Flint said.

"Hmm," Hyperion said, thoughtfully stroking his chin. "Those vehicles are only for official DSA use and authorized personnel. The brigade has several cars on loan from the department, but it's not like there are that many of them that an escaping supervillain would just happen to stumble across one to steal."

Charlie shrugged. "Unlikely."

Blend scratched his head and said, "Well, this is embarrassing."

"What, it's just been a wild goose chase?" Sledgehammer Sue snarled.

The brigade and the pair of task force agents broke off to talk among themselves. Charlie turned to give the sheriff a smile. "Sorry about all this, but believe it or not, they do mean well."

"I've got to tell you, Mr. Harris, what I've

just witnessed does not fill me with confidence," the sheriff said, shaking his head in disbelief.

Charlie nodded. "I understand. But what we've got going in our favor is that most of the bad guys aren't even *this* smart."

And at that moment, as if to prove Charlie's claim, the bad guys launched their attack.

IN WALLY'S ABSENCE, MIKE Brewer had declared himself leader of the Crumbly Patrol, with the snickering Abel Schotz and Nick McCain as his deputies, despite Benny telling him no such thing existed, and, oh, by the way, what did he know about supers, anyway.

"Man, you're gonna be surprised how much I know," Mike said with a nasty laugh that set off Abel and Nick, even though they had no idea what he meant. What other reason could the Justice Brigade have for coming to Crumbly besides his email? They would all find out soon enough. When he collected the reward for turning in the Accelerator.

"Where's Wally? I can't believe he's missing this," Lulu Yeung said.

"I wonder where Brenda and him ran off to," said Kit Truman.

"They should be back by now," said Kat Truman.

"You don't even know where they went," said Kit.

"How far can they go?" said Kat.

Jocko Mullins pointed to Main Street and said, "Hey, here comes Brenda."

"But no Wally," Olivia Snyder said. She called out to the auburn-haired girl and waved her over.

"Your dad and Mr. Harris are still inside with the supers and some other people," Benny said. "Where's Wally?"

"Doesn't matter; I'm giving the orders," Mike said.

Brenda, winded from her race from Wally's house, ignored Mike and said, "Grounded. His mom won't let him come."

"That's not fair," Lulu said. "She knows what this means to him."

"Man, the first chance he gets to meet a real super and the Whiz Kid just chickens out," Mike said with a derisive snort.

"Shut up, Mike," Benny said. "You don't know what you're talking about."

"Yeah? Then how come he's not here?"

"Because of his mom," Benny said, clenching his fists and taking a step towards the other boy. "You know what happened to his father in Lincoln City. His mom is the one who's afraid."

Mike threw up his hands, "Yeah, yeah, I

forgot, okay?" He turned and gave Abel a slap on the shoulder, growling, "Why didn't you remind me?"

When Benny looked at Brenda, he found her smiling at him.

"What?" he said, suddenly self-conscious that his hair looked goofy or his pants were unzipped.

"Nothing," Brenda said. "I'm just sort of surprised. But in a good way."

"Because of that?"

A drop of water fell on the top of Brenda's head, but she just brushed it off, saying, "Well, admit it, Benny, sometimes you can be sort of insensitive."

"Even an idiot could figure out what's bugging his mom," Benny said. He waited a moment, then grinned at her. "C'mon, this is where you're supposed to say that any idiot *did* figure it out."

Brenda rolled her eyes. "And we're back to normal," she said, as another drop of water hit her shoulder. Then another, and a few more, the beginning of a summer shower. All around, people were glancing up at the sky, coming to the same conclusion, but the novelty of what they were watching far outweighed the inconvenience of a few raindrops on a summer day.

But attitudes changed in an instant when, a

moment later, the scattered droplets gave way to hard little balls of icy hail that turned, in an instant, into a downpour that sent everyone racing for cover.

23

AS SOON AS STORMCLOUD gave her the nod, Manika took off, a nearly invisible streak of blue that threaded its way up, down, and across the streets of Crumbly, zipping into doors and out, speeding through basements and attics, storefronts and garages. She left a wake of stirred up dirt and debris in the streets and blew up storms of loose papers and small objects as she whisked through homes and businesses. It took her less than a minute to make her first inspection of the town, passing the lot where the side-walks ended several times to witness the results of Stormcloud's precision strike hailstorm.

The painful storm of stinging ice fell only over the lot, the hard little pellets bouncing off the *Screaming Eagle*, while all around it people scattered, arms thrown protectively over their heads. From her supersonic point of view, the moment looked frozen in time.

Her first pass through town failed to turn up any sign of the Accelerator. With the doc's psychic abilities on the fritz, it fell to the speedster to get a visual on their target and, if she thought she could manage it alone, grab him and bring him back to the van at the edge of town. If she needed help taking him down, Sledgehammer Sue and Crosshair were standing by.

For her second circuit through town, Manika took a much more leisurely pace. The moment the *Eagle* had announced its booming presence, Brendan would have moved, either to set up a defensive position or, more likely, to get away. Either way, he'd take pains to camouflage his movements.

As she began her third race through town, Manika's hopes were falling. She had checked behind every door in town, peered into every corner hidey-hole, but still no Accelerator. Brendan McMahon didn't have a reputation for subtly. He grabbed hold of stuff and made it age until it decomposed. He didn't move through the shadows or avoid detection at superspeed, so either he'd learned some new tricks or, more likely, he had never been here in the first place.

Manika widened the parameters of her search, racing in ever-larger circles from the town center, into the marshlands that surrounded it on three sides, and onto the sandy beaches to the east. She smiled when the old concrete concession building and the rest of the remains of the never-built amusement park came into view.

"Gotcha now," she told herself and ran straight toward it.

But before she reached her destination, Manika tripped.

WHILE HE WAITED FOR William to suit up, Swift glanced out the window to see a gust of wind dragging a tail of dirt and debris down the center of Kane Street. He didn't give it a second thought, except a second gust of wind followed almost immediately after the first... but from the opposite direction.

"That's no wind," he muttered and raced into the other room, slung William over his shoulder, and then ran out of the house and down to the beach.

"Sorry for the detour, but there's another speedster searching Crumbly. It's gotta be Manika," Swift said, his tongue racing. "She's running a grid pattern. I gotta get ahead of her."

Mr. Justice nodded.

"That means the league's close at hand. Don't worry, I can find my way back to town."

Swift nodded and, with a buzz like a swarm of bees, ran off.

VIBRATING TOO FAST TO be seen, Swift waited for the slipstream of sand to pass where he crouched in the tall sea grass, before launching himself into pursuit and falling into pace in its wake. As long as he remained behind the speeding figure, he would be undetectable.

He didn't bother to count the number of races he and Manika had run over the years. When it came to sheer speed, sometimes he would win a leg of the relay, sometimes she would, but in the end, the race always belonged to Swift.

He put on enough extra speed to pull up behind her, closer and closer, and then stuck out his foot.

MANIKA TUMBLED THROUGH THE air in an uncontrollable spiral before she splashed down several hundred yards from shore.

Sputtering and wiping the stinging salt water from her eyes, she instantly knew that someone, not something, had caused her to trip, a feat only the fleet-footed Swift could pull off.

She started to superspeed swim back to the beach, but Swift came racing across the top of the water as effortlessly as he did on solid ground. She could do that too, running so fast her feet didn't have time to break the surface tension of the water and sink, but she couldn't get up and running from a dead start *in* the water.

Manika began beating her arms at super-speed, churning up a great wall of water in Swift's path between them. Swift exploded through the liquid barrier, but the waters churning under his feet made him momentarily lose his balance, and Manika used that instant to grab his arm, pulling herself out of the water, yanking him down into it, and then used his back as he started to go under to push herself off and race back to the beach.

Swift let himself be shoved beneath the waves, then kicked his feet until he shot through the water like a human torpedo. The instant his feet touched bottom, he took off after Manika.

TO CHARLIE, IT SOUNDED like a mob gone crazy, screaming and pelting the *Screaming Eagle* with a barrage of rocks. And almost before he could react, he heard a not-too-distant series of sonic booms cracking the air.

"Where's Swift?" Hyperion snapped, as he raced to the hatch just as another boom boomed closer, rattling the ship.

"He's gone," Aquina said.

"Old fast-feet must've slipped out when we weren't looking," Fakeout said.

Charlie and the sheriff were closest to the

hatch and got there first to see the large hailstones falling from the sky and the townspeople running for cover.

"Okay, somebody's making this happen, right?" the sheriff said, his voice an angry rumble. "No way it's hailing by itself in the middle of a cloudless summer day."

"Yeah, someone's doing this," Charlie agreed. He looked over his shoulder at Hyperion. "This is Stormcloud's doing."

Another sonic boom shook the *Eagle*. Hyperion nodded. "And Manika, if the sonic booms we're hearing are any clue."

"Which means the league is close behind," Blend said. "But why?"

"They must have picked up the same internet chatter you and the task force did," Charlie said. "They're looking for the Accelerator too. It's no secret he ripped them off on the Vegas job."

"Then what are we waiting for?" Ms. Muscles said. "Sounds to me like it's finally go time."

The sheriff said, "You mean a bunch of those lunatics are on the loose in town?"

"Sorry to say, but yeah," Charlie said.

The sheriff had reached his boiling point. He whipped off his cap and started to whack it angrily against his thigh. "I don't believe this. *You* people," he snarled, waving an accusatory finger in the faces of all the heroes, "get *those* people," his finger whipping around to point out the hatch, "out of *my* town before anyone gets hurt!"

"It's not that easy, Sheriff," Hyperion started to say, but when the sheriff turned his red, angry face in his direction, the Mighty Mortal backed down and meekly said, "Yes, Sheriff."

With a nod to his teammates, Hyperion led the brigade through the hatch and into the hailstorm, which at the moment felt a lot warmer and more inviting than the sheriff.

HIS COSTUME A RIOT of turbulent gray roiling clouds that grew even darker and flashed with lightning, Stormcloud crouched on the roof of a tool shed in a backyard half a block from the vacant lot, from which he had whipped up turbulent weather conditions around the *Eagle*. He enjoyed watching the civilians scatter like pigeons in the park to find shelter from the hail, but now that they'd all escaped the zone of the localized effect, he ended the storm.

The Master of Meteorology took a moment to catch his breath. Manipulating the weather took a lot of effort. Take that hailstorm. Sure, he'd gained the power to manipulate the elements after being struck by a bolt of lightning focused through a magical Egyptian gemstone, but it took years of practice before he'd acquired the knowledge to use it properly.

First, he had to create a microclimate in the form of a cold front, feeding it a crazy amount of atmospheric moisture, then sustain it under the proper conditions until the hail formed. And now, follow that up with a major lightning strike. He hoped he had the strength.

Hyperion led the charge from the ship, two bounding steps down the ramp before he went into a crouch and sprang straight up into the air as if shot from a cannon. But as fast as Hyperion was, he couldn't outfly a bolt of lightning traveling at two hundred and twenty thousand miles an hour.

Stormcloud sucked in a deep breath as his costume flashed with lightning and—

Strike!

HYPERION'S HYPERSENSITIVE NOSTRILS TWITCHED. He detected the scent of ozone in the air, like swimming pool water and electricity, which formed, he thought, from oxygen by electrical dischar—

Stormcloud's bolt of lightning slammed Hyperion back to the ground, his entire body jerking and writhing under a power hotter than the surface of the sun.

Fakeout reached him first. Hyperion didn't move and his body smoked from the energy. With a thought, Fakeout moved himself one minute into the future and, seeing that

Hyperion would already be staggering back to his feet by then, returned to the moment.

Blend vanished from sight and made a fast reconnaissance of the area, hoping to get the drop on some of their opponents. By the time he found Stormcloud on top of the shed, the villain had rained several more bolts of lightning down on the heroes. Blend willed himself to appear to Stormcloud's clouded mind as the top hat-wearing Professor Lamplighter.

"Come with me, quick," Blend/Professor Lamplighter called to the villain. Stormcloud saw him, gave a thumbs-up, and nimbly leapt from the shed.

"I nailed Hyperion good, Professor. What's next?" Stormcloud said, joining the other man.

"You take a nice long nap," Blend/Professor Lamplighter said and knocked Stormcloud cold with a solid right jab.

24

AFTER SWIFT ZOOMED OFF in pursuit of Manika, Mr. Justice headed back to town to join up with the brigade. His lack of enthusiasm surprised him. His dedication to the pursuit of justice hadn't dimmed, but he'd been enjoying his little vacation from the cause; the first vacation he had allowed himself since taking up the mantle of Mr. Justice.

He told Charlie he thought the brigade could handle things without him for a few days. Apparently, he'd been wrong. So wrong, that even without knowing they were doing it, they had followed him here to Crumbly. He wanted to curse the burdens of his natural leadership qualities, but he had no time for that. His comrades and the citizens of Crumbly needed him.

Running back to town and the distant sounds of combat and sonic booms and lightning strikes, Mr. Justice passed Handelman the Handyman's with little more than a cursory glance. Even without thinking, he had taken in the structure and its surroundings in a mental snapshot that his subconscious reviewed and analyzed even as he ran. And a few steps later, it screamed its conclusion in his head:

Antennae!

They were expertly masked and integrated into the rusted steel girders rising from the old concrete pads, but his trained eye could pick them out as plain as day. The area was bristling with an array of sophisticated antennae and scanners, including the sixty-foot-tall flagpole capped by an oversized brass ball. Unfolding the digital binoculars from a pouch in his belt, he zoomed in on the ball. As he suspected, that was no ornament; breaking the gleaming surface were sensor vents and scanner holes, and the whole thing rotated slowly on its base.

Mr. Justice put away his binocs. Considering what this place had going on, whoever had set this all up had probably had him under surveillance from the moment Swift deposited him on the beach. Which meant he didn't have to bother sneaking up on whoever manned the bunker. A good thing too since, judging by the sounds of combat coming from town, there was no time for it either.

Waiting for Mr. Justice at the door to Handelman's was a very old man in overalls who held an old World War I rifle at port arms.

"Stand and be identified," the old man ordered.

The masked hero ignored the order and continued walking.

"Friend or foe?" the old man said.

Mr. Justice stopped in front of him.

"I suggest you hand over the gun, sir. I'd hate to have to hurt you," he said.

"Happy to say I don't have the same problem with you, son," the old man said and brought the stock of the rifle crashing up into Mr. Justice's jaw.

The lawman's head snapped back and he saw stars. He didn't know what stunned him more, the blow or how fast the old man struck it. Willie had faced expertly trained foes a quarter this one's age who could never have taken him by surprise like that.

The old man may be fast, but he didn't stand a chance against Mr. Justice, one of the world's leading experts in unarmed combat. The black-clad guardian of justice sent a flurry of strikes at him, but the old man flicked away every blow and kick with the rifle, seeming to tag Mr. Justice whenever and wherever he wanted.

Mr. Justice had been holding back out of fear of hurting the old man, but now he found himself having to use all his skills just to keep up with his opponent.

The old man, on the other hand, seemed tireless, almost robotic in his ability to strike at will without leaving any openings for Justice to get in any blows of his own.

Then, as Mr. Justice parried a savage jab to his stomach with the rifle barrel, he saw an opening to slip a fist past the punishing weapon. Before he could act, though, the old man surprised him with a one-two punch so out of nowhere that, just before he blacked out, the crime fighter wished he could have seen them coming so he'd know how it was done.

MANIKA KNEW TWO THINGS for sure. The first: the Accelerator was nowhere in, near, or around Crumbly. She had been over every square inch of the town, inside and out, and unless that big, grim gorilla had found a way to make himself invisible, she would have found him.

The second: she had to lose Swift. Bad enough the search hadn't turned up Brendan, but it would be humiliating to get caught and sent back to prison because they'd gone on a fool's errand.

Manika came to a sudden, dead stop in the middle of someone's front yard. Swift blew right past her, freeing Manika to streak off in a different direction before the rival speedster could put on his brakes.

By the time Swift came back around to where he had passed her, Manika had sped away, the dust from her passage still swirling in the air. After a split-second pause, Swift raced off.

WALLY BLINKED.

He saw a woman in a blue costume standing in his front yard.

Wally blinked again.

Gone.

Then a man in a white and yellow costume appeared in another part of the yard. This time, even before Wally could blink again, *he* vanished.

He couldn't be sure he hadn't imagined it, but if it had been real, he couldn't have mistaken the costumes and colors of Manika and Swift. Which meant that, in addition to the brigade, the League of Villains had also come to Crumbly...

...with Wally *grounded*!

For the first time in his life, he understood what it meant to be unable to stand something. He thought there had been times before in his life when he couldn't stand it, like waiting for Christmas or his birthday, or the anticipation of the next part of a continuing story in his favorite comic, but they were nothing compared to what he felt now.

The greatest superheroes in the world and their archenemies were all together in Crumbly, and what always happened when heroes and villains ended up in the same place at the same time?

They fought!

A genuine clash of the supers right here in his hometown! Two of the supers had already been in his front yard. *His* front yard! Could anything be more awesome than that? Only one thing he could think of... to be a witness to a supers battle!

But the Whiz Kid remained shackled to the house and porch by his promise to Super-Mom.

He wanted to scream. He could hear the tantalizing sounds of people screaming, sonic booms, and crashing thunder, just a few streets over from where he sat. But the screaming, booming, and crashing would have to happen without him.

No one in Crumbly cared about the supers except for Wally and he would be the one not to see them. He almost wished Hyperion would come crashing through someone's house and go bouncing down the street. Not that he wanted anybody to get hurt or their homes wrecked or anything, but, yeah, that sure would be cool to see, wouldn't it?

Wally heard a sound like the boom of a big cannon from above and, when he looked up to see what had caused it, he remembered something his mother once told him: “Be careful what you wish for, honey. It might come true, but not in the way you expect.”

He should have been more careful!

“Mom!” he screamed, running for the front door.

HYPERION FOUND THAT WHILE his ears were still ringing from the lightning strike and he saw two of everything—*three* if he moved his head too fast—he felt otherwise more or less . . . okay. Not exactly invulnerable, his super-tough skin and bones were usually more than sufficient when facing guns or the average super-weapon or power-blaster. But he did try to avoid things like lightning.

But he couldn’t let a little thing like dizziness and nausea get in the way of his going after the bad guys. Just when he thought he had led the brigade on a useless mission to nowhere, the tables had turned, and they were given the opportunity to round up the entire League of Villains all in one neat package. Heck, he wouldn’t be worthy of the sobriquet “hero” if he couldn’t put aside a little head-to-toe tingling and numbness in order to do his duty.

"Justice Brigade," Hyperion called to his teammates. "To me!"

"What did he say?" Fakeout asked.

"I can't understand him. He's slurring his words pretty bad," Ms. Muscles said.

"Poor Guy," Aquina said. "The lightning affected him worse than we thought."

With the help of a running start, Hyperion took to the air, waving to the others to follow him. He couldn't work up very much altitude or speed, but he could still lead the brigade into battle. With looks ranging from concerned to amused, Fakeout, Ms. Muscles, and Aquina followed.

MANIKA FOUND CROSSHAIR AND Sledgehammer Sue making their way carefully up Main Street. Crosshair held projectiles at the ready in both his hands, while Sue clutched the leather-wrapped handle of her twenty-pound sledge tightly in her fist.

"This whole thing's a bust," Manika said, before they knew she had arrived. "If Brendan was ever here, he's gone now. Let's get back to the van and go. No point taking on the brigade if we don't have to."

Crosshair nodded in agreement. "Yeah, let's find Stormcloud and blow this place."

Suddenly, a voice boomed a stream of gibberish at them from above.

Confused, Crosshair looked up and groaned. He should have known. Hyperion hovered over their heads, hands on his hips, cape fluttering, doing his superior goody-goody Boy Scout thing. There were also three of his brigade buddies racing up the street to join the fun.

Receiving no response from those on the ground, Hyperion repeated his slurred words, but that only made the villains look at one another, baffled.

He had warned them: "Not so fast, you felonious fiends! The only way you're going anywhere is in power-dampening handcuffs." If they chose to ignore his words, he would have to let his fists do the talking instead. With his teammates still half a block away, Hyperion dove at the villains at what he judged to be a speed beyond any of their abilities to exceed.

Sledgehammer Sue didn't know what made Hyperion stutter through the air like a moth with a damaged wing, but she didn't question her good fortune. Instead, she told her friends to stand back, then whipped her hammer over her shoulder and, swinging from the hips, batted Hyperion up into the air with a thunderous boom, sending him sailing out of sight over the rooftops like an out-of-the-park home run.

"Nice!" Sue said with a satisfied nod.

CHARLIE WENT HOME. HIS plan should have been to go home and hide in the darkest corner of the basement until the supers invasion ended and everybody went away.

That *should* still have been his plan.

Instead, he would run home, grab his Knave gear, and join his teammates fighting the league.

He should have just burned it all before he left New York. The costume, the flying shoes, the Knave's bag of tricks, and the tricks therein. The whole kit and caboodle. But he thought they'd make nice souvenirs, or maybe he just got sentimental, and anyway, he never could have imagined that he'd ever be tempted to use any of it again.

Willie had gone by the time Charlie slammed through the door. Mr. Justice had probably tripped over himself getting into his Kevlar tights and racing out to join the fracas. Sure, why not? If the bad guys were going to wreck the town anyway, crazy Willie didn't want to be left out.

Charlie ran upstairs to his bedroom and took a small hard-shell suitcase from the back of his closet and unlocked it. He had modeled the blue, red, white, and yellow costume after the image on the jack, also known as the knave, in a deck of playing cards. It had puffy sleeves and he'd always felt a little silly wearing it. He did ditch the poofy hat and feather after his first outing when a couple of bank robbers had laughed at it, but he'd kept the ridiculous mask with the red cheeks, large nose, and mustache, which did an excellent job of hiding his true features.

Suiting up now would take too much time, so, after checking they were still adequately charged, he slipped on the shoes, did a quick inventory of his bag of tricks, and grabbed the mask. Maybe if he got real lucky, he could get through this without any of the residents of Crumbly tweaking to the fact of his Knave alter ego.

Yeah. And maybe Willie would break out in a song and dance routine.

"But this is the *last* time you do this!" he said to the image of himself in the mirror.

Sighing, Charlie hung the bag of tricks over his shoulder and stepped out his bedroom window.

25

"MOM!" WALLY SCREAMED. "GET out of the house! Mom!"

Wally's head twitched back and forth, like watching a high-speed tennis match, looking from the rapidly growing body hurtling in what seemed to be a straight line for them to the doorway. He yanked open the screen, still screaming "You gotta get out! Mom!" but when he didn't get an immediate answer, he raced inside.

Just then, Jamie came striding out of the kitchen, frowning. "What, Wally? You don't have to yell, I can—" she said, but the look on her son's face stopped her cold.

"Mom!" he screamed, "let's *go*!" She started to run toward him. He looked back out the door. The figure plummeted toward the house, closer and closer, close enough for Wally to make out Hyperion's distinctive blue costume, and he wondered what happened when

Hyperion fell on your house. Well, he'd know in just about two secon—

Wally was airborne.

He'd been swept up from behind, grabbed around the waist, and whisked out of the doorway and into the air in a dizzying rush of sight and a whoosh of wind. "No, my mom's in there," he screamed, struggling against the arms holding him dangling twenty feet above the yard.

"Relax, kid," Charlie Harris's voice said in his ear, just as Hyperion went crashing like a meteor from space through the front porch and front of Wally's house. The concussive force of the impact made the walls and porch explode outward, showering the yard and sidewalk with debris.

Wally screamed in horror, but Charlie held him tight and yelled, "She's okay, Wally," pointing to the porch of the Robinson house, across the street.

His mother, disheveled and confused but otherwise unharmed, stood alongside Swift.

"See? I got you; Swift got your mom," Charlie said. "Sorry we couldn't do anything about the house."

Wally didn't know what to start to geek out over first, being airborne, being airborne with the Knave, that his mom had been saved by Swift, or that his house had been trashed by Hyperion.

Or that the Knave is . . . ?

Wait!

Wally twisted his neck for a look at his rescuer, but all he could see was part of the mask. "Charlie?" the boy stuttered. "Is that you?"

"Yeah," Charlie's voice said from under the mask. "It's a long story and I'll explain later, but for now, don't tell anyone who I am, okay?"

"Wow," Wally said. "Your shoes really do fly. How do they work?"

"Antigravity, inertial guidance, toe controls in the shoes. Listen, about you keeping my secret . . . ?" Charlie stepped down from the sky, walking on thin air in his antigravity shoes to bring Wally over to his mother.

"Heck yeah!" Wally practically shouted. "Does that make me like, your sidekick or something?"

"No, I don't do sidekicks. Anyway, I'm retired. C'mon, your mom's waiting. We got a deal?"

Wally nodded vigorously, a sappy grin on his face. He'd been excited just being in the same vicinity as the heroes and, all of a sudden, he found himself in the middle of one of their adventures. Because he and the Knave were neighbors . . . and he trusted him with his secret identity!

His feet had barely touched the ground before his mother had him in her arms, crying. "It's okay, Mom. I'm okay. We're okay," he said, hugging her awkwardly back. "Did you see? We were flying. Well, Ch—I mean, the Knave did the flying but with me flying *with* him. Did you ever think you'd see anything like that?"

Jamie gave him an extra hard squeeze and said, "No, honey, I never thought I would," then let him go, wiping tears from her eyes. She turned to Charlie and said, "Thank you so much. It all happened so fast I didn't know if Wally had . . . ," but she had to stop there when her voice cracked, and the tears returned as Wally hugged her

"That's what we're here for, ma'am," Charlie said, trying to disguise his voice by making it deeper. He thought he sounded like a pompous goon, and then he made it even worse by tossing her a stupid little salute before turning and stepping, no, running, up into the air to get away from them before he did anything else lame.

"You folks be careful," Swift said, looking at Charlie in confusion. "Um, I better check on Hyperion. Excuse me."

Swift vanished and Wally watched the Knave running across nothing over to his house. It looked pretty bad. The porch had collapsed and a big chunk of the front of the house had blown into the street, causing the second floor to sag down into the first floor, leaving the house looking like a sadly pouting clown.

"Oh no, our poor house," Jamie groaned.

"Yeah, it's pretty bad," Wally admitted. "I'm so sorry, Mom."

Jamie found some tissues in her pocket and dabbed at her eyes.

"Sorry for what, honey?" she said. "There wasn't anything you could do to prevent what happened."

"Well, yeah, sure," Wally said. "But that's not what I mean. See, before that, a couple of days ago, when Charlie first came to town? And his friend too, the one helping him at the house? And he drove this car. A gray one. With New York license plates? Well, I thought Mr. Williams might... you know they lock up super-villains at a special prison in Trenton, right?"

Jamie nodded.

"Well, see, the Accelerator escaped from Trenton, like, that same day," Wally said, plunging ahead at breakneck speed. "In a car he stole. Exactly like the one Mr. Williams drives and... and, you know, I went into one of my supers chat rooms, with everybody talking about the escape, so I said I had seen one like his, the Accelerator's car, I mean." He paused for a deep breath. "And I think that's why everybody's here... and why the house got smashed."

Jamie shook her head and smiled. "None of this is your fault, sweetie. I can't imagine what an eleven-year-old in Crumbly could possibly have posted in a chat room that would bring this kind of response."

"But the sheriff said—"

"Wally, I'm sure Sheriff Cunningham doesn't believe any of this is your fault."

"I'm not," Wally said sullenly. "You'll see."

Across the street, Swift and the Knave were leading a dust-covered and dazed Hyperion out of the gaping wound that had minutes before been the front of their house. The teammates conferred for a few moments while the Man of Might caught his breath, the Knave pointing a couple of times in Wally and Jamie's direction. Hyperion straightened up and threw back his shoulders and twisted his head around a few times, loosening the kinks, then he shot straight up into the air in a trail of dust and landed seconds later, as light as a feather and shaken clean of dust, on the walkway at the foot of the porch in front of Wally and Jamie.

"I'm sorry about your lovely home, Mrs. Crenshaw," he said in his most reassuring superheroic tone. "Please be assured the Justice Brigade carries ample insurance for just such tragic incidents. We'll take care of everything."

With a smile and wink to Wally, he rocketed

skyward again and circled out of sight, off to rejoin his teammates. Swift and the Knave were already gone.

Wally turned to check on his mother's reaction. She didn't have to be a fan of the supers to be impressed by Hyperion in person. But her gaze wasn't at the airborne hero. Instead, she frowned at the ruin of her house, her lips pressed tight.

"Mom?" he said. "What're you thinking?"

Without looking at him, she said, "I'm wondering why your friend Charlie is wearing that mask?"

Wally swallowed hard.

"Um," he said.

RUSSELL CUNNINGHAM MAY HAVE spent the last few years as a small-town sheriff, but he had been trained in police work by the US Army and the Newark Police Department, neither of which could be described as easy duty. He had been in plenty of difficult, sometimes even dangerous, situations serving in both uniforms and had even seen his share of super battles, usually at a distance, working crowd or traffic control.

It had been precisely because of the things he'd seen as a cop that he had moved back to his hometown to safely raise his daughter. He used to watch reruns of an old television show with his father about a sheriff and his nervous deputy in a small southern town full of colorful characters where everyone knew everyone else. His father would laugh and say, "I swear, whoever came up with this must have been to Crumbly." Nothing had changed here in generations. Even the internet couldn't find a way to bring the twenty-first century into town.

And things would stay that way if he had any say in the matter.

Which he didn't, at least not where the supers were concerned. The moments after the lightning had been a free-for-all. The citizens of Crumbly had scattered like frightened rabbits, the supers took off, and he found himself reaching for a holstered gun that he hadn't worn in years.

He turned the corner and raced up Main Street, relieved to find the street deserted. As he passed the shops along the way, he saw that small groups of townspeople had taken refuge inside, some peeking cautiously out from doors and windows.

A new round of nearby ominous-sounding impacts and crashes made the sheriff pick up his pace. He could feel the ground trembling under his feet and he dreaded catching up with whatever waited ahead. Following the sounds and the flashes of light, he passed Cole

Lane and what he saw there made his blood run cold: the Crenshaw house, looking as though a bomb had gone off inside it.

The supers' brawl momentarily forgotten, the sheriff ran toward the house, his heart racing more from fear than exertion. He didn't remember seeing Wally or his mother in the crowd around the *Screaming Eagle.* He knew all about Jamie's past and her feelings about the supers. She would have stayed away. She would have kept Wally home too...!

The closer he got to the house, the clearer the damage became. If either of the Crenshaws had been inside when it happened, he didn't see how they could have escaped unharmed. Or worse.

"Russell!"

Jamie Crenshaw called to him from the porch of the Robinson place, Wally at her side.

The sheriff felt lightheaded with relief.

"I've never been so happy to see anyone in my life," he said. "Even you, Wally. What happened?"

"We got rescued by Swift and the Knave," Wally babbled excitedly.

"But we only *needed* rescuing because Hyperion fell on our house," Jamie added.

"Just as long as you're alright. Houses can always be rebuilt," the sheriff said. "You think it's safe to stay here?"

Jamie shrugged and looked over at her

house. "I suppose. Don't they say that lightning never strikes twice in the same place?"

"I'm not so sure that applies where these people are concerned," the sheriff said. "But I guess this is as safe a place as any. Just stay off the street. Take cover down in the basement if you have to, okay?"

Jamie nodded and then flinched as a series of loud blasts from several streets away shook the windows around them.

The sheriff said, "I gotta go. Stay safe." He pointed a finger at Wally. "And you! Stay right here and listen to your mother."

"Yes, sir," Wally said dully, wishing he could have been running toward the sounds of the fight with the sheriff instead of being stuck behind the lines with his mother.

Sometimes, his life just sucked.

26

SOMETIMES, CROSSHAIR THOUGHT, HIS life just sucked.

He'd become a supervillain in the first place to avoid hard work. He had been born with an unusually highly developed sense of aim and great reflexes. He never had to practice throwing or honing his super-accuracy. He could just naturally pick up an object of any size or shape, select a target, and hit any point on that target at will.

Early on, he tried using that ability to make his fortune in sports, but no matter which one he tried out for—football, baseball, javelin, shotput, even bowling, anything that required throwing—there were always groups of coaches demanding he put in endless, exhausting hours of practice when practice had nothing to do with what he did. Isn't the whole point of having a superpower that you didn't have to work at it?

He somehow found himself, years later, performing in a traveling circus. In his act, he threw stuff at ever-smaller stuff from peoples' heads, mouths, and hands, like a sharpshooter, except he used jellybeans and gumdrops instead of bullets. It had been easy work, no one ever telling him to practice or rehearse, but throwing jellybeans at a marble on top of some guy's head was humiliating. A few months of wandering the Midwest entertaining screaming kids and bored parents for three shows a day in a place that always smelled like elephant poop proved to be way more work than he wanted to do, so one Sunday night he robbed the box office, and thereafter would only go out and pull a job when he needed the money. He liked to think of himself as a gentleman of leisure.

He later joined up with Doc Psycon and the league, believing it would make being a crook easier. Not only did the bulbous-headed criminal genius plan all their crimes, but his jobs usually ended up in great big fat paydays, like the Vegas job. That had been worth millions to each of them. Crosshair couldn't help smiling every time he thought about how long he could do absolutely nothing at all with *that* prize in his pocket. Plus, Doctor Psycon supplied the cool costumes and, Crosshair had to admit, despite all their bickering, he sometimes liked having a place to hang out and talk shop with his fellow villains.

Stealing the sixty million bucks from the casinos had been surprisingly easy. The doc had planned it out to the split second and, for once, there had been no mistakes. Until Brendan stole all the money. Which, one thing leading to another as it always did, brought them to one of those moments that his life sucked the most: when the League of Villains got into a fight with the Justice Brigade.

Not even the entire league. Just him, Sledgehammer Sue, and Manika. Doctor Psycon and Professor Lamplighter were back with the van, outside of town, incommunicado because of the weird radio interference. He had no idea of Stormcloud's location.

So that left the three of them against the brigade's Hyperion, Ms. Muscles, the Knave, Swift, Fakeout, Aquina, and Blend. But no Mr. Justice? That was strange, he thought.

The odds made this a battle that wouldn't last very long or end up well for the league. The villain's harassment of the townspeople seemed the only thing keeping Hyperion from swooping in and taking them out by himself. Busy rescuing civilians and property, the Mortal of Might hadn't yet gotten to them. Manika and Swift could be seen flailing at one another as they blipped in and out of sight at superspeed. Sue swung her sledgehammer at anything that moved.

Crosshair scored a direct hit on Ms. Muscles's forehead with one of his steel throwing pellets as he dove behind a row of hedges, narrowly avoiding Knaves' knockout gas whoopee cushion. He rolled to his feet and kept running, but Blend blocked his way. Crosshair had been here and done this before, however, and he knew that Blend could almost never be counted on to be where you expected him to be. His hands filled with pellets, he let loose a shotgun-like barrage at Blend and the empty air all around him. The visible Blend kept running for a second even after he heard the crack of steel against skull and a groan a few feet to the visible figure's left. Then that Blend blinked out of sight, and the real Blend appeared six feet to the right, collapsing to the ground.

One down, he thought, but he didn't like the odds against the rest of them.

"We're getting slaughtered here, Doc Psycon," he said through gritted teeth, concentrating as hard as he could on the little man. Their comm devices were useless here, but he might be able to get through via the psychic connection the doc maintained with his teammates. He had said that whatever caused the electronic interference also affected his mental powers so

Crosshair could only hope the doc might still pick up his message through the static.

THE WHITE VAN CREPT into town along Old Crumbly Road. In the driver's seat, Professor Lamplighter sat hunched over, clutching the wheel in his white-gloved hands and peering cautiously through the windshield at the empty pavement ahead.

"Can't you go any faster, Professor?" Doctor Psycon said impatiently, his fingers massaging his throbbing bald dome. "Our fellows need us. Curse this interference, everything is so muddled. I can only hear them as though from a great distance."

"You know I am not comfortable piloting internal combustion engine conveyances, Doctor," the professor said testily. "If you feel you could do a better job than I, then, by all means, have at it."

"You know my feet don't reach the pedals, Professor," Psycon said sullenly.

"Then why don't you continue your cerebral efforts to locate the larcenous Mr. McMahon and allow me to drive?"

The doctor closed his eyes tight and began humming as he rocked back and forth in his seat.

"Something," he whispered in a strained voice. "I cannot say if it is him or merely the echoes of our thoughts." He winced and started slapping himself on the forehead. "It." Slap. "Is." Slap. "So." Slap. "Confusing." Slap. "So many thoughts." Slap, slap, slap. "Must." Slap. "Focus." Slap, slap.

Professor Lamplighter could not recall ever seeing his colleague this distressed. He depended almost entirely on his advanced mental abilities and when they were being thwarted as they were now, he had nothing else to fall back upon. Lamplighter, no intellectual slouch himself, possessed great knowledge and expertise in many fields, though none, alas, in the psychic realm, and he had no advice to offer his companion.

The old road finally turned into the town and they were crawling slowly up Main Street. That it was deserted didn't surprise the professor. He could hear the sounds of the battle even with windows closed and the air-conditioning blowing. Anybody with their wits about them would be taking cover wherever they could.

The doctor stopped slapping himself, but he still had his eyes closed and he rocked steadily back and forth, holding his head in his hands and humming.

As they rolled to the end of Main Street, the professor let out a laugh.

"If you are mocking me, Professor, I swear I shall—" Doctor Psycon started to growl, but

Lamplighter said, “Not at all, my friend. In fact, I give you… victory.”

“What the dickens are you babbling about?” the doctor snapped, opening his eyes.

“That, dear Doctor,” the professor laughed, pointing to the empty lot at the end of Main Street where the Justice Brigade’s *Screaming Eagle* sat, unattended.

“Oh. That *is* good, Professor,” he said, smiling. “Very, *very* good.”

WALLY’S MOOD PERKED UP when Swift and Manika appeared suddenly, skidding to a dead stop and trading blurred hyperspeed blows in the middle of the street. Manika did something and Swift twisted around at the hips as he fell to the ground, only to disappear and then reappear in almost the same instant behind her. His next move happened too fast for Wally to see, but it sent Manika skidding across the street like a hockey puck over ice, straight at the Robinson’s front porch. It all happened so quickly Wally had no time to shout a warning to his mother.

But, once again, he found himself swept up in a dizzying rush of wind and noise, this time in the arms of Hyperion, who had sped in just ahead of Manika to move Wally and Jamie before the villain smashed into the porch with a deafening crash.

Mother and son staggered as the hero deposited them at the end of the street and then leapt back up into the sky, swooping away to handle the next life-threatening emergency. In the time it had taken Hyperion to save them, Swift and Manika had sped out of sight.

Wally's head spun in both directions at once from the speed of the rescue and with the knowledge of who had performed it.

Hyperion!

"We've got to go, Wally," Jamie said, grabbing the stunned boy's hand. "It's too dangerous out here."

Wally nodded. It was weird, though. He wasn't afraid. Well, he was . . . but not really, not like a hide-under-the-bed scared. If he still had a bed to hide under. But this didn't even feel as frightening as sneaking into Charlie's backyard to spy on Mr. Williams. He felt the way he had in Washington, DC, when he'd been a kid. A combination of excitement and fright, but with the scary part being what made it so exciting, like riding a monster roller coaster. When he'd been younger, he didn't understand the danger, but now that he did, it didn't seem to matter.

"This way," Wally said. He had to get his mom to safety. It sounded like most of the fighting had shifted a few blocks over to the west side of town. He went east, toward Main Street.

But when they turned the corner, they were confronted with an obstacle to Wally's plan.

The *Screaming Eagle*, flying at street level, and screaming straight at them.

"I FIND IT INCREDIBLE that you are unable to operate a simple motor vehicle but are perfectly comfortable piloting unfamiliar jet aircraft," Professor Lamplighter said over the roar of the *Screaming Eagle*'s powerful engines.

"Elementary, my dear Professor. This craft has no foot pedals," Doctor Psycon said. "All the controls are on the joysticks."

"Joy indeed," the professor agreed. "I'm *over*-joyed we shall be able to extricate ourselves from this debacle after all."

"Not entirely a debacle. We are coming away from this episode in possession of a new jet aircraft, are we not?"

The professor chuckled. "As ever, my friend, you are correct. Now, let us pick up our companions and be away from this vile place."

The doctor peered at the instrument panel before him. "Mmm, yes. I'd best familiarize myself with the weapons systems before we engage with the brigade—"

"Doctor!" Lamplighter cried. "Watch where you are going!"

* * *

IN HIS HEART, WALLY knew they would be saved again. That's what the supers did. They fought bad guys and saved people like him and his mother. They'd already proved that twice today. So why not a third time?

Please.

He squeezed his mother's hand and started to say something, but, yes, yes, and, oh, *yes*, Wally had gone from being in the path of the *Screaming Eagle* to being up in the air as it blasted by beneath his feet.

"Hyperion's got your mom, kid. He'll drop her on Main Street, which is where I'm taking you," Charlie said in his ear over the rush of the wind. "We've been trying to contain the fighting on the other side of town, away from everybody."

"That's what I figured," Wally said. "We were going there when—Hey! Who's flying the *Eagle* anyway? They could have killed us."

"Wasn't one of us," Charlie said. "But I think I might know how we can find out."

"How?"

"We can ask them. They're coming back this way!"

27

"WHAT'S GOING ON NOW?" a gruff voice said from the darkness.

A second man said, "They're still fighting. But at least they're keeping it away from us."

"Good," the first voice said. "Sooner or later, they've got to get tired and go away."

"I don't think it's going to be that simple, Sarge," voice number one said. "Look. The league's van just drove into town. Looks like the doctor's joining the fight."

"Uh-oh, I don't like that," said a third man, a voice Mr. Justice recognized as belonging to the old man who had kicked his butt.

But why were they talking in the dark? He wished someone would turn on the lights, until he realized that he still had eyes closed. He groaned, then cursed himself. There went his element of surprise.

Mr. Justice put his hand to his aching head

and slowly blinked his eyes open. He had been dumped in a wheeled office chair, facing a corner, his hands and feet untied.

What kind of foe didn't tie up their captive?

He slowly spun his seat around until he faced the voices. They belonged to his old guy… and two *other* old guys. His old guy and one with a buzz cut were standing on either side of the third one, seated at the controls of a large bank of monitors.

"Who are you?" Mr. Justice said, pushing himself to his feet. He felt a little wobbly.

"I'm Morris Handelman. This is Boomer," he said, nodding over at the old man who had beat him up. "And that's Sarge."

As unsteady as he felt, Mr. Justice couldn't help but react to the name. "Handelman? You're Giz-Mo," he said. "I thought you were supposed to be dead."

"Just retired," Morris said, "but it makes it easier if everybody thinks I'm dead."

"Nobody's heard from you in thirty years. And why didn't you tie me up after you had your goon take me down?"

Morris laughed. "Tie you up? You're the world's greatest escape artist. Why would I waste my time tying you up if you're just going to escape in two seconds?"

"I suppose. It's just that people usually do," Mr. Justice said, sounding disappointed.

"Anyway, I never heard of these two and the whole world thinks you've been dead for thirty years. Did you think the entire Justice Brigade came here for you?"

Morris shrugged, "When you put it that way, it does sound silly."

"We got a tip about the Accelerator hiding out in Crumbly," Mr. Justice said, not mentioning that he had already been in town when McMahon escaped. No reason to give up even the tiniest hint to his alter ego.

"The Accelerator's not here," Morris said. "And I would have seen him if he were."

"No doubt," Mr. Justice said, eying the rows of monitors

"Look, we're not the bad guys here," Sarge growled.

"Sarge is right. We've been living in Crumbly for decades, just minding our business, until you and the others came along."

"You call having the whole town under surveillance minding your business?" Mr. Justice said. Not that he didn't wish he could have a cool surveillance system just like it back home. He just didn't care for Giz-Mo's hypocrisy.

"Oh, I don't always watch everybody," Morris said with a chuckle. "I activated the system today when people started showing up. Otherwise, I rarely fire this baby up."

"Except for jamming enemy radar," Boomer added.

"What enemy radar is that?" the Detective of the Night asked.

"It's nothing, it doesn't matter," Morris said with an unconvincing chuckle.

His friend's curt dismissal seemed to confuse the old soldier. "But you said you had to keep it on twenty-four seven to scramble the enemy's radar or they'd be able to locate our base."

With a guilty glance at Mr. Justice, Sarge put his arm around the other man's shoulder and said, "You hungry, Boomer old buddy? Let's grab some chow," and led him away.

But the damage had been done. Mr. Justice had already put two and two together and exclaimed, "You're jamming the electronics!"

Morris took a deep breath and let it slowly out. "Guilty as charged."

"What kind of a monster are you, denying these good people their right to cable television and cell phones?" Mr. Justice snarled.

The question made the old man, once known as Giz-Mo, the Master Engineer of Crime, hang his head.

"Because I'm afraid," he said, his voice scarcely above a whisper, unable to meet the other man's eyes. "What do you know about Project Commando?"

The question caught Mr. Justice by surprise,

but his encyclopedic memory quickly pulled up the details. "You mean the secret World War II-era project designed to turn ordinary soldiers into super-soldiers? I've only heard rumors, of course, but it's said our scientists tried everything from some of the earliest known experiments in gene splicing to cybernetic bone enhancement and replacement. As best as I've ever been able to learn, the project's records were destroyed at the end of the war and anybody directly involved in it is long dead."

"You're right. Except there are still four project members alive. My two friends and me, and this man," Morris Handelman said, pointing to a monitor showing one of the heroes locked in a struggle with Sledgehammer Sue. "Colonel Darwyn Flint."

"So that's how the old man beat me so easily," the detective said with relief.

Morris nodded. "Old Boomer's about 75 percent man-made parts under those overalls. Sarge and me had a few electronics implanted and our DNA tinkered with, resulting in some interesting mental and physical improvements. The colonel—a lieutenant then and our platoon leader—got dished up a combination of some of everything. We're all of us within spitting distance of one hundred years old but you could never tell it."

By habit, Mr. Justice whipped the communicator from his belt to relay this new information to his teammates, before remembering the device wouldn't work.

Morris glanced at the array of screens and said, "That's not good." He tapped some keys and brought the image of the *Screaming Eagle* in the empty lot up onto the main display. He zoomed in on the hatch in time to catch sight of Doctor Psycon and Professor Lamplighter before it slid shut.

"You're causing the interference, Giz-Mo," Mr. Justice said. "You can also shut it down and allow for normal communications."

Morris nodded. "Yes, but—"

"Don't 'but' me, mister," the Master of the Night said. "Two of the nastiest criminal masterminds in the world have just taken possession of one of the most advanced airborne weapons platforms known to man. This town will be lucky to survive the next five minutes, but if it does, it will be thanks to that thing we call... *justice*. Now, do it!"

Morris looked over at Boomer and Sarge. Boomer chewed contentedly on a stick of beef jerky, leaving Sarge to cast the deciding vote.

"The man's right, Morris. Do it."

Morris did it.

* * *

DOCTOR PSYCON WORKED THE controls as he hunched forward in his seat, watching the Knave race ahead of them through the *Eagle*'s windshield. A simple twist of his wrist and the aircraft would pass harmlessly over or around the airborne hero, but the doctor wanted to wait until the last possible moment to make the maneuver. Of all the heroes, he had always found the Knave to be particularly obnoxious and it amused him to make the pointy-shoed buffoon sweat a bit before he veered off.

The instrument panel gave off a sudden loud alert tone, and then a soothing female robotic voice said, "Target acquired."

"Target? What have you targeted, Doctor?" Professor Lamplighter said.

As Psycon watched, a swatch of the instrumentation that had been dark began lighting up. Then, as if by magic, a targeting sight in glowing red lines appeared on the windshield before him, the crosshairs on the heads-up display centering on the fleeing Knave. Psycon jiggled the control stick but the *Eagle* didn't respond, except for the robot voice to say, "Target locked. Automatic command and control activated."

"GANGWAY!" THE KNAVE HOLLERED, racing through the air as fast as he could, a whole lot faster than he could have run on the ground thanks to his antigravity shoes. But as fast as he was, he couldn't run faster than the *Screaming Eagle*. Especially with an eleven-year-old kid hanging on to him for dear life.

The *Eagle* stayed on them like they were attached by a string. He caught a glimpse of Doctor Psycon at the wheel before turning to run. He had no idea that bulbous-headed runt could handle a ship so well.

First thing first. Charlie had to ditch his passenger.

"When I hit the ground, I'm going to let you go, Wally," he yelled in the boy's ear. "You drop and roll and stay down. The *Eagle*'s going to follow me. Okay?"

Wally swallowed hard and nodded.

"Here we go, kid," the Knave said, and raced for the ground like running down a steep hill. Even though it made his stomach flop, Wally forced himself to watch a patchy green and brown front lawn hurtle up toward him. He could feel the impact as Knave's feet touched the ground at the same moment Charlie yelled, "Now!"

Wally went limp and let himself drop, hitting the ground with a jolt. But as Charlie started to run up and away from him, Wally felt his left arm being pulled up along with the masked man. His arm had was entangled in the strap of Knave's bag of tricks. With a startled cry, Wally yanked on the strap as the hero climbed away from him. It snapped, sending Wally tumbling to the ground with the bag in his hands just as the *Eagle* blasted by over his head.

"NOTHING, I DID NOTHING," Doctor Psycon stammered. "All the electronics have come back online, and the systems have reacquired contact with outside sources. Satellite. GPS. Targeting radar. Whatever caused the interference has ceased and now the ship has locked on the Knave and is executing a pre-programmed attack protocol."

"Make it stop," Lamplighter groaned, his fingers clutching the armrests of his seat for dear life. The *Eagle* swerved and swooped like mad in its radar-guided pursuit of the Knave, who ran through the air for dear life, zigging and zagging wildly.

"Abort, abort," the doctor yelled at the ship.

The *Eagle* ignored him and edged closer to its target.

"Intercept in five... four..."

"Stop, don't," Psycon screamed.

"... three... two..."

"I demand you cease this instant, you infernal machine," Lamplighter commanded, slapping at the controls with his gloved hand.

"... one," the *Eagle* said, and the doctor and the professor could only close their eyes and turn their faces away in horror.

The control panel beeped and the heads-up target display disappeared.

"Weapons system reboot initiation complete," the *Eagle* said. "Have a nice day."

THE JET SWEPT PAST the airborne Charlie, the blast of air from the powerful craft sending Charlie tumbling out of control, his legs churning and spiraling wildly before he slammed into the side of a house across the street and slid to the ground.

The *Eagle* rose above the surrounding rooftops and banked sharply, sliding off in search of a different battle to fight.

Wally raced across the street and dropped to his knees next to Charlie. He shook him by the shoulder, shouting his name.

Charlie groaned.

"You okay?" Wally said. "Charlie? Can you hear me?"

The masked head nodded slowly. With some more groans and assorted other sounds of pain and discomfort, Charlie pulled the mask off his face.

"Ow," he said. "How about you?"

"I'm okay, but, man, when I saw you hit that house..."

"Is that what I hit?" Charlie said through gritted teeth. He started to push himself into a sitting position but stopped and howled in pain, his pale face twisting in agony.

"What? What?" Wally jumped back, frightened.

"My leg," Charlie gasped. "I think it's broken." Gingerly, he reached down with both hands to grab his left thigh, ever so slightly moving the leg, producing a new howl of pain.

"Oh, yes. Broken. Definitely broken," he gasped.

"*Attention, Justice Brigade. Can you hear me?*" the Knave mask lying next to him on the grass suddenly said.

Wally jumped again, and even Charlie looked at it with surprise through his pain.

"It's the radio," Charlie said. "There's a headset built into the mask."

"Radios don't work in Crumbly."

"*This is Mr. Justice to the brigade,*" the mask said. "*The electronic interference has been disabled; all systems are operational. Repeat, all systems are operational! Converge on my signal. Justice, out!*"

"Well, what do you know," Charlie said with a weak laugh. "Score one for the big guy." He put his hand to his forehead and laid back down flat on the ground. "Hoo boy. Hey, kid, I don't want you to worry or anything because I'm going to be just fine, but I think I may be in a little bit of shock and I might just have to pass out for a few minutes here, okay?"

"Huh? But what am I supposed to do?" Wally said, but Charlie had already passed out cold before he finished the question.

28

MOMENTS AFTER THE *Screaming Eagle*'s displays flashed to life, the lights in Doctor Psycon's mind came back on as well.

The little man laughed with delight. Ever since they had entered the influence of Crumbly's mysterious interference, he had felt as though his head had been stuffed with cotton. It had no effect on his intelligence, but it threw a dark and heavy blanket of static over the psychic abilities that enhanced his already brilliant mind. Now, with the static lifted, all those smothered psychic emanations were coming through as clearly as a mother's lullaby in her baby's ear.

He could feel them all. The mental links with his criminal cohorts were as strong as ever, but he could also sense the presence of each of the members of the brigade, some closer than others. He extended the reach of his mental probing, flitting over the scores of ordinary minds he touched belonging to the besieged citizens of the town, most of them scrambled with questions and fear. He sensed a psychic dead zone somewhere below, but he hadn't the time to seek it out now.

"Are you still with me, Doctor?"

"I'm with you all," the doctor responded. "My powers are working again. We will rendezvous in thirty seconds—"

"We have commandeered the *Screaming Eagle*, my friends! Meet us at the original landing zone," the professor said, hearing the mental message in his head the doctor had sent out to the entire team.

Then something in Doctor Psycon's brain said: *Accelerator.*

"He's here," the doctor exclaimed out loud. "I can't quite pinpoint him yet, but Brendan is near, just beyond the reach of my thoughts."

"Excellent. Then, by all means, let us stop dallying with the brigade and get on with reclaiming our stolen booty."

"My sentiments exactly, dear Professor," he said out loud, and in his mind, he told the others, "Prepare to board, my friends. And be quick about it. I have a surprise for you."

"THIS IS MR. JUSTICE *to the brigade. The electronic interference has been disabled; all systems are operational. Repeat, all systems are operational! Converge on my signal. Justice, out!"*

Hyperion gently eased the large oak tree that Sue's sledgehammer had sent toppling toward a house to the ground when Mr. Justice's message crackled in his headset.

"Hyperion to *Screaming Eagle.* Activate emergency shutdown protocol," he snapped.

"*Awaiting voiceprint confirmation,*" the ship's electronic voice replied. "*Confirmed. Please state command execute code.*"

"Command code prime alpha prime."

"*Command code accepted.*"

Hyperion launched himself skyward. Several blocks over, he saw the *Screaming Eagle* stop dead in the air and drop toward the ground.

DOCTOR PSYCON'S VOICE IN his head woke Stormcloud up. Surprised to find himself still on the ground, face down, where Blend had left him, he wondered why he hadn't been hauled away and locked up somewhere. The hero must have gotten distracted before he could finish the job.

But the moment he tried to roll over onto his back, he realized that the hero hadn't been quite as sloppy as he had hoped. Stormcloud's hands were locked behind his back in a pair of power-dampening handcuffs. Stormcloud groaned and switched his efforts into pushing himself up onto his knees and staggering to his feet with his hands cuffed behind him.

In his head, Doctor Psycon announced, "*Prepare to board, my friends. And be quick about it. I have a surprise for you all.*"

The only surprise Stormcloud cared about would be being left behind if he didn't meet up with the doc and the rest of the league on time. He took off in a clumsy run.

AFTER BEING DEPOSITED IN front of the general store by Hyperion, Jamie Crenshaw waited for Wally and Charlie Harris. Or the Knave. Whatever he wanted to call himself. She assumed they would be right behind her and that she and Wally would wait out the end of this craziness with their friends and neighbors. But a minute passed. Then another. And another. The sounds of combat and the scream of that jet plane overhead continued unabated, with still no sign of Wally.

Ma O'Casey had to practically drag Jamie into the general store and physically restrain her to keep her from running back outside.

"If he's with one of those super fellas, your Wally's just fine," Ma said. "You know they'd never let anything happen to a child."

"I... I know you mean well, Ma," Jamie said, her voice choked as she peered out the store window, hoping desperately to catch sight of her son. “But I’ve been out there in that, and we were almost killed three times before Hyperion brought me here. And now Wally’s out there, alone...”

“He’s not alone, and you were also *saved* three times, weren’t you?”

“They’re not perfect, Ma,” Jamie said. “They can’t be everywhere at once. They couldn’t save Lincoln City.”

“No,” Ma agreed sadly, “they couldn’t. But this isn’t Lincoln City and those aren’t invading alien warriors trying to conquer the planet. They’re just a bunch of crooks in costumes, not killers.”

“Unless you happen to get in their way,” Jamie said.

MIKE BREWER HAD FOUND the perfect spot to plant himself in the crowded general store. Directly in front of the counter, right beside an arrangement of large glass jars filled with a variety of loose candies ranging from bubble gum to miniature chocolate bars to lollypops. Several wooden kegs of nails were stacked in front of the counter, at just the right height to make for comfortable seating.

From his perch on one of those kegs, flanked by Abel Schotz and Nick McCain, he easily and unobtrusively plucked and pocketed treats from the glass jars behind them. Mike figured with everyone so caught up with the events outside they wouldn't be paying attention to a few jars of candy, but the last time he had glanced Pa O'Casey's way, he thought the old man might have given him a funny look.

Mike let his eyes wander away and pretended to ignore the candy. Instead, he looked around. He saw Wally's mom at the window with Ma O'Casey.

"Hey, you guys seen the Whiz Kid lately?" Mike whispered to his friends.

Abel and Nick looked at each other, then around the store, and then at Mike, shrugging.

"Me neither. You don't think he's still out there, do you?"

Abel shrugged. Nick scratched his head.

"Because if he thinks he's gonna get *my* reward," Mike started to say, before he remembered that he hadn't told his friends about the tip he had sent to the Super-Villain Task Force. He knew it had been his tip that had brought the Justice Brigade to town.

His friends were waiting for Mike to finish his thought, but instead he said, "I gotta use the bathroom. Save my seat." He left the two of them fighting to see which of them would sit on the keg until he got back.

Mike tried to look casual as he lumbered to the rear of the store where, with a glance back to make sure the coast was clear, he walked past the restroom and slipped quietly out the back door.

PENNY POTTER JUMPED IN surprise when her smartphone began to beep and buzz. She hadn't had any cell or internet reception since hitting town, but she had been using the device nonstop once the action began to take pictures and videos of the fighting and dictate notes for her story.

The young researcher for the *National Mask* had waited a long time for the opportunity to prove herself as a journalist, and now on her very first assignment, she'd been handed the chance to deliver an exclusive.

Penny looked at her phone. She had twenty-two missed calls and thirty-nine missed texts. One of the calls had been her mother. The rest were from her editor, Mr. Taylor. All the texts were from her friends and colleagues at the *Mask* warning her of Mr. Taylor's growing anger over her continued silence.

Taking cover behind a backyard tool shed, Penny decided to not even try and explain her absence in words. Instead, she emailed her photos, videos, and notes directly to the angry editor under the subject, "Dateline: Crumbly-by-the-Sea, New Jersey."

If Mr. Taylor still had a problem with her after that, she assumed he would find a way to let her know. But until she heard otherwise, Penny still had a story to cover. She could worry about whether or not she still had a job when she got back to New York.

Meanwhile, the *Eagle* screamed over her head; she raced out from behind the shed and chased after it, because wherever it went, that's where the story would be.

"WAS THAT WALLY?" BENNY Sachem said.

Up until a minute ago, he and Brenda had been in the Cunningham's basement where they had taken refuge when some of the fighting came crashing down her street. Now that the sounds of combat and the big jet fighter that had been buzzing the town had passed, Benny led them cautiously back upstairs and now peered through the curtains to check for further danger outside.

Brenda looked surprised. "It can't be. His mom grounded him."

"Either that's Wally or he's got an evil twin. Check it out," Benny said.

Brenda joined him at the window.

"That is Wally," she said, confused. "What's he carrying?"

"I can't tell. Looks like shoes . . . and a pouch and some other stuff. Maybe they sounded all clear and we didn't hear it down in the basement."

"Maybe," Brenda said skeptically. The world outside her window seemed to be back to normal without a superspeedster or flying man in sight. "I guess it couldn't hurt to take a look."

Before they went out, Brenda ran back to the kitchen where she'd earlier set Wally's souvenir on the counter. She hadn't been able to get close to Hyperion, much less have the hero autograph it for her friend, but she knew he'd understand. She pocketed the plastic cube with the fused nut and bolt and left the house.

HE COULD HEAR EVERYTHING!

All the chatter between the supers as they coordinated their attacks and rescue efforts, then came Hyperion's commands to the *Screaming Eagle*. Wally heard the Man of Might give the order over the radio in the Knave mask and, in the next second when he looked up at the jet, it had come to a sudden halt in mid-air, the engines swiveling into position for a vertical landing. From where he stood, it looked to Wally like it would land back down pretty much where it had started, in the lot at the end of Main Street.

Juggling the Knave's mask, flying shoes, and bag of tricks had slowed him down some, but he didn't have far to go. You never did in Crumbly, a town too small for anything to be far from anything else. He felt bad about leaving Charlie, but Wally didn't know what to do for him and he didn't seem to be in any immediate danger. Besides, without his Knave accessories to give him away, a passing villain wouldn't know about his alter ego and leave him alone.

He also figured he should safeguard the Knave's equipment. He didn't want to think what someone like Doctor Psycon could learn by reverse engineering the shoes or cracking the secrets of the brigade's comm-link.

From the radio, Wally heard Hyperion say, "*They're all converging on the lot. Stand by. Wait for my signal.*"

One after another, the heroes acknowledged the command.

"*That's everyone but Knave,*" Mr. Justice said.

"*Hyperion to Knave. Acknowledge, Knave.*"

Wally waited.

Hyperion said, "*If you can hear me, link up with us when possible, Knave. We can't wait. Out.*"

"Oh, man," Wally muttered and ran down the street, the dangling shoes banging against his leg with every step.

29

DOCTOR PSYCON WRESTLED WITH the unresponsive joystick controls as, without warning, the *Screaming Eagle* hit the air brakes. The sleek ship shuddered to a dead stop and started its vertical descent.

"The controls are useless," the little man growled. "With the electronic interference gone, they must have been able to activate a remote-controlled override. We are coming in for a landing, whether we like it or not."

"I am taking it for granted that you have a backup plan to see us successfully through this sad turn of events," Professor Lamplighter said, craning his neck to watch the ground rise up to meet them through the windshield.

"I believe I might. Now, when you say 'us,' Professor, are you are referring to the entirety of the league, or . . . ?" the doctor said, leaving the question dangling.

The professor smiled. “Well, as much as I shall miss the company of our criminal cohorts, if it came to *their* capture being the price for *our* freedom, I would be quite satisfied if ‘us’ were just you and I, Doctor.”

“Then we are in agreement,” the doctor said. He closed his eyes and brought his hands up to massage the temples of his swollen head. “Ah, I sense that the others are gathering below. Unfortunately, the heroes are out there as well, concealed, waiting to pounce no doubt, as soon as they have us all in one place.”

“And you have a plan to save us from being pounced upon?”

“Indeed,” the doctor said.

THE TREES RINGING THE backyard Wally raced through momentarily blocked his view of the *Screaming Eagle* as it lowered into the empty lot at the end of Main Street. The heroes didn’t seem to have much to say in those last moments as they waited anxiously in hiding to spring the ambush. Hyperion would say things like, “*She’s holding steady*,” and “*Wait if for it, my friends*,” but they were all frozen in the moment, waiting for what came next.

Wally knew he had to stay off Main Street if he wanted to avoid being seen and stopped, but he struggled to carry his load through backyards and over hedges and bushes. The shoes were heavy, and the bag of tricks' shoulder strap, which he had clumsily tied together, kept slipping. The mask, too big for him to wear, kept trying to slip out of his grasp. He wished he had a pair of flying shoes so he could just go running unseen over everyone's head.

Wait!

He *did* have a pair of flying shoes. Okay, maybe they weren't exactly his, but at the moment they were hanging around his neck, with the guy they belonged to in no shape to use them.

Wally dropped to his knees to examine the shoes. On the outside, they were kind of clunky, like clogs, but they were shaped like the pointy-toed slippers worn by clowns and jesters he had seen in old drawings, narrowing to a point that curved up and around at the tip.

He peered inside the shoe, reaching in to feel around. Charlie had said there were buttons he could operate with his toes that controlled the shoes. Yeah, there they were, three little bumps under the lining.

"Wonder which button does what," Wally muttered. He decided it made sense that the largest button, under where the big toe would go, would be the on/off switch. Holding the shoe at arm's length in case something went wrong, he clicked the button.

Nothing happened.

At least not right away. Then he felt the shoe vibrating ever so faintly around his hand and, when he brought it closer, he could hear it give off a soft mechanical hum. With nothing disastrous resulting from his first experiment, he pressed the middle button and immediately the shoe and his hand started to rise, as if released from the pull of gravity. Wally laughed and pressed the last button, which returned some sense of weight to his arm but not enough to let it drop to his side.

He clicked up again, this time banking his hand this way and that, feeling the shoe shifting and adapting to the movement of his hand. It reminded him of riding a Segway scooter he and his mother had taken on a tour of Boston while they were on vacation last year. The scooters were self-balancing, making it almost impossible to fall, and you had to just lean slightly in whatever direction you wanted to go.

Wally quickly kicked off his sneakers and jammed his feet into the antigravity shoes. They didn't have laces, but the elastic opening closed snugly around his ankles so there was no danger of them slipping off his feet in flight. Only his feet were a couple of sizes too small to fill the shoes and allow his toes to stay in contact with the control buttons.

He pried his feet out of them and pulled off his socks. Then he shoved his bare feet back into the shoes, stuffing a rolled-up sock behind each heel to push his feet forward. He stood up and took a few experimental steps. It worked. His toes were positioned over the buttons.

Wally draped the strap of the bag of tricks over his shoulder and tucked the Knave mask into the waistband of his pants at the small of his back.

Then he took a deep breath, trying not to think about what came next, because if he thought about it, he wouldn't be able to do it. But didn't thinking about *not* thinking about something have the same effect as actually thinking about it?

"Stop it," he told himself and made himself not think about it this time. He clicked the *on* buttons in both shoes, tapped the middle buttons, and slowly rose several inches off the ground.

It felt like he was standing on solid ground but different. Not unlike balancing on a Segway, but while his body swayed unsteadily in all directions, the shoes continuously adjusted to keep him upright. After a few moments of wild gyrations with his arms and legs, he finally got the hang of staying vertical.

Then he tried to take a step, sliding his right foot forward, arms extended out to his sides for balance, like a tightrope walker. One step. Good. Then another, slowly sliding his left foot to catch up with the right. He found that if he kept his legs loose and knees slightly bent and didn't fight the shoes, he could take shuffling baby steps while suspended inches off the ground.

Now he tapped the middle buttons to rise higher. Nothing happened. He clicked again, but still no response. He bounced up and down at his knees and flapped his arms, first a little, then a lot, but he still didn't move. He frowned down at the shoes for a moment, then lifted his foot, like walking up a step, and when he pushed off on that foot, he lifted several inches higher and stayed there. He repeated the move and got the same result.

The brigade had been mostly silent during Wally's efforts, but while he walked in ever-higher circles around that backyard, the radio in the mask whispered in Hyperion's voice, "*The* Screaming Eagle *has landed. Wait for my signal.*"

That made up Wally's mind. He'd taken all the practice he had time for if he planned to do this.

Wait. *Was* he going to do this?

Yes.

"Whiz Kid to the rescue," Wally cried out in his deepest and loudest supers voice and bound up, up, and away into the air, tripping and almost losing his balance twice before he gained enough altitude to jitter nervously over the treetops and race, with shuffling, measured strides, to the empty lot.

Wally had every reason to be proud of himself. He had only screamed in terror two or three times on the way up, but it would be smooth sailing from now on.

As long as he didn't look down.

THE FOUR VILLAINS WATCHED the *Screaming Eagle* touch back down on the empty lot. Manika, Sledgehammer Sue, Crosshair, and Stormcloud kept shifting their gazes from the descending ship to the skies and streets around them, anticipating an attack from the supers at any moment. If they moved fast enough, the doctor could set the ship down, pick them up, and be airborne again in a matter of moments.

But the moment the aircraft settled on its landing gear, the engines cut off and the *Eagle* went silent.

"What's he waiting for?" Stormcloud said.

"Why doesn't he open the hatch?" Manika groaned.

"Something must be wrong," Crosshair said.

INSIDE THE *EAGLE*, DOCTOR Psycon and Professor Lamplighter stood opposite one another on either side of the closed hatch.

"This is going to happen fast, so stay close by my side," the doctor said.

Lamplighter snapped off a quick salute. "Where you go, I go, my friend."

"Very well," Psycon said. He closed his eyes, rubbing his broad brow with delicate strokes of his fingertips. "Now, I just need to sort through this jumble of minds and find what I seek. I won't be but a moment."

HYPERION KNELT NEXT TO the chimney on the roof of a house that offered him an unobstructed view of the empty lot half a block away. The villains were regrouping there, expecting to be picked up by Doctor Psycon in the stolen *Eagle*, but the rest of the brigade had already taken up positions around the lot. His remote override of the *Eagle* had set it in lockdown mode from which it could only be released with voiceprint-authorized passwords from two of the heroes, so the leagues' only possible escape would be on foot. But as soon as the bad guys showed themselves, the heroes were set to spring from hiding and scoop them up.

"Steady, people," Hyperion said into his radio.

The dust settled around the *Screaming Eagle*, but the hatch remained closed.

"Wait for my signal."

Hyperion's left ear began to itch. He tried to ignore it, but it quickly got annoying enough that he had to pull his mask aside and wiggle his pinky finger around in his ear to scratch. It didn't help.

If anything, the itch grew worse. It felt like something wiggling its way into his ear canal, a sensation that went from merely annoying to maddening in a matter of seconds. It kept spreading, filling his left ear then his right, and then his entire brain felt as though a million worms were wiggling around in it, and he had to grab his head in his hands and try to scream but the worms wouldn't let him, calling urgently in the voice of Doctor Psycon, "*Come quickly, Hyperion! We need you!*"

THOUGH WALLY COULDN'T REMEMBER what it had been like learning to walk, he had seen the videos his parents had made of those early efforts and imagined he probably looked every bit as awkward and goofy now as he did then. It was all he could do to keep his legs from flying out from under the rest of him; no easy trick with the control buttons for the shoes right there under his toes. He had to be very careful or he could accidentally click on one, as he'd already done once, switching off the power to the right shoe, which left him momentarily dangling upside down by his left leg until he got it turned back on.

Trees were the main problem, especially tree*tops*. Up here, they were everywhere, giant masses of leafy greenery at all different heights bobbing and swaying in the breeze. They were hard to avoid, but he didn't want to go up too far above them for fear he might be spotted.

Thankfully, with the destination of his air-borne stroll in sight, he could start to make his way back down to the ground. He clicked on the descent buttons in the shoes and leaned forward, feeling the slight tug of gravity. He took one step down, then another, his arms held out from his sides for balance.

The Knave mask tucked into his waistband started to slip as he heard Hyperion's voice say, "*Steady people.*"

Without thinking, Wally twisted around to grab for the mask, but the sudden, violent movement sent him tumbling head over heels, out of control.

"Stop!" Wally yelled. His toes must have hit the off buttons because the next thing he knew, the shoes had shut down and he had nothing to keep him up anymore.

He fell like a stone, dropping the mask just as Hyperion said, "*Wait for my signal.*"

At the last moment, as he plunged into the full canopy of a large old oak tree just past the empty lot where the *Screaming Eagle* sat, he got the shoes turned back on. They slowed him as he dropped through the treetop, grabbing desperately for a handhold. Greenery whipped wildly past his eyes and branches scratched his arms and legs, but the dense foliage slowed his fall until he came to a jarring stop on a very hard and very unyielding tree branch.

"*Oooofff!*"

Wally gratefully wrapped his arms and legs around the sturdy old branch and hung on for dear life. After catching himself, he needed a few seconds to also catch his breath, before hauling himself carefully into a sitting position, his legs straddling the branch with his back against the tree trunk.

"Wow, talk about close," he muttered, and then said "Wow" again when he took a look at the scene spread out below him.

The tree grew at the edge of the vacant lot, overlooking the *Screaming Eagle.* Wally wished he hadn't lost the mask because he wouldn't be able to hear the conversation between the heroes. But he still had the Knave's bag of tricks hanging on his shoulder. Maybe it held some kind of backup communications device.

Keeping one eye on the still silent aircraft,

Wally opened the black, leather, drawstring pouch and looked inside. As expected, it held an assortment of the Prince of Pranks' gag weapons, many of which Wally had seen featured in magazine articles. Little round bomb-shaped concussive grenades. Tear gas whoopee cushions. Explosive itching powder pellets. Expanding snakes-in-a-can restraint devices. Small plastic soldiers, full of super-sneezing powder, on parachutes. The bag also contained a few other devices he didn't recognize and the slingshot that the Knave used to deliver his tricks to his foes.

Movement down below caught his eye.

The *Screaming Eagle*'s hatch started to slide open.

And as it did, Crosshair, Sledgehammer Sue, Stormcloud, and Manika came bursting out of concealment and ran toward it.

They had only just shown themselves when Hyperion streaked down from above and dove into the opening hatch. He emerged a moment later with Doctor Psycon and Professor Lamplighter in his arms.

The Man of Might paused just outside the *Eagle*'s hatch, hovering over the landing ramp, while Psycon called out to his stunned criminal comrades, "Our apologies, dear colleagues, but this escape route only has room for two. Let's be on our way, shall we, Hyperion?"

"Yes, Doctor Psycon," Hyperion said in a halting, flat voice, and then rose into the air and flew away on the wind.

30

DOCTOR PSYCON FELT A twinge of guilt about leaving the league behind, especially Crosshair, who had always been his most loyal and reliable henchman. But simple logic dictated that if only one of them could escape, that one be him. And to be fair, his continued freedom was to their advantage; who else possessed the super-intellect to devise their eventual escape?

It took every bit of concentration the little man had to maintain his mental control over Hyperion's mind and keep the rest of the heroes and villains frozen where they stood. Leaving them briefly paralyzed was easy, just a quick, low-level mental pulse that momentarily stunned the nervous system. Getting Hyperion to do his bidding took something else entirely.

He had used this trick a few times before

on the members of the brigade—one time, thanks to a power boost from a psychic amplifier, he had even gotten them to turn against one another and fight—but they had all learned to recognize the early signs of his mental tampering and how to counteract it, which mostly consisted of yelling and jumping around like crazy people to distract him and themselves. This time, he didn't try to be clever or sly. He just sent everything he could muster slamming all at once into Hyperion's brain before the hero knew what had hit him, and overwhelmed him with psychic shock and awe.

It had been an exhausting effort, and even now he could feel a small part of Hyperion's mind resisting his mental control. Gritting his teeth, Doctor Psycon pushed back against it. He just wanted to be gone from here as fast as possible, before his paralytic strike against the heroes and villains wore off.

"What is the delay, Doctor?" Professor Lamplighter whispered desperately.

"Need silence," the doctor hissed. "Must. Focus."

"Of course," Lamplighter said, before he started sneezing loudly and uncontrollably.

UP IN THE TREE, Wally let loose a loud, victorious shout and gave the slingshot in his hand a big, wet kiss. He had spent hours studying the plastic reproduction of this very weapon on the shelf over his desk at home, never dreaming he would ever get to hold the real deal. *And use it.*

Against *real* supervillains!

Down below, Professor Lamplighter's explosive sneezes made Doctor Psycon cry out in alarm before he too erupted in a spasm of sneezes. And when he did, Hyperion jerked awake, as if from a nightmare, and dropped them both as he too started sneezing. None of them had yet noticed the remains of an exploded little green army man dangling from a plastic parachute drifting down toward them in a cloud of fine sneezing powder.

Wally would have jumped for joy if hadn't already been thirty feet up in the air. Instead, he allowed himself a muttered "So cool! What else is in here?" and reached into the bag of tricks.

THE DOCTOR'S SNEEZES WERE so violent he had no hope of maintaining his control over Hyperion. Fortunately, his super foe seemed to be in the same predicament, his mighty frame bent over and convulsing with each explosive exhalation of air.

Meanwhile, the effect of the doctor's mental pulse had worn off and the heroes were moving again.

"You lousy rat! Thought you were gonna

leave us behind, huh?" Sledgehammer Sue growled, hefting her hammer as she ran toward the sneezing little man. "I think it's about time someone pounded a little respect into you."

"You'll get your turn at him after me," Manika said, racing past Sue.

HYPERION RECOGNIZED THE EFFECTS of the Knave's sneezing powder, but for once, he couldn't be angry at being dosed with it. From what little he could remember of those hazy moments he had been under the sway of Doctor Psycon's mental control, he would still be the villain's unwilling puppet if not for the violent sneezing fit that broke the spell.

To cleanse the irritant from his system, Hyperion rocketed straight up into the air, as fast as he could, then dove back toward the ground, leveling off at treetop level to streak around and around in a circle. The force of the wind blasting into his face whipped the tears from his eyes and he sucked in great lungs full of air that he blew out of his nose to clear away the last of the powder.

Only then did he turn his attention to the villains.

* * *

AFTER DITCHING EVERYONE BACK at the general store, Mike Brewer crept down the short alley alongside it, then through some hedges. He crouched there wondering which way to go when the super guys' jet shot by overhead and dropped down for a landing in the empty lot.

"Guess that's where I'd be if I were Whiz Kid," Mike said and went in that direction, keeping low behind whatever he could find for cover. He made his last stop behind the big, old oak tree at the edge of the empty lot. From there, he could see the whole thing. The *Eagle*'s door opening, Hyperion flying out with a couple of guys before they all broke into those insane sneezing fits.

It was pretty cool, but Mike wanted to find Crenshaw and make sure the little twerp didn't try to steal the credit and the reward from him. Then Hyperion flew off, right in the middle of a thunderous sneeze, zipping around like a crazy bird with its tail on fire. Mike took a step back to follow the hero's progress through the sky and tripped over something.

He picked it up. A facemask. And not a cheap toy either. It looked like the face of one of those guys on the playing cards.

As he stared into the masks' blank eyes, it said, "*You need some help there, buddy?*"

Surprised, Mike dropped the mask and looked around, wondering if he'd been pranked. Then he heard several dull explosions and a lot of confused shouting from the empty lot and the mask answered itself, but in a different voice, saying, "*No thanks. I've got this covered.*"

Then someone, not the mask, let out a shout of victory. It came from right over his head.

Mike looked straight up into the tree as a wind blew past his face.

"Crenshaw?" he said.

IT TURNED OUT THAT launching the Knave's gag weapons with the slingshot didn't require much aim or skill. As long as he could lob a steady stream of them in the general vicinity of the bad guys, the barrage of deafening noises, blinding lights, showers of sneezing and itching powder, and entangling glue-covered, expanding snakes-in-a-can were still effective against their targets. He stuffed a handful of the little weapons into the pocket of his shorts for easier access and got to work.

"So cool," he muttered after each launch, a big grin on his face. The slingshot had some gizmo built into it that activated the weapons when they were placed in the sling, making a little red light come on when ready to be released.

The villains didn't know which way to turn. Not that it mattered. Thanks to Wally's random peppering of the scene, every direction held danger. The heroes seemed to understand that. They had all come out of hiding, but none of them were in any rush to race into the fire zone. Instead, they gathered around the lot to watch the show.

"Looks like old Charlie came through for us," Fakeout said. He glanced skyward. "Think this will hold them until Hyperion gets back?"

Ms. Muscles laughed. "Look at 'em running around like chickens without heads."

"Someone want to get Doctor Psycon a Kleenex?" Blend said.

"You ever get a whiff of Charlie's sneezing powder? It's brutal," said Swift.

Aquina pointed overhead. "Here comes Hyperion."

Fakeout saw a streak of bright blue and yellow speeding down toward the lot. He activated his radio and said, "You need some help there, buddy?"

"*No thanks,*" Hyperion responded. "*I've got this covered.*"

HYPERION SWEPT PAST THE incapacitated Doctor Psycon and Professor Lamplighter, leaving them sprawled flat on their backs, unconscious on the ground.

Stormcloud, already locked in a pair of power-dampening handcuffs, posed no threat; a tap on the chin from the Mighty Mortal dropped him to the ground.

Hyperion just smiled at Crosshair's volley of explosive pellets, which he made no effort to evade. He slapped them away with his bare hands as fast as Crosshair could throw them, scattering them everywhere. One exploded in Sledgehammer Sue's face as she charged forward with her hammer swinging, sending her flying backward before crashing to the ground.

Manika didn't wait for Hyperion to come for her. She would never be fast enough to outrun him. She needed an edge, some sort of advantage.

Her speeded-up senses caught the arc through the air of another of the Knave's incoming weapons; to her eyes, they were moving in slow motion, like helium-filled balloons floating on the breeze. It had started its journey from high up in the branches of a tree.

She remembered all the times she'd suffered sneezing or scratching fits thanks to Knave's stupid little toys and thought how much fun it would be to shake the annoying little twerp off his perch and watch him splatter on the ground.

But business before pleasure. Maybe by taking one of his teammates hostage, she might be able to avoid sharing their fate.

She raced up the side of the tree, past some townie kid hiding behind it, running so fast gravity didn't have a chance to keep her grounded.

But, as usual when it came to the Knave, the joke turned out to be on Manika. Instead of the Prince of Pranks, she found a kid.

"Who are you?" Manika demanded, appearing as though from out of thin air when she stopped in front of the boy.

He looked at her and hollered in surprise. He lost his balance and toppled from the branch. Manika rolled her eyes and raced back down the tree.

WALLY SCREAMED AS HE fell, arms and legs flailing wildly. He needed to stop that. Supers shouldn't scream, not even while plummeting to certain death. Or even toward certain numerous broken bones.

But not being a super, he couldn't stop screaming because if he got killed it would kill his mother too, and he wished he could apologize for being so stupid, but then he remembered the shoes but the socks wedging his feet in place had slipped and, uh-oh, he didn't think he could reach the buttons, but he felt himself slowing down anyway but he probably just imagined it and—

Wally stopped.

Caught by Manika, who had run down the tree ahead of him, slowing his fall with a cushion of air she whipped up with the superspeed spinning of her arms before catching him, safe as a baby.

And there, looking right at Wally and Manika, stood Mike Brewer, with a dumber than usual dumbfounded look.

"Uh, hey, Mike," Wally said before he disappeared in a blur and cloud of dust.

MIKE BREWER BLINKED, WONDERING if that had really just happened. But it had. Lying at his feet were a slingshot and drawstring bag that hadn't been there before Wally dropped them.

With a quick look around, Mike gathered up Knave's mask and weapons. He had no idea where Wally and the superspeed lady had gone, but he had an idea of a way to help himself. To the reward, that is. It belonged to him legitimately to begin with, but he figured this stuff should make it a slam dunk.

"Sorry, Crenshaw. Finders keepers, losers weepers, dude," Mike said.

31

EVEN AFTER THEY'D LURCHED to a stop, it took Wally's stomach a couple of seconds to catch up with the rest of him. He thought he'd been moving the times Swift and Hyperion had saved him earlier, but those rides felt like a walk in the woods compared to Manika's pace. Fortunately for him, superspeedsters gave off some kind of aura that surrounded them and anyone they were in contact with, protecting them from the heat, friction, and punishing forces of their velocity. At least that's what he'd read.

Protective aura or not, he didn't think anything could have prepared him for the unreality of super speed. It felt like being in one place and then being in another, without having to move to get there. Except he could still feel the speed, right there in the pit of his stomach, and he hoped he got through this without barfing.

Or, you know, getting killed.

When his head stopped spinning, he saw that they were at the opposite end of Main Street from the vacant lot. Manika paused long enough to get a better grip on Wally and sling him over her shoulder for easier carrying, like a baby being burped. Kind of embarrassing, but he didn't think complaining about it would do any good.

"What's the fastest way out of town, kid?" Manika said.

"Old Crumbly Road?" Wally stammered. "I mean, it's the only way."

"No good." She nodded to the east. "The beach this way?"

He nodded.

Then they were on the beach, Wally's stomach doing more flip-flops.

"I hope you don't get seasick," she said, and the next thing Wally knew, Manika raced into the water.

"No! Not the ocean!" he screamed, starting to struggle in her arms.

"Stop squirming," she said. Running on top of water only looked easy, but it required precision and balance. The way the kid kicked and waved his arms, she worried he might upset the delicate balance she needed to maintain her stability. Defying gravity was harder than it looked.

WALLY'S FRANTIC KICKING JARRED the rolled-up sock in the right antigravity shoe loose and it lodged under his heel, forcing his foot forward, pushing his toes into simultaneous contact with all the control buttons.

HYPERION HAD VISUAL CONTACT with Manika and waited for Swift to catch up to them and take over the pursuit. The speedster acknowledged his rapid approach, but when Hyperion's super-vision showed him Manika had taken a child hostage, he knew he didn't have even a split second to lose.

Without warning, Manika leapt straight up in the air before going into a series of aerial somersaults, bleeding off speed with every roll.

At first, Hyperion thought she might be executing some sort of new superspeed attack until she plunged straight down into the waves, before shooting back up into the air for another series of loop the loops.

As he drew closer, he could hear Manika and the boy screaming, her demanding he let go of her, him pleading she not drop him into the ocean. The youngster's right leg acted like it had a mind of its own, sticking straight out from his hip, jerking first straight up then straight down and then to this side or that.

Hyperion narrowed his eyes, focusing his hypervision on the boy's leg, magnifying the sight as though looking through binoculars. He almost laughed at what he saw.

The boy had on the Knave's antigravity shoes. And, except for that wandering right leg, he had his other three limbs wrapped so tightly around the hapless Manika that it looked like they'd need a crowbar to pry him loose. As long as they were locked together like that, Manika would remain a hostage to antigravity.

"*Coming up behind you now, partner,*" Swift's voice crackled in Hyperion's ear.

"No hurry, Swift. Looks like Crumbly has its very own hero… and Kid Knave doesn't need our assistance."

"Help me! I hate the ocean!" Wally screamed as he and Manika corkscrewed up into the air.

"Well, maybe a little," Hyperion said with a chuckle.

SOMEONE SLAPPED HIM GENTLY across his cheeks and called his name and Charlie Harris wished whoever did it would go away and stop bothering him. He didn't know how long he'd been lying out here on the lawn, awash in the warm glow of the summer sun, but it had been such a nice rest and he didn't want to wake up yet. Something told him that if he did open his eyes, he'd regret it.

Slap. Slap, "Charlie?" Slap. "Wake up, Charlie." Slap.

Unable to stand it any longer, Charlie swatted the hand from his face and started to roll over on his side, mumbling, "Go away, I'm napping," when a bolt of electric agony shot from his left leg up through his body and he just screamed instead.

"My leg," he groaned through clenched teeth. "I broke my leg."

"I know," Mr. Justice said. "I hope you don't mind, but I took the liberty of setting the bone and putting your leg in a makeshift splint with some scrap wood I found behind the house here, but you should get that looked at by a professional, ASAP."

It all came back to Charlie in a rush. Doctor Psycon trying to run them down with the *Screaming Eagle*, his getting all tangled up with Wally, then hitting the wall and busting his leg. And, just before that, he remembered Willie radioing the brigade that he had disabled whatever caused the electronic interference, and Charlie had said to Wally—

"Wally," Charlie gasped.

"He's not here."

"Where is he?"

"I haven't seen him."

Charlie carefully raised himself on his elbows and looked around.

"Do you see my mask and shoes anywhere?"

Justice shook his head. "Nothing. You were in your stocking feet when I found you."

"No, no, no," Charlie groaned, dropping back down, a move his left leg made him instantly regret. "He's got them. Wally must have taken the mask, the shoes, my bag of tricks, the whole shebang."

Mr. Justice grunted and said, "Hmm. The rest of the team assumed that was you."

"What me?"

"One of them reported that a barrage of your gag weapons kept the league busy until Hyperion could take them down." Mr. Justice pointed his thumb back over his shoulder. "The brigade's got them all locked up tight in energy-dampening cuffs and are loading them into the *Eagle*. Except for Manika, but Hyperion and Swift should have her in custody any second."

"I didn't barrage anybody," Charlie said.

"You don't think Wally took your stuff and did it, do you? He seems like an alright kid, but I didn't think he's got what it takes, *here*," the Detective of the Dark said, pushing a fist against his stomach, "for something like that."

"Man, I hope you're right," Charlie said. Mr. Justice stopped him.

"Incoming messages," Justice said, and peeled back his mask so Charlie could hear the voices over the radio.

Swift: "*Coming up behind you now, partner.*"

Hyperion: "*No hurry, Swift. Looks like Crumbly has its very own hero . . . and Kid Knave doesn't need our assistance.*"

Charlie and Mr. Justice looked at each other in confusion. "Kid *who*?" they said.

Wally (from the distance): "*Help me! I hate the ocean!*"

Hyperion: "*Well, maybe a little.*"

Charlie's eyes were wide with horror. "That's Wally! What's going on? Where are they—?"

"Sounds like Manika tried escaping by sea. Don't worry about the boy. Hyperion and Swift have everything under control. Yes, they've just reported that Wally is safe and Manika's in cuffs. They're on their way back to the *Eagle*."

Charlie blew out a great big gust of air in relief. "Wow."

"Yes. Justice is triumphant once again."

Charlie rolled his eyes. "Yeah, that's what I meant. Okay, you think you can help me up without causing my leg to fall off or something?"

A hurt expression creased Justice's lips. "You don't have to be mean, Charlie. First of all, I'm a fully trained and certified emergency medical technician. Second, if I hadn't gotten rid of the radio interference, the league would have gotten away in the *Eagle*."

"Yeah, you did. And thanks. But I still can't

help feeling that somehow this whole mess is your fault to begin with."

"Me? What did I do, except come to visit a friend?"

"I'll let you know when I figure it out, Willie."

Charlie reached up his hand and Mr. Justice grasped it firmly. Together, the former teammates worked to get the injured man up and balanced on his one good leg, resulting in a scream of pain that could be heard several streets away by the citizens of Crumbly as they cautiously emerged from shelter all along Main Street.

32

JAMIE CRENSHAW HURRIED OUT the door of the general store. She stood in the middle of the street, turning in circles searching the faces spilling out onto the sidewalks for Wally.

When she saw Brenda and Benny walking through the crowd, she raced to them, calling their names.

"Have you seen Wally?" she asked breathlessly. "I can't find him, and the last time I saw him, he—he—" but she had to stop.

"I'm sure he's okay, Mrs. Crenshaw," Brenda said. "We just saw him, a little while ago on my street."

"Yeah, he seemed fine," Benny said. "It looked like he was headed this way."

"And he was okay?" Jamie asked, just to be certain.

"Yeah, just fine, really," Benny said.

Brenda took Jamie's hand and said, "Come on, we'll help you find him."

"Yeah, you know Wally. He's probably bugging the brigade to let him fill out a job application or something," Benny said.

Jamie felt relief flooding through her. "You're probably right, Benny. We better find him before they hire him."

"WE ARE GOING TO be packed terribly tight in here," Aquina said dubiously at the hatch of the *Screaming Eagle*.

"You can sit on my lap if that'll help make room," Blend said behind her.

Aquina glanced over her shoulder and said, "On second thought, I believe I'll swim home. It has been too long since I was fully immersed in mother ocean's rejuvenating embrace."

"And because you don't want to sit on my lap, right?"

"Mostly that," the She-Devil of the Sea agreed.

Ms. Muscles muscled her way past Blend into the ship. "Be a good boy, Normie, and maybe I'll let *you* sit on *my* lap."

Swift vibrated to a stop at the foot of the ramp, a dripping, dazed, and handcuffed Manika slung over his shoulder.

"Room for one more?" he grinned.

Fakeout poked his head through the hatch and said, "It's going to be standing room only, but bring her aboard."

"She can have my seat," Swift said. "One slow ride a day in this thing's more than enough for me. I'm just going to stretch my legs on the open road."

"Where do you think you're going with those prisoners?"

Colonel Flint's deep baritone boomed across the lot, just ahead of himself and Agent Marrs.

"I thought we'd take them out to dinner and then maybe a movie," Blend said. "Why? What's your idea?"

Flint fixed Blend with a hard stare. "Are you trying to be funny, son?"

"Usually, but seldom with much success according to the critics," Blend said with a sigh.

"I'm claiming custody of the league for the Super-Villain Task Force," Flint told them. "If you'll hand them over, we'll see to it they're returned to the proper authorities in Trenton."

Blend put his hands on his hips and looked around the lot. "How? You have secure transport for them?"

"We have an armored task force vehicle," Flint said defiantly.

"The battery's dead. Remember, sir?" Agent Marrs whispered near his ear.

"And all we need is a little boost to get it started," he added, with somewhat less bluster.

"Good luck with that," Swift laughed.

"You need a jump start, call Hootie down at

the station and he'll send his truck," Sheriff Cunningham said, stalking angrily toward the heroes outside the *Screaming Eagle*. "Whatever it takes to get you lunatics out of town as soon as possible."

"I don't think you realize who you're talking to, Officer," Flint said. "And if you have any idea of claiming jurisdiction over these prisoners yourself, I assure you as an officer of a high-level federal agency that I will—"

The sheriff shoved his face close to the colonel's and snarled, "It's *sheriff*, Mr. Federal Agency. And I don't care who you are, you start threatening me, I'll lock you up so fast your head will spin."

"I like this guy," Blend snickered.

"Thanks, but you'll pardon me if I don't return the love," said the sheriff. "I moved my family to Crumbly to get away from this kind of craziness in the city. Luckily, no one got hurt today, but a lot of folks had their homes pretty badly damaged."

Fakeout handed the sheriff a card. "We're insured for that, Sheriff. Have anyone with a claim get in touch with this number and they'll take care of everything."

That seemed to calm Sheriff Cunningham down a bit, and he nodded his grudging thanks as he tucked the card in his shirt pocket.

"Hey, wait! Don't let 'em go yet," Mike Brewer yelled, racing around the corner. "They can't go until I get my reward!"

The sheriff hung his head in exhaustion.

"What now?" he moaned.

Panting heavily, Mike stumbled to a stop at the foot of the ramp, hugging something to his chest. "Man, I'm glad I caught you guys. I'm the guy," he gasped. "You know? The tip about the Accelerator? Online?"

Colonel Flint nodded. "Thank you for saying something when you thought you saw something, young man, but you were wrong. The Accelerator isn't here."

"Yeah, but you caught all those other bad guys," Mike said with a big grin. "You never would've found them if you didn't come here looking for the Accelerator, right?"

The sheriff raised an eyebrow and nodded slowly. "Let me get this straight, Mike; you're saying this is all *your* doing?"

Mike pumped his head emphatically up and down. "Yes, sir. Just me. Nobody else had anything to do with it. Especially not Wally, no matter what he says. Which means I get the reward and don't have to share it with anybody, right?"

"There are no current rewards posted on the League of Villains, son," Colonel Flint said. "Sorry. But at least you can take satisfaction in knowing you've done a service for your community."

"Bu—bu—bu—but . . . I did it, I caught 'em," Mike stammered. He opened his arms and showed them the Knave's mask, slingshot, and bag of tricks. "See? Who do you think threw all that junk at them so you guys could stop them, huh?"

Swift plucked them out of Mike's hands. "Where did you get these, kid?"

"I, uh, you know. Found them."

"These belong to the Knave. *Where* did you find them? You sure you didn't see him?"

Mike shrugged and pointed vaguely over his shoulder. "I didn't see anybody. I just found that stuff, you know. Back there. And then I saw you guys were in trouble, so I tried to help."

The grown-ups exchanged skeptical looks.

"Fine, don't believe me," Mike whined. "Nobody ever does."

The sheriff rubbed his chin. "Well, now, you're not exactly known for public service, Mike."

Mike shrugged again and put on a guilty smile. "Okay, so maybe at first I just wanted to see if I could make any of them explode and stuff."

"That," the sheriff said, "sounds more like the Mike Brewer we know."

"Whatever his motives, I'd say the lad's

actions make him the hero of the day," Colonel Flint said.

"But that other kid had the Knave's antigravity shoes," Swift said, confused. "I thought for sure it had been him laying down that cover fire for us."

"Yeah, sure. The shoes. Right. Uh, I guess Wally must have taken the shoes and left this stuff behind. Maybe he couldn't carry it all." He shook his head in disbelief. "Crazy, huh?"

Swift looked dubious, but shrugged and said, "Well, I'd say that deserves an honorary membership in the Justice Brigade. What do you say to that, kid?"

"Sure, why not?" Mike said, but learning there would be no reward, he had already lost interest in the whole thing. Until a blonde woman with a cell phone in hand came running over to them.

"Hi, hello, glad I caught you," she said, speaking fast. "Wow, my battery's almost dead. So yeah, anyway, I'm Penny Potter. I work for the *Weekly Mask*." She flashed them her company ID, a magnetic passkey for getting through the doors in the office. "You guys were great today. Did I hear that *this* young man had a part in saving the day?"

"You're a reporter?" Mike's interest flashed anew.

Penny started snapping pictures of Mike, the sheriff, and the heroes with her phone.

"Sure am. Would you move closer to . . . right, just like that. And could you let him hold the slingshot . . . I'm sorry, young man, I didn't get your name."

Mike eagerly snatched the slingshot back from Swift to pose for Penny. "Mike Brewer. Yeah, I found the Knight's stuff . . ."

"The Knave," Blend corrected him.

"Yeah, him. I found his stuff and when I saw the heroes were getting beat—"

"We were not getting beat, you little liar," Ms. Muscles snarled. "We had everything under control. We were just waiting to spring the ambush when you opened up on them."

"Yeah, well we'll never know how *that* would've worked out, will we?" Mike replied with a sneer. "Maybe I saved you guys from a major stomping."

"Who's gonna save *you*, big mouth?" Ms. Muscles clenched her fist and took a step toward Mike, who flinched and jumped behind the sheriff.

"That's enough," the sheriff said. A glance down Main Street showed him just about the entire population of Crumbly coming their way. "I think it's time you moved this vehicle of yours before I'm forced to start ticketing you for just about every traffic and parking violation on the books."

"Hyperion," Swift said, speaking into his

radio. "We're being invited to leave, the sooner the better."

"Roger," Hyperion replied. *"You get going. You can pick me up on the way."*

"You heard the man," Swift said to his teammates. "Everybody load up if you don't want to be left behind."

"Mind if I hitch a ride back to the city with you guys?" Penny said.

"I guess it'll be okay," Blend said. "But we've got a full load. I hope you're okay with standing?"

"I don't mind sitting on someone's lap," the young reporter said and skipped through the hatch, smiling sweetly at Blend. "And maybe you could give me a little interview, if you don't have anything else you have to do."

Blend grinned. "Nothing that can't wait, Ms. Potter."

"Call me Penny."

Sheriff Cunningham, Mike, Swift, and Aquina stepped away from the *Screaming Eagle.* The landing ramp slid back into the fuselage and the hatch hissed closed. Moments later, the big jet engines roared to life and, with a high-pitched whine, built up power and lifted from the ground. When it had gained enough altitude, the sound of the engines changed as they swiveled on their mounts and the *Eagle* shot off into the sky.

Swift turned to the sheriff and held out his hand. "Sorry for all the trouble, Sheriff. I know it doesn't always seem that way, but we truly are here to help," he said.

The sheriff accepted the offered hand and shook it.

"Just the same, I hope never to see any of you in Crumbly ever again."

Swift laughed. "I can't imagine any reason we'd have to return, sir." He turned to Aquina. "You ready? I can drop you off at the beach."

Aquina smiled her thanks and, with a wave to Mike and the sheriff, she and Swift were gone in a swirl of dust.

"Man," Mike breathed. "Did you hear that, Sheriff? I'm a hero. I bet I'm gonna be all over the news."

The sheriff nodded. "Uh-huh. And you're sure you did it all by yourself? Nobody helped you? Not Nick and Abel? Or Wally?"

"Naw. Those dweebs just stalked the new guy who moved in on Kane Street. I came up with the idea to tip off those task force guys all by myself."

"You caused a lot of trouble, Mike. A lot of homes and town property got damaged. We're just lucky nobody got hurt."

Mike blinked, confused. "Huh?"

"I think we'd better go have a talk with your father about this," the sheriff said.

"But," Mike said, "I'm a hero. The Justice Brigade said so."

"The Justice Brigade doesn't know you the way I do," the sheriff said. "Let's go."

They passed Colonel Flint and Agent Marrs, both loitering helplessly on the edge of the lot. "If you turn left here, the service station is at the end of the road. You can't miss it. Ask for Hootie. He'll be the only one there."

"Thank you, Sheriff," the agent said. "Don't hesitate to call on the task force in the future if you ever need us again."

"What makes you think we needed you this time?" the sheriff asked.

33

MR. JUSTICE HELPED CHARLIE lower himself onto a folding chair that had been left out on a front lawn. They had made it this far without being spotted, but Charlie's leg was starting to hurt too much to go on.

"I'll get the car," Justice said. "It'll give me a chance to get out of costume before anyone sees me dressed like this."

"What difference does it make? They saw a lot of supers today and besides, you're leaving soon too, right?"

"Well," Mr. Justice said, slowly drawing the word out. "I've been thinking about that, Charlie."

"No, don't think, Willie. Every time you do something bad happens in my life."

"Your leg is broken. You're going to need help just getting around and taking care of all the normal stuff."

"I'll hire a nurse."

"And then there's your house. You know me, once I start a project, I like to finish it."

"I'll hire a carpenter."

"I couldn't do that to you, Charlie. No, I'm staying and that's final."

Charlie groaned. "This can't end well. I'm going to look back on today and my broken leg is going to turn out to be the best part of it."

"Gentlemen," a voice from above said. "I hope I'm not interrupting anything."

"Please interrupt," Charlie said, glancing up to see Hyperion floating down from the sky. Perched on his shoulder, wet but smiling and waving like the grand marshal of a parade, sat Wally.

"Hi, Charlie," he yelled. "Did you hear what happened?"

"I heard. You captured your first supervillain. Congratulations."

Hyperion touched down and helped Wally down from his shoulder, the still damp boy splashing Charlie with drops of water. "It's so cool! You can't imagine. Like, Manika had me hostage, right? And we're running over the water, and I'm like, how do I stop her? Then I remember." He lifted up his leg and wiggled Charlie's pointy shoe at him. "Ta-da! Man, you should have seen it."

Charlie said, "Wish I could have. But I did

hear part of it, over Mr. Justice's radio headset. That would be the part where you were screaming for help."

"Oh, yeah," Wally grinned. "I guess maybe I got a little freaked out. But, man, these antigravity shoes are so cool."

"Speaking of which, take them off," Charlie said. "Now. Before you accidentally wind up in orbit. I don't think you understand how dangerous this stuff is, kid. You could've been hurt."

Wally plopped down on the lawn to pull his feet from the tight collar around his ankles.

"Yeah, I know. I'm sorry, Charlie. I didn't mean to use your stuff. At first, I just took it because you were unconscious and I didn't want to leave it lying around where anyone could take it. But then, I don't know, it sort of made sense for me to put them on, and then I flew up in this tree with your slingshot and bag of tricks and starting shooting at the League of Villains and then things just sort of got out of hand."

Charlie shook his head in disbelief. "Oh, *that's* when things got out of hand, huh?"

"Uh-huh. When Manika showed up," Wally said, working on the second shoe.

"You were the one firing those gag weapons at the league?" Hyperion said.

Wally looked up and nodded.

"Swift reported another kid in town claimed

credit for that," the Man of Might said. "Mike Brewer?"

Wally jumped angrily to his bare feet and shouted, "He's lying."

"But he had the Knave's slingshot and mask."

"Uh-uh," Wally said, shaking his head. "I dropped that stuff when Manika grabbed me. He must've picked them up and—"

"Slow down. Maybe Mike taking credit's not such a bad thing," Charlie said.

"What do you mean? Mike's a liar."

"I can give you a whole lot of reasons, pal, but I think they're all best summed up in one word: your mom."

The fight went out of Wally.

"That's two words," he said.

"I'm a writer, not a mathematician," Charlie said. "We'll talk later, okay?"

"You were the last person I ever expected to find here, Mr. Justice," Hyperion said to his teammate. "Where were you keeping yourself while this all went down?"

The Detective of the Dark gestured vaguely and said, "Around, keeping an eye on things in case you guys needed me."

"Pretty slick work knocking out that electronic interference when you did. Psycon almost got away with the *Eagle*."

"Mmm, yes, about that," Mr. Justice said. "I'm afraid my solution to the interference is, um, only temporary. I wouldn't be surprised if it started up again at any moment."

"Yeah?" Charlie said. "What's the problem?"

"How much do you know about subspace quasars, magnetic ley lines, and reverse quantum fields?" Mr. Justice said.

"Absolutely nothing," Hyperion said.

"Less than zip," Charlie agreed.

"Well, there's your problem then," Mr. Justice said.

"Wally!"

Everyone turned in the direction of the shout.

"It's my mom," Wally exclaimed. "Oh, man, I'll bet she's been worried."

Hyperion tousled Wally's hair and smiled. "You tell your mom she doesn't have to worry about you, Wally. Or should I call you Kid Knave?" Then, with a wink and smile, he rose up into the air and flew away.

"I best be moving on too," Mr. Justice said, drawing his dark cape tight and moving quietly to blend with the shadows around the foundation of the house. "Farewell, my young friend."

"Okay. See you later, Mr. Williams," Wally said.

Mr. Justice looked back at Wally, rattled. "Who? My name's not Williams. It's... Justice!"

"Give it up, Willie," Charlie said. "The kid's too smart for you."

"Great," Mr. Justice growled to himself as

he slunk away. "Why bother even having an alter ego?"

"I guess that's why they call me Kid Knave, huh, Charlie?"

"Nobody calls you that," Charlie said.

"Hyperion did."

"Hyperion sometimes doesn't realize the effect his words might have on others and speaks without thinking."

"Wally!" His mother's shouts were coming closer.

Wally grinned and said, "Kid Knave. I like it," and before Charlie could object, he shouted, "Here I am, Mom!"

Jamie came rushing around the house, Brenda and Benny behind her.

"Wally, oh, honey," she sobbed, smothering him in a hug. "Where have you been? I thought you were going to be right behind me when Hyperion dropped me at the general store."

"I'm afraid that's my fault," Charlie said before Wally could answer. "See, I had an accident and the Knave saw me on his way to drop Wally off, so he stopped to lend me a hand..."

Jamie turned on Charlie and snapped, "Do you always refer to yourself in the third person, Mr. Harris?"

Charlie blinked. "Excuse me?"

Wally slapped his forehead and groaned.

"She knows you're the Knave, Charlie. I'm sorry, I didn't get a chance to tell you—"

"You told your mother my secret identity?" Charlie said in disbelief. Then he looked over at Brenda and Benny and threw his hands up in the air. "And now they know too. Great!"

"Wally didn't say a word," Jamie said. "He didn't have to, you idiot. I recognized your voice through the mask, and even if I hadn't figured it out then, I would know because you're wearing the same T-shirt as he did."

"Oh."

"Yes, *oh*. How could you let my child get involved in this?"

"Speaking as the guy sitting here with a broken leg, yeah, I think I've got an idea about the danger," Charlie said, gritting his teeth against the pain. "And *I* didn't *let* Wally do anything. I broke this leg keeping us both from being squashed on the *Screaming Eagle*'s windshield."

"It's true, Mom. Charlie saved us both."

"Nobody would have needed saving if they hadn't come here in the first place, Wally. They bring the danger with them wherever they go. They *are* the danger."

Charlie groaned in pain, holding his leg. "Stop yelling at me, okay? I agree with you. That's why I quit. I'm not the Knave anymore. I quit the Justice Brigade and moved here, ironically enough, so stuff like being thrown against houses and breaking bones would stop happening to me."

Jamie's said, "Oh." With a shake of her head, she turned to Brenda and Benny. "You'd better get your father, Brenda. He can help us get Mr. Harris over to Doc Steinbeck's." Brenda nodded and ran off with Benny.

"I'm sorry, Mr. Harris. I've been so worried about Wally, I didn't realize you've been hurt."

"No, I get it. I'd have been crazy worried too if it was my kid. If I had a kid," Charlie laughed, instantly regretting it and wincing in pain. "Ow."

"Doc Steinbeck will take good care of you," Wally said.

"Thank you," Charlie said. "Uh, wait. This Doc Steinbeck's a real people doctor, not a veterinarian or a chemist or something?"

"No, he's a genuine people MD" she assured him.

"Okay, just checking."

Jamie shook her head and put her arm around Wally's shoulder. "I can't believe the day this has been."

"Yeah, you got to fly with Hyperion, Mom," Wally said.

"Not exactly what I meant," she said. "I'm just glad no one else got hurt." She turned at the sound of a car horn from the street. "Oh, good. Here comes Sheriff Cunningham."

The next few minutes were spent helping the injured man up and maneuvering him comfortably into the sheriff's car, stretched across the back seat. Jamie volunteered to go along to help unload the passenger at his destination, leaving Wally and his friends on the sidewalk.

As soon as the car turned the corner, Wally's barely contained excitement erupted.

"Okay, look, it's supposed to be a secret between me and . . . me and the Knave, right? But I gotta tell you guys and you can't tell anyone, okay? Okay. You know that stuff about Mike Brewer saying *he* helped stop the supervillains? He didn't." Wally laughed. "I did that! I flew up into a tree in Knave's antigravity shoes and I had his slingshot and, boom! I fought supervillains!"

"We know," Brenda said when she could finally break get a word in.

"Yeah, you ran past Brenda's house carrying all of the Knave's junk and we saw you. We tried following you, but—"

"But you couldn't," Wally laughed. "You know why?"

"Because you took off flying in the Knave's antigravity shoes?" Brenda said, hazarding a guess.

"Yes!" Wally laughed and did a little happy dance in front of his friends.

Benny shook his head in disbelief. "I don't believe this."

"It's true, I swear," Wally exclaimed. "And I haven't even told you how I helped Hyperion and Swift capture Manika yet."

"I believe you, Wally," Benny said. "It's just… I know you've been wishing for something like this to happen, but I kind of figured if it ever did, you'd probably be too scared like most of us to, you know, *do* anything."

"Yeah, that's the weird thing. The whole time I was doing that stuff, it was scary but," Wally shrugged, "I don't know, it's like my being afraid made me do what I did so I could make the thing that frightened me stop." He scratched his head. "Does that make any sense?"

"Sounds nuts to me," Benny said.

"Benny!" Brenda said.

"But what do I know? I'm not the one who fought supervillains like my pal the Whiz Kid here," Benny said, socking Wally playfully on the arm.

Wally laughed and said, "But don't call me Whiz Kid anymore. That's just some dumb name I made up a long time ago."

Brenda and Benny looked surprised.

"From now on," Wally said, assuming a heroic pose, "you can call me… Kid Knave!"

34

"I THINK IT'S SAFE to stand down," Morris Handelman announced as he switched between the cameras located around town from his seat at the command center. "Everyone's returning home. The *Screaming Eagle* has left our airspace, carrying both the Justice Brigade and League of Villains with it. Hootie is driving Colonel Flint and his associate back to their vehicle on Old Crumbly Road even as we speak, and they too will soon be on their way out of our lives."

"Then all's well that ends well," Sarge said.

"It would seem," Morris said. "All that remains is to hear from Mr. Justice. He might still be a wildcard in this situation."

"What'd you mean, Morris? I thought we were teaming up with Mr. Justice," Boomer asked.

"He means," Mr. Justice said in his gravelly voice from the shadows by the doorway, "he doesn't know if I can be trusted with your secrets."

"Welcome, Mr. Justice," Giz-Mo said, a hint of awe in his voice. "I see you've worked out how to bypass my perimeter sensors and defenses."

"It's a hobby," Justice said. "And to answer your question, you can trust me. Whatever your pasts, you're not wanted now and, as far as I can tell, you're not hurting anybody."

"What about our electronic interference zone? You seemed to have a problem with that earlier."

"I did, but the more I think about it, the more I like it."

"Oh, yeah? What's in it for you?" Sarge said.

"Peace and quiet," Mr. Justice growled, slamming a fist into his open palm. "A place where the real world can't find me and I can relax!"

"You do sound tense," Boomer acknowledged in sympathy.

"You're sure you're not just hiding from the world?" Morris said.

"Justice hides from nothing!" the Knight of the Night exclaimed. Then, in a softer voice, added, "But sometimes it needs a quiet place to rest."

"You won't get any argument from us," Giz-Mo said. He turned back to the control panel and began typing. "The Commando

Project may have been a long time ago, but there are people out there with long memories and the three of us would just as soon put as much distance and as many barriers as possible between us and them."

"That's your business," Mr. Justice said.

"That it is . . . Mr. Williams," Giz-Mo said, turning to face the masked hero. "Don't be so surprised. You practically told me yourself who you are. You say you're planning on staying in town, and there are only two newcomers in Crumbly. One is Charlie Harris. The other is his friend, William Williams. I just ran images of all three of you through identification analysis software and you and Mr. Williams are an exact match."

"Touché," Mr. Justice said with a nod of appreciation. "Now we both have something to lose."

"A satisfying balance of power," Morris agreed.

Mr. Justice and Giz-Mo shook hands.

"Welcome to Crumbly, Mr. Williams."

"Call me Willie," Mr. Justice said.

HOOTIE'S PICKUP TRUCK DIDN'T have springs. At least not the kind that gave a vehicle's passengers a reasonably comfortable and smooth ride. On this bumpy road, the ride could be a torture that brought tears to the eyes of even the bravest of men.

Colonel Flint knew this to be true because he had tears in his eyes, although not just from the lack of suspension. Indeed, what the truck lacked in suspension, it more than made up for with what felt like dozens of sharp metal springs poking up through the threadbare seats. Every little jostle brought a stab of pain to his rear and every bump a moan of agony. Hootie, a thin man in a red plaid shirt and no expression on his face, seemed immune to the experience, while Agent Marrs, on the seat between them, suffered in silence with Flint.

Hootie had never seen anything like what the task force-issued SUV had under its hood. Flint didn't know what to make of it either, but Agent Marrs pointed out the battery to the mechanic and he hooked it up to the jumper battery he kept in the back of his truck and give them a start.

The SUV fired up as soon as she pressed the ignition, but it caused Hootie's jumper battery to explode. To Flint's irritation, Hootie didn't accept credit cards, but fortunately Agent Marrs had enough cash with her to cover their bill.

"Too bad we came away empty-handed, sir," she said once they were on the road again.

"I'm not so sure we did," he said slowly. "There's something going on in that town. Didn't you sense it?"

"I don't know, sir. It's just coincidence and dumb luck that we all wound up here in the first place."

"I don't believe in coincidence or luck. No, there are secrets being kept there. *Dark* secrets. Something tells we haven't seen the last of Crumbly-by-the-Sea, Agent Marrs," Flint said. "Mark my words."

"Yes, sir," Tracy Marrs said, taking one last look at Crumbly in her rearview mirror.

THE NEXT MORNING, MR. Williams showed up at what had been, before yesterday, the front door of Wally's house on Cole Lane. Jamie and Wally had gotten an early start sorting through the wreckage, salvaging what they could. A lot of what had once been inside had been blasted outside by the concussive force of Hyperion's impact, but most of the living room furniture, except for a coffee table that Jamie admitted she never much cared for, had miraculously survived. Her bedroom upstairs hadn't been so fortunate, but as Wally pointed out, they didn't have a floor up there anymore for furniture to sit on anyway.

Wally's room in the rear of the house had suffered only minimal damage, mostly books and smaller items knocked off of shelves, and one dresser of drawers that had toppled over.

Mr. Williams introduced himself and offered to help with the cleanup.

"That's very nice of you, Mr. Williams," she said. "I appreciate any help I can get. It's a bit overwhelming as you can see."

"Charlie wanted to come himself, but obviously he can't, so he made me come instead."

"I see," Jamie said. She didn't know whether to be insulted or amused. "How is Charlie doing?"

"Sleeping a lot."

"Understandable given all of the excitement yesterday and his broken leg."

As the morning progressed, other people wandered over to offer their assistance. By noon, she had a full crew of friends and neighbors pitching in to clear the house, lawn, and street of debris. Manny Brewer from the town dump rolled around with his sanitation truck, which he and an unhappy Mike Brewer filled to the top. Ma Casey came by with sandwiches and lemonade to feed the work detail, and Mrs. Pinchot, the librarian, brought her homemade cupcakes, half a dozen of which a very contented Mr. Williams consumed for lunch. Ma reported that neighbors all over town were out helping those whose homes had suffered damage in the brawl.

Wally asked his mother if it would be okay if he took a break and went over to check on Charlie and have lunch with him. He'd already wrapped up some sandwiches and cupcakes in paper plates.

Jamie gave her permission. “But promise me, no flying shoes.”

“Promise,” he said, and ran off.

He met Brenda on his way.

“I wanted to give this back to you,” she said, holding out the plastic cube with the fused nut and bolt from Washington, DC, to him. “I'm sorry you didn't get it signed by Hyperion.”

“Yeah, that would have been cool. Almost as cool as getting to fly with him,” Wally said with a grin.

“Anyway, maybe you can get Charlie to get him to sign it for you one of these days.”

“Maybe. But check this out.” Balancing the plate of food against his chest with one hand, he dug into his pocket with the other and pulled out a small green object.

“What is it?”

“It's one of the Knave's gag weapons, from his bag of tricks. I put a bunch of them in my pocket yesterday and this one's a leftover. I'm gonna ask Charlie if it's okay to keep it.”

Brenda took it from his hand to examine it. “It's a little toy soldier on a parachute. What does it do?”

“It explodes and spreads super-sneezing powder over a ten-foot radius. Cool, right?”

Brenda laid it carefully back in his hand.

"Not the word I'd use."

"It's okay. It can only explode if it's shot from his special slingshot."

"I'd rather not take any chances. Make sure it's okay for you to have that, okay?"

"Yeah, yeah."

"And one more thing, Kid Knave," she said, and kissed him on the cheek.

His face flushed red-hot, and he almost dropped his cupcakes.

"I—heh—yeah, thanks. What—?" he stammered.

"I didn't want to embarrass you in front of Benny or your mom yesterday, but I'm very proud of you," she said. "And a little jealous. I mean, you got to live your dream. You're a *real* superhero."

"Yeah?" he said. He could still feel the spot on his cheek where she had kissed him.

"And you know what that makes me?" she said.

Please, please, *please* say it makes you a superhero's girlfriend, but even knowing she would say something else, he had to ask anyway, "What?"

"Kid Knave's best friend," she said, imitating his supers voice.

Wally smiled weakly. "Ta-da!"

WALLY FOUND CHARLIE SET up in the living room on the sofa, his leg, now encased in a new plaster cast from just below his knee to his ankle, resting on a mound of pillows on a footstool. On his foot he wore one of the Knave's antigravity shoes. He had surrounded himself with papers, books, and magazines, and he had his laptop open before him. He greeted Wally with a smile.

"Hey, how's it going, kid?"

"Good. How are you?" he said.

"This old thing? No worries, my little friend. Hurts like the dickens, but thanks to the meds kindly old Doc Steinbeck gave me, it doesn't seem to bother me that much. And since I'm stuck here anyway, I figured why not get started on my writing project." He pointed to the plates in Wally's hands. "What you got there?"

"Oh, I brought over lunch. I thought you might be hungry." He uncovered the plate and said, "There's turkey or ham sandwiches. And Mrs. Pinchot made cupcakes."

Charlie laughed. "Better hide those from Willie."

"He ate practically the whole tray," Wally said. He took a sandwich for himself and handed the plate to Charlie. "Do you want me to get you some socks?"

"Why?" He followed Wally's gaze to the foot in the Knave shoe. "Oh, that. No, my foot's not cold. I'm just wearing it to keep the weight off my leg when I go to the bathroom or something. It's easier than the crutches the doctor gave me, at least inside, where no one can see me."

"Speaking of Knave stuff." Wally pulled the sneezing powder soldier from his pocket. "Would it be okay if I kept this? You know, as a souvenir of my debut as Kid Knave."

"You're not Kid Knave," Charlie said. "And, yeah, you can have it. Just let me take the powder capsule out of it so you don't accidentally make the whole town sneeze to death."

"Thanks, Charlie."

"You're welcome."

They ate in silence for a while.

"How much did you tell your mother about yesterday?" Charlie said, swallowing the last of his first sandwich.

"Um, most of it," Wally said.

"The part where you put on my shoes and flew by yourself?"

Wally shook his head.

Charlie held up the green soldier. "The part where you were up in a tree shooting at supervillains with semi-lethal weapons?"

Another shake.

"Grabbed by Manika and chased out into the Atlantic Ocean by Hyperion and Swift?"

Wally thought it over and said, "I might have skipped that too."

"So basically . . . nothing?"

"Pretty much, but," Wally added quickly, "you saw how upset she got, and I thought if I told her what really happened, she'd totally lose it, and by the time I figured she'd gotten over it, I'd waited too long, and then I thought she'd be mad that I didn't tell her right away. And then she'd *totally* lose it."

"You can't lie to your mother, dude," Charlie said.

"I didn't lie. Not exactly. I mean, it's not like she *asked* me if I flew with your shoes and fought supervillains and I said no, right? I just didn't tell her something. She didn't ask and I didn't tell. That's a thing, right?"

"Yeah, but not this thing."

"Besides, it's all over and I'm okay, so why tell her now and get her upset all over again?" Wally said, but he didn't sound like he believed himself. "You're not gonna tell her, are you?"

"It's none of my business. Besides, I don't think she's that crazy about me to begin with," Charlie said as he reached for another sandwich. "And you're the one who's got to live with the lie."

"It's not a lie," Wally insisted.

"Whatever."

They went back to quietly chewing their food.

Then Charlie said, "I mean, I'm assuming she doesn't like me. Because of the whole supers thing."

"Beats me. She hasn't said anything to me about it," Wally said. "When I asked if I could come over to see you, she said okay. She just made me promise not to put on any flying shoes."

Charlie grinned. "Yeah? That's all she said?"

Wally nodded. "So, I should tell her, huh? All about being Kid Knave?"

"For the last time, you are *not* now nor will you *ever* be Kid Knave. You start calling yourself that and your mom will really hate me."

"Why do you care if my Mom hates you or not?" Charlie asked suspiciously.

"Why do I want anybody to hate me? I live here now. I want to get along with everybody, including your mother."

Wally slowly nodded. "Or maybe... *especially* my mother?"

"What? No." Charlie's denial didn't sound very convincing.

"Like you said. Whatever," Wally said. "But, you know, if you *did* marry her, then I really would be Kid Knave."

"Yeah, right, very funny. And even if I did marry your mother and you got cloned and were trained from birth to be a sidekick, I *still* wouldn't let you be Kid Knave."

"Okay, if you say so," Wally said.

"I do," Charlie said with a firm nod. "Now, let's have dessert and speak of this no more."

Wally took a strawberry frosted cupcake from the plate and bit into it.

"So how long do you think it'll take me to get good with the flying shoes?"

Charlie just stared at him.

Wally Crenshaw took another bite and, licking strawberry frosting from his upper lip, said, "Brenda believes I'm a real superhero, Charlie. I think I want to believe it too."

Charlie sighed and picked up a chocolate cupcake.

"You're killing me, kid," he said, raising his pastry in salute. "But welcome to the club."

CPSIA information can be obtained
at www.ICGtesting.com
Printed in the USA
LVHW011925290122
709583LV00002B/136